# CONTACT

# CONTACT

Written By
LAURISA WHITE REYES

# For Stuart,
## May this be the one book you'll want to read.

# I

I'M ALIVE?

Yes. Still alive…

Again.

A tube runs from an IV bag into my arm, the plastic needle burrowing under my skin like a tick. Thank God I was unconscious when they put that in. I cringe at the thought of being deluged with so many psyches at once—paramedics, nurses, doctors, all of them touching me.

Where are my clothes? They must have taken them off when I was out. This flimsy gown can't protect me. I want to tear off the tape securing the IV tube to my skin, rip it off like a Band-Aid. I want out of here, but then I see Mama sleeping beside me, her body sloped in a plastic chair. I shouldn't have done this to her again. But I had to try.

A plastic clamp pinches my finger, connecting me to a heart monitor. Three inches further up, my wrist is wrapped in gauze. Two months ago I would never have had the courage to do this—or any reason to. But now, feeling the staples beneath the bandage, I wonder how deep someone has to cut in order to die?

The curtain jerks back, the metal rings dragging across the ceiling rail. Mama snaps to attention. I half expect her to stand and salute.

"Miranda Ortiz?" says a woman in a beige linen suit and crisp white blouse. She is thin, stiff, and colorless. She reeks of gardenias.

"I'm Dr. Walsh from Mental Health," she continues. The plastic laminated nametag hanging from her neck confirms this.

Dr. Walsh extends her hand, but instead of taking it, I grasp the edge of my sheet and pull it up to my chin. Other than this stupid hospital gown, it's the only barrier I've got right now.

Mama stands up and reaches over the bed to shake the doctor's hand. "I'm Mira's mother, Ana," she says wearily. She starts to sit back down, but Dr. Walsh interrupts.

"It's a pleasure to meet you in person, Mrs. Ortiz. However, I'd like to speak to your daughter alone, if that's all right."

Dr. Walsh is insistent, in a polite sort of way. Mama leans toward me, and for a split second I think she's going to kiss me goodbye. Though deep down I almost wish she would, instead she offers me her gentle smile and tucks the sheet under my shoulder.

"Please don't go," I whisper.

"It'll only be a few minutes," she says. "I'll be just outside, all right?"

Mama brushes a strand of hair from my eyes with her manicured fingernails, careful to avoid contact with my skin. She smiles at me, but her eyes are wistful. As she walks out, my insides tighten up, and I suddenly realize how much I've missed her touch. My instinct is to cling to her like when I was small, but instead I press my arms stiffly to my sides like a corpse.

A security guard opens the door and accompanies Mama out into the hall. Dr. Walsh takes Mama's empty chair, crosses one leg over the other, and lays a clipboard on her knee. "So," she begins, "you cut yourself last night. Is that right?"

Her voice is casual and smooth, as if she's just asked me what I ate for dinner. She waits for me to respond. When I don't, she glances down at her clipboard. "I understand it's not your first attempt. You were here a couple of weeks ago, I see. Overdose, but no permanent damage done."

She glances up at me, pausing in case I have something to say.

I don't.

"Miranda—"

"It's Mira."

"Mira, what happened that made you want to die?"

Her perfume hangs heavy around her. I rub the sheet against my nose, trying to block out the overpowering smell and the awkward silence between us. It's obvious she's going to sit there for as long as it takes. I want her gone, so I might as well talk.

"My boyfriend wants to dump me," I tell her, and it's true. Sort of.

3

"I see," she says. Her eyebrows lift a little. "Things aren't going well between the two of you?"

"Something like that."

Her eyes narrow as she looks at her clipboard again. She thinks she's got me all figured out. She's met a hundred kids like me, maybe more. To her, I'm just like all the rest.

Only I'm not.

"Mira, do you mind if I ask you some questions?" She looks up at me, a trace of a smile on her lips. "Your answers will help me understand what's happening with you, all right?"

She begins with the same questions Dr. Jansen asked me the last time I was here: Do you have trouble sleeping? How's your appetite? Do you feel anxious or sad more often than usual?

She's so pale with her white skin and bleached hair. Craig's skin is light like hers. I used to relish his touch and let his lips linger on mine as long as he wanted. My skin tingles just thinking about him, but I shove the memories back, burying them down deep inside me where they belong.

Dr. Walsh shifts in her chair, drawing my mind back to the present. "Mira," she continues, "do you believe you have special powers?"

Beneath the sheet my arm jerks, and the clip on my finger pops off. The monitor lets out a loud, piercing beep. I pat around the mattress, but I can't find the clip. Then I see it dangling over the side of the bed. I reach for it, but Dr. Walsh gets to it before I do.

"Here," she says, smiling. "Let me help you."

"No, don't!" I say, grabbing for the clip.

4

Too late.

Oh God. Please God, not again.

I squeeze my eyelids shut, bracing for impact as she grasps my wrist in one hand and replaces the clip with the other. It takes only half a second, like those commercials where a crash test dummy rockets forward at high speed and slams into a wall. In that instant every thought in Emma Lynn Walsh's head collides with mine—every thought, memory, hope, disappointment, and dream. They come at me like a hailstorm, assaulting me at random. I see her as a child falling off her bike and scraping her knee, and her father scolding her for forgetting to brake. I see the wedding ring slide onto her finger—her yanking it off and flushing it down the toilet. I feel despair at her mother's funeral and relief at her father's. She masks so much pain with poise and self-assurance, but beneath it all she's a mess.

"Mira? Mira."

I open my eyes to see Dr. Walsh peering at me, a puzzled expression on her face.

"Let—go—of—me," I order though clenched teeth.

Dr. Walsh releases my wrist. I turn on my side, rolling up in the sheet, attempting to disappear into my cocoon. I hear the chair legs scrape against the floor as Dr. Walsh slides it closer to my bed.

I stare at the bottom of my IV bag, watching clear drops form, preparing to fall into the tube. One by one they hang there for a moment suspended in time, and then *plop!*

I glance over my shoulder and look at Dr. Walsh. Her smile is gone. Both feet are on the floor, and she's holding the clipboard up now, like a shield. There's a yellow Sponge

Bob sticker on the back, staring at me with a goofy, wide-mouthed grin.

"Okay, Mira. Why don't we get back to your boyfriend? You said he wants to break up with you. Why?" Dr. Walsh's tone has changed. It's softer now, more sympathetic, but what can I tell her that won't sound crazy?

"I won't let him touch me anymore."

"So he told you he wants to break up with you?"

"No. He hasn't said anything—yet."

"Hasn't said anything." Her voice holds a note of confusion. "Then, how do you know?"

She dangles the question in front of me like the proverbial carrot, hoping to draw me out. I don't want to talk anymore, but something inside me needs to. Maybe part of me believes there is a chance, no matter how slight, that this woman might be able to help. That's how desperate I've become.

I open my mouth to say something, but I can't. Instead, I just lay there wrapped up like a mummy, someone who's dead inside. Only I'm not dead. I'm alive. Too much alive.

Just then a nurse comes into the room to check my IV. "Are you comfortable, Ms. Ortiz?" she asks. "Your father called a bit ago. I assured him that if you needed anything, anything at all, I'd see to it myself."

The nurse, a plump middle-aged woman wearing purple scrubs, glances at Dr. Walsh and reacts as if the good doctor had just magically appeared there.

"Oh my, I'm sorry, Dr. Walsh. I didn't mean to intrude."

"Not a problem. We're finished here," says Dr. Walsh, offering a nod.

I hear the snap of the clipboard's metal clasp as she tucks her pen into it. Walking around the side of my bed, she gives me a conciliatory smile. "All right, Mira," she says. "I'm going to have a word with your mother about getting you admitted. I need you to be somewhere safe, where we can keep an eye on you for a few days."

As Dr. Walsh turns to leave, I find my voice again. "If you hate them so much, why smell like them?"

"Pardon?" She turns, pausing at the door.

"Gardenias. You hate gardenias."

Her lips turn pale as she presses them together. I don't want to do this, but I need her to believe me. My voice chokes when I say it. "It's your mother's perfume."

Dr. Walsh's eyes glisten, and hurt and confusion fills her face. Without a word, she turns and walks through the door, taking the invisible gardenia cloud with her.

# 2

THE FIRST TIME I TRIED TO KILL MYSELF I sucked down half
a bottle of Advil. Turns out you can't OD on Ibuprofen, but
it can sure as heck make you feel like you're dying. I puked
every ten minutes for six hours straight. Even when there
wasn't anything left to puke, my stomach convulsed and
heaved until I expected to see my toenails drop into the bowl.

Dr. Jansen must have felt sorry for me then because he
sent me home with a prescription of oral Gaudium and
instructions to take the rest of the week off from school. I
guess the obligatory injection I got on my sixteenth birthday
wasn't enough.

"The first few days you'll feel a little dizzy, so I'll start you
on a low dosage," he'd explained. "We'll increase it over the
next few days, and in two weeks or so we can start weaning
you off. By then your production of dopamine and serotonin
will have reached optimum levels. Your depression will be
permanently cured."

Of course, I already knew all about the miracles of
Gaudium, named after the Latin word for *joy*. As the CEO of
Rawley Pharmaceutical, Papa never failed to take credit for

the creation. But not anymore. Not since he was blamed for those women dying.

Dr. Walsh doesn't let me off as easily as Jansen did. For the next three days I lay curled up on a bed in the adolescent psyche ward serving time on a seventy-two hour hold. How anyone can *not* want to kill themselves while being in here is beyond me. Frankly, though, I haven't minded it. It's the most isolated I've been in months.

I ask the staff to leave me alone and they do, not to mention, the ward is practically empty except for a handful of thirteen or fourteen-year-olds who mostly steer clear of me. Apparently nobody anywhere near my age has been admitted in months thanks to Gaudium, and the statewide policy of inoculating teens with it when they turn sixteen.

On the third day of my imprisonment, Dr. Walsh stops by after breakfast. "How are you holding up?" she asks, sitting across the table from me. The smell of gardenia is noticeably absent. "I'm releasing you today, you know. Your mother's waiting in the lobby."

Behind us, a couple of kids are draped on the couch watching a recorded episode of "Psyche."

"What if I don't want to be released?" I challenge her, stealing a glance at the TV screen.

"Don't you?"

"No."

At the end of the table is a box with an assortment of puzzles and board games. I fish out a pair of dice and toss them onto the table. Two and six.

"I had considered extending your stay here," she replies. "But when I suggested it to your father he said he wanted you to come home."

"Papa was here?" I glance up from the dice.

"No," she answers. "We spoke over the phone."

Of course. Mama has visited every day, but not Papa. I throw the dice again. Three and two.

"I looked at your medical report. Your wrist is healing nicely." Dr. Walsh reaches for my hand as if to touch me, but I withdraw and slide both hands under the table. When she retreats, I pull them out again and rub the dice between my palms.

"Mira." Her voice is quiet and calm. "Do you still have thoughts about killing yourself?"

"I always feel like killing myself."

Snake eyes.

Dr. Walsh drums her fingernails on the table. "I wish you'd talk to me," she adds. "Three days and you haven't said much at all. It's against my better judgment to let you go home. But your father—" Her voice cuts off. I can hear her frustration. "I need to know you're not going to try anything."

I clasp the dice tightly in my fist. "Then let me stay here."

I try to lift my gaze again to look at her so she'll know how badly I mean my words, but I know it won't do any good. Papa practically owns this hospital. He's got more clout than just about anyone. If Dr. Walsh refused to sign the release papers, he would just go over her head and get someone higher up to get the job done.

The doctor sighs heavily. "You're coming to see me at my office tomorrow. In the meantime, if you feel like you want to hurt yourself again, you need to tell someone—your mother or your father."

I snicker at the thought.

"You can always call me, but is there someone else at home you can talk to?"

*Is* there someone? I think. There's our cook, Helen. There's Papa's chauffeur. And there's Jordan. Not what I'd call the ideal lineup, but I nod my head anyway.

Dr. Walsh gives a half-satisfied smile. "All right then," she proclaims, getting to her feet. "I'll tell the nurse to let your mom in while I sign the forms."

A buzzer sounds, and the wide double doors barricading me from the rest of the world swing open. Mama comes in, her face pinched with worry. With her is Jordan Cummings, Papa's closest friend and *my* self-appointed bodyguard. Unlike Papa who retired from Rawley to run for office, Jordan divides his time between the pharmaceutical company and managing Papa's campaign. At a lean six-feet with a hint of gray at his temples, he's a perfect fit for political life.

"Hey there, Sunshine," he says, offering his familiar smile. "Ready to go home? The car's waiting, but so is every news station this side of the Rocky Mountains."

"The media's out there?" I ask, suddenly petrified. "Who told them?"

Mama sets something down on the table in front of me. An Abba-Zaba. She knows it's my favorite candy. "A nurse, a custodian, a parent of some other patient—what does it matter who told them?" she replies with an exasperated shrug. "The sooner we get you home, the better."

I can see it now: *Daughter of Medical Mogul Has Mental Breakdown—Story Tonight at Ten!* Glancing down at the purple, flannel pajama bottoms and t-shirt I'm wearing, I think about the press parasites waiting outside, the way they always push and shove to get a mic in my face—I feel so exposed.

Jordan seems to know just what I'm thinking, as he holds up a plastic grocery bag and reaches his arm into it like it's a magic hat. "Voila!" he says, pulling out my favorite hoodie, the black one he bought me in Venice Beach last summer. He then retrieves some jeans and my pair of Converse and drops them into my lap. "Better hurry. Your carriage awaits, my lady." He winks.

Dr. Walsh returns with paperwork in hand. "Don't forget about our follow-up appointment tomorrow, all right?" Drawing a business card from her pocket, she holds it out to Mama along with her copy of the release form. "In the meantime, call if you need anything." Mama's busy with me, so Jordan takes the information and shoves it into a pocket, and Dr. Walsh walks away.

I head for the restroom where I tug on my jeans. Then I slip into my hoodie, pulling the hood onto my head and the sleeves down past my fingertips. When I step out of the bathroom I ask a passing nurse for some surgical gloves, but her caustic expression is enough to make me regret asking. "Never mind," I say. Then I join Mama and Jordan at the door where we all share apprehensive glances, like Gladiators preparing for battle.

Mama whispers in my ear, "Remember the drill. Face down, hands up, *silencio*."

Slipping the Abba-Zaba in my pocket for later, I follow her and Jordan through the double doors and into the elevator. It's only the next floor down, but the ride seems to take forever. When the doors slide open, my stomach lurches. The front of the hospital is all glass, and from here I can see hordes of reporters and photographers congregating outside where several police officers are attempting to hold them at bay. Parked at the curb is Papa's black Benz. For a split second I wonder if he's come for me himself. But of course Papa wouldn't be here. More bad press is not what he needs now.

As the hospital doors open to the nightmare, I'm hit with a blast of heat that can only be delivered by a So Cal afternoon in July.

The barrage of questions begin:

"Did your father's investigation have anything to do with your suicide attempt?"

"How do you think this will affect your father's campaign?"

In an instant, Jordan is beside me, fielding questions while Mama bundles me into the backseat of the Benz.

"Ladies and gentlemen of the press," Jordan calls out to the frenzied pack in a smooth voice, "Mr. Ortiz has no official comment to make at this time but requests that you respect his family's privacy. He will be available tomorrow to discuss his campaign and the investigation."

"But, Mr. Cummings," shouts one female reporter wearing black rectangular glasses. "Under the circumstances, will Mr. Ortiz consider withdrawing his bid for governor?"

"We have no further comment at this time."

A moment later, Jordan slips into the backseat of the car beside me and Mama. As he shuts the door, I catch a glimpse of the 1911 Colt pistol he carries beneath his jacket. Not that I know much about handguns, but this one's his pride and joy, something he shows off whenever he has the chance. I don't mind. Despite everything I've done to myself, I feel safer when he's around.

Jordan tells the chauffeur to head out. "That wasn't so bad, was it?" he asks me, brushing off the lapels of his suit coat.

"Not bad?" I reply, tucking my hands under my knees. "In a few minutes my face is going to be all over the news."

"Now, Mira," says Mama, "don't worry about it. It will all be forgotten tomorrow."

Mama. Always the optimist. I guess that's what I love about her. She's managed to weather the first stretch of a gubernatorial campaign, a federal investigation of her husband, and a lunatic daughter who shrivels at the slightest touch ... still, she smiles.

"Your dad's sorry he couldn't meet us at the hospital," Jordan says. "But with everything going on, he thought it best to wait for you at home."

Mama squeezes my knee through my jeans. "I'm sure he would have come if he could," she adds. I cringe at her touch, even though the denim keeps her skin off mine. And yet I long to feel her warmth again. It seems like forever since I've let her touch me.

As we pull out of the hospital parking lot, I glance back at the media mob packing up their gear and retreating to their respective vehicles. Behind them, the hospital's new ten-story Rawley addition juts skyward. Like the older complex in Bakersfield, the outer walls are polished, red granite with wide, reflective windows. The bottom floor will house a cafeteria and patient lounge, while the upper floors will be home to medical offices and the laboratory. The first four floors have been complete for a while, but the top floors are not much more than steel girders and scaffolding. It looks more like a giant erector set than a hospital. It should have been finished by now, but construction stopped when the investigation began. It reminds me of myself—empty, broken, abandoned.

# 3

THE CHAUFFEUR TAKES US THROUGH our gate and up the gravel lane, stopping at the front entrance to the house. Papa had it built a few years ago. It looks like that southern plantation in *Gone with the Wind*: tall, scalloped columns out front, a massive circular drive, and a sprawling lawn. Inside, the floors are white marble, and all the wood trim and banisters are maple. It cost a bundle, but as Rawley's former CEO, Papa's got plenty.

As promised, Papa meets us at the door.

"So, how'd it go?" His question is directed at Jordan, not me.

"Not a hitch." Jordan gives Papa a brief report on the media frenzy at the hospital, then excuses himself, saying something about needing to call Papa's attorneys. Once Jordan's gone, Papa turns to Mama and kisses her on the cheek. He starts toward me, but I take a step back.

"That's right," he says. "Sorry."

He's dressed in a dark suit and tie, which he loosens before sliding it out from his collar. Papa's not a tall man,

16

barely five-and-half-feet, but he's strong and good looking. His black hair is combed back from his face, a face adorned with dark eyes and a sculpted jaw line that has captured the hearts of Californians. A Latino JFK.

"How was the inquiry?" Mama asks, taking Papa's tie and draping it over her arm. She heads for the sitting room and mixes him a drink.

"Those damn piranhas just want to take any bite out of me they can," Papa replies. His back is turned to me like I'm not even here. But in this house, not here is the best place to be.

"I keep telling the commission that being a CEO was all about the money, marketing, and international distribution. Rawley Pharmaceutical eradicated Autism, for God's sake. We're on the brink of curing Alzheimer's *and* schizophrenia, yet they want to gut me like a fish because some basement level researcher tested a couple of volunteers without Federal authorization. Volunteers, mind you! It's not like the corporation raided villages and slapped them in chains."

"Of course not, Beto." Mama remains calm, handing him his glass. She glances at me over his shoulder. "Mira, why don't you go upstairs and get some rest?"

Papa turns to look at me as if noticing me for the first time. "I'm sorry, Pumpkin," he says, wiping the condensation from his glass with the thumb of his right hand. His fingers are thick and strong, but soft. No calluses because he's spent most of his life behind a desk or in front of TV cameras and microphones.

"I didn't mean to be insensitive," he tells me. "You know, you really gave us a scare this time."

*This* time? So the first time was child's play?

Beneath the fleece sleeves of my hoodie and the white gauze taped around my wrist, my wound still throbs. The staples are out now, replaced by a bunch of tiny butterfly strips. It'll heal eventually, leaving only a scar behind as evidence. But will the reason I did it ever go away?

Mama grasps my shoulders and steers me toward the staircase. "I'll be up in a minute to tuck you in."

"Mama, I'm sixteen."

"So? Go on. I'll be right up."

I obey—mostly. The staircase starts wide at the base and narrows as it curves around a huge Greek pillar toward the landing on the second floor. About halfway up I pause, concealed by the pillar, and listen.

Papa sets his glass down on the foyer table with a little more force than usual. "I am sorry, Ana," he begins. "I'm just so aggravated about this unwarranted investigation. What evidence do they have anyway? Hell, the guy who supposedly conducted those drug trials has been dead for years. What was his name again?"

"Stark." Mama sighs. "Gregory Stark. We were introduced at an office party once, don't you remember?"

"So this Stark guy is dead, and now they need someone to hang in his place. And I'm the perfect target, of course. The first Hispanic candidate for governor in this state with a helluva good shot at winning. They'll stop at nothing to tear me down. Nothing!"

Everything goes quiet. Mama's probably removing Papa's jacket, rubbing his shoulders the way she does when he gets worked up. They continue talking, but with softer voices.

18

"What about Mira?" Papa asks. His tone is calmer now, more concerned. "Did the doctors say anything more?"

I try to picture their faces. I know Mama's looking hopeful, nodding her head, smiling as if everything's going to be okay. "Dr. Walsh wants to evaluate her again tomorrow," she says.

"Evaluate her? What for? She's depressed. Give her Gaudium."

"She received her immunization on her birthday two months ago, just like the policy requires."

"And that policy is in place for a reason, Ana. Gaudium is still relatively new. Supplies are limited at this point, which is why we've only distributed it to children with Autism and teenagers. But once this investigation is over, Rawley can go into full production, making it available to everyone. Mira's fortunate to have received it when she did."

"I agree, Beto, and Dr. Jansen even prescribed a booster. But it has had no effect on her."

"Impossible."

"But what if Mira doesn't have depression or any sort of imbalance? Gaudium couldn't help her then. Beto, what if she's telling the *truth*?"

A silent pause. When Papa speaks again, his voice is strained. "She won't let anyone near her. Jesus, Ana ... she thinks she can read people's minds."

Mama's probably looking into Papa's eyes, searching for the right words to say. "I know it seems improbable—"

"*Improbable?* Ana, it's crazy!"

"I just think that after what's happened, we should take what she says more seriously. Maybe she should have stayed at the hospital a while longer like Dr. Walsh suggested."

"No." My father's answer is firm, final. "Thanks to some anonymous tip, the press has already spread this thing all over the place. They can attack me all they want, but they'd better leave my daughter out of it."

At this point their voices drift off, presumably into the dining room. I can't hear them anymore, but Papa's words resonate in my mind. *It's crazy*. Or, more accurately, *she's crazy*.

I don't want to hear any more. So I head for my bedroom at the top of the stairs. It doesn't matter that it's never really felt like mine. The decorators Papa hired insisted on painting the walls a swirly pink and green, Hannah Montana theme. It was fine when I was twelve, but that was four years ago—and I hate the color pink. I've hidden most of it beneath a collage of posters from my favorite Broadway shows, like *Wicked*, *Once*, and *Memphis*. There are more posters on the ceiling over my bed stuck up with thumbtacks, and a floor to ceiling bookshelf filled with my favorite novels. Papa bought me the latest iPad for Christmas, but I still prefer real books.

I slip into my room and close the door behind me. Then, pressing my back against it, I sink to the floor and pull my knees up to my chest. If only I could stay here in my own little sanctuary, maybe I'd have a shot at survival. I wrap my arms around my legs and lay my cheek against my knees. I try to coax back the tears, but despite all my efforts a few drop onto my jeans leaving three dark, damp spots behind.

MORNING ARRIVES, DRAGGING ME FROM what I like to call 'outer darkness'. The term is one of endearment. I sleep deeply. I don't dream. At least, if I do have dreams I never remember them when I wake up, which is a good thing since I've got so many other people's dreams to worry about.

At night my mind somehow files away all the other psyches I may have uploaded during day. Not that I forget. I never forget. But my brain sorts itself out, I guess, archiving memories, emotions, and everything else, so that when I wake up all that's left are vague impressions. Kind of like waking from a dream that evaporates before I can grab hold of it. It is the one thing about my condition that is bearable.

My *condition*.

That's what Mama calls it—like I'm pregnant or mentally ill. I know she's just trying to be sensitive, but it irritates the heck out of me.

After a quick shower I throw on my jeans and tank top, with the familiar hoodie over that. Papa says I dress like a

21

bum, but it's become my ritual garb, my ultimate defense against the outside world.

I head down the hall to Mama's room and find her sitting on the side of her bed with her blood sugar monitor in hand. From a distance, it kind of looks like a cell phone. It's the same size and shape, with a large LED screen and some little white buttons. Mama groans as she tries to slip the tiny plastic testing strip into the reader and misses.

"Mama, your hands are shaking. Let me do that."

I pull a pair of silicon surgical gloves from the box on the nightstand and tug them on. Then I take the strip from her and slide it into the monitor. Retrieving a clean lancet from the black plastic container, I prick the tip of her finger and hold the bead of blood to the protruding end of the test strip.

"You shouldn't have to do this for me," Mama says, running her shaking fingers through her disheveled hair.

"Don't worry about it," I tell her. "It's all good." The red LED numbers blink on the tiny screen. "Seventy-two. Pretty low."

"No wonder I woke up. I always feel like crud when it gets that low. Hand me some juice, will you?"

Mama keeps a case of juice boxes on the bookshelf beside her bed. She likes apple best, so I grab one, insert the straw, and hand it to her.

"I may need two this morning." She sighs. Finishing them both off, she sets the empty boxes on her nightstand before lying back down and pulling her comforter up to her chin. "I could sure go for a Double-Double right about now."

"You want a hamburger at—" I glance at her digital clock, "seven-fifteen in the *morning*? I'm pretty sure In-N-Out doesn't open until ten."

"Mickey D's has been open since five."

"You really want a burger?" I roll my eyes at the pout Mama offers. "Okay… I'll send Jordan to pick one up for you."

"Jordan is Papa's campaign manager, Mira, not my personal gofer."

"You know he doesn't mind," I tell her. "He'd get you a burger if I asked him to."

Her shoulders slump in an intentional effort to look disappointed. "I think he left with your father already."

"Then I'll have Helen make one in the kitchen."

"It's not the same. I'm craving something greasy and salty. *And* I want French fries."

Mama grins. I don't have to touch her to know what she's thinking. She's trying to make me want a burger, too—and it's working. After spending three days in the hospital, a burger and fries sound like heaven. When I close my eyes and draw in a slow, deep breath, both she and I know she's got me hooked.

"How much time do you need to get ready?" I ask, surrendering to my now growling stomach.

"Half an hour to get my blood sugar stable, and a few minutes to shower. We'll go at eight?"

"My appointment with Dr. Walsh is at nine."

"Perfect," says Mama. "We'll grab some burgers on the way."

# CONTACT

AT TWENTY AFTER EIGHT, Mama and I climb into the front seat of her little aqua VW Bug with a giant daisy painted on the front hood. She's promised it to me once I get my driver's license.

"It's a classic," she says, touching two fingers to her lips and then the dashboard. She follows the same ritual every time she drives and claims that it is her best disguise from the paparazzi. "They haven't caught me yet," she adds, pulling into traffic.

After a quick jaunt through the nearest drive-thru, we head for Santa Monica, gleefully stuffing our faces with hot, crispy fries. Just as we pull into the parking lot of Mercy Medical Plaza adjacent to the hospital, Mama's cell phone rings. She swipes a stray smear of ketchup from the corner of her mouth and then answers.

"Can't this wait?" She pauses for a minute before saying, "No, it's fine. I can be there in twenty."

She ends the call. "That was your father. There's a problem at the convention center. Something to do with the seating arrangements for Sunday night's fundraiser." She sighs loudly. "Politicians! They all act like twelve-year-old girls. This one refuses to be seated next to that one..." She rolls her eyes and huffs. "Anyway, your father wants me to talk to the event coordinator and smooth things out."

"Papa knows about my appointment, right?" I ask, already knowing the answer.

She throws an apologetic glance my way. "I'm sorry, Mira. This fundraiser comes at a very precarious time for your father. He's counting on this event to fund the last leg of his campaign. With all the bad press about the investigation, everything has to be perfect."

She pauses, carefully studying my face.

"You know what? It can wait." She starts to dial. "I'll tell him I'll swing by in an hour or two."

"No, Mama. I'm good. I can go on my own." I open the car door and step out onto the sidewalk to prove it.

Mama leans over the emergency brake to smile up at me. "Are you sure?"

"Yes, I'm sure." I'm really not, but I smile anyway.

"I'll call Jordan, all right? He'll come by in an hour to pick you up." Mama reaches for my sleeve. She pinches the fabric between her fingers and rubs her thumb back and forth a little. "Everything will be all right. Okay?"

She says this to reassure herself rather than me. I can read it in her face: *You're wearing a black sweatshirt in the middle of summer. You just got out of the hospital after trying to kill yourself. Of course you're not okay.* And she's right. But instead of answering her, I simply nod and close the car door. My stomach clenches as I watch her drive away. Then I reach for the office door and step inside.

# 5

"SO, MIRA, HOW ARE YOU feeling today?"

Dr. Walsh sits on an avocado-green loveseat with her legs crossed at the knee. She's wearing blue slacks and a nautical-style blouse. Perched on her lap is the familiar clipboard.

"Better, I guess." I take a seat on the matching sofa. My hands, still sheathed in the surgical gloves from Mama's room, are tucked in my pockets. On the wall above Dr. Walsh's head hangs a large canvas smothered in brown and yellow brush strokes. It looks like an overripe banana.

"Were you able to sleep last night?"

"Yes."

"How's your wrist?"

"Fine."

We stare at each other for a few uncomfortable seconds before she speaks again. She leans forward and searches my eyes. "Are you ready to talk about what happened?"

"Not really."

Trying unsuccessfully to mask her sigh, she leans back in her chair. "All right." She offers me a nod, pressing her pen into the metal clip at the top of her clipboard. "It's your nickel, she adds with a little laugh. "What I mean is, it's your hour. I'd like to discuss why you ended up in the hospital, but that's really up to you."

I gaze at the banana painting, the clock on the wall, the trophy on the bookshelf—all of it is unsettlingly familiar.

"It's for bowling," says Dr. Walsh, proudly.

"What?"

She nods at the shelf. "The trophy. My team won first place last Saturday."

It's a gaudy, cheap-looking thing with a gold-toned bowling ball cradled by a pair of angel's wings. The whole thing is mounted on a thick, dark green marble slab. Hideous.

"Nice," I tell her. This is going to be a very long hour. If I don't say something soon, she just might tell me more about it, so I speak up. "You really want to know why I tried to kill myself?"

Do I *really* want to do this? I mean, she *is* paid to listen to other people's problems and all, but this is well beyond the normal stretch of the human imagination. Then again, what have I got to lose? I'm already here in a shrink's office. How much worse could it get?

"In the ER you mentioned your boyfriend," says Dr. Walsh. "Why don't you start by telling me about him?"

How much worse? I could get locked away in some institution for the mentally insane. And this time they might not let me out.

"It started a couple of months ago, around the first week of May," I begin. "I had spent a week home in bed—sick. I'd been back for a few days, but was trying to stay away from everyone. Keeping to myself. Craig got mad. Accused me of avoiding him, and I guess in a way I was. He tried to kiss me, but I wouldn't let him. I didn't mean to embarrass him or make him angry. But he grabbed me, saying he was going to kiss me whether I wanted him to or not. And then he did."

My voice sounds so thin and weak. I try to keep the memories of that day—mine and his—pushed down deep, but they force themselves to the surface, elbowing for room in my already overcrowded brain.

I continue.

"When Craig kissed me, I *saw* him."

I look at Dr. Walsh hoping for some hint of comprehension. Instead her eyebrows press together, forming tight lines above the bridge of her nose. "I don't understand."

"I mean, I saw how he really feels about me." I try my best to explain. "He never really loved me. It was—I don't know—horrible? But that was just a sliver of everything, one moment out of millions. He wanted to dump me. I took some pills to save him the trouble. When that didn't work, I tried something more drastic."

When I stop talking, Dr. Walsh just looks at me. Her eyes are narrowed and intense, like she's studying something written on my face. After a few moments, she clears her throat.

"Let me see if I understand what you're telling me," she begins slowly. "You didn't want your boyfriend to kiss you, and that's why you attempted suicide. Seems a bit excessive, don't you think?"

"It wasn't just because of that," I tell her, my frustration mounting. "It was *how* I knew ... what I saw. You see, when people touch me—"

I stop talking. This is all too crazy. If I can hardly believe it, how can I expect Dr. Walsh to? But what choice do I have?

"When people touch me," I start again, "I know things about them."

"You know things about them." The sound of Dr. Walsh's pen scratching across the clipboard tears at my brain. "Like what?"

"Everything."

The scratching stops. "You know, Mira, unrealistic perceptions of one's abilities can be a sign of a chemical imbalance in the brain, a symptom of one of several types of disorders."

"I don't have a disorder." The clipped words come out harsher than I intended, but I need her to understand. "It started the week after my birthday—some vague impressions popped into my head when people touched me. I thought it was just some bizarre déjà vu thing, but it got stronger as the weeks passed. I saw—I *knew* what people were thinking and feeling, though it was kind of muddled ... unclear. Then the memory thing hit just before summer break."

"Memory thing?"

"Yeah. The first time it happened it freaked me out. I was in Trigonometry and my friend, Krista, leaned over my desk to tell me something. I didn't hear a word she said because her lip brushed against my ear, and suddenly it was like her entire life got dumped into my brain, a million fragments of memory all jumbled up. Throwing snowballs at her brother

29

when she was three, her dad calling her stupid because she couldn't remember seven times nine, her first kiss. And what was especially weird was that they weren't *her* memories. They were *my* memories, as if all of those experiences had happened to me. I left school that day, went home and curled up in my bed. I stayed there for a week before Mama finally coaxed me into coming out.

"Then the thing with Craig happened. It's impossible to explain, but it's horrible. I do everything I can to stay away from other people, to avoid contact. I can't stand it, Dr. Walsh. Sometimes I'd rather be dead."

Then, just like that, I'm done. I hadn't realized how revved up I was getting. It is the first time I've actually articulated any of this to anyone. I mean, I tried to explain it to Mama, but how can I really put something like this into words?

"I know you think I'm crazy," I add quickly, shifting uneasily in my seat. "Dr. Jansen didn't believe me either. You both think I'm nuts. But if I were, that would make things a lot simpler, wouldn't it? All the Gaudium I've been given would have made this go away. But it hasn't."

What have I done? I've just proven myself to be a certifiable loon.

"I gotta go." I jump up from the couch and make a beeline for the door.

"You're not crazy, Mira."

My hand pauses on the door knob. Her calm, sure words send a flitter of excitement through my body. I glance up at the banana painting and back to Dr. Walsh. She's watching me intently.

30

"You believe me?"

"Why shouldn't I believe you?" Picking up the clipboard, she flips over the first page. "I admit it all sounds a little … far-fetched. But from what your mother told me about you, you're a model student. You've never been in any trouble, nor have you given your parents any cause for concern—until recently. Taking everything into consideration, and the fact that you knew about my mother's perfume," she adds, with a half grin, "I don't see any reason why I should doubt you. Now, why don't you come sit back down, and let's talk about it?"

To have someone, anyone, believe me is like having a stack of bricks lifted off my chest. For the rest of the hour I tell her as much about my life as I can. I tell her how I was adopted at birth because my parents couldn't have any kids of their own, and how even though they're great, being the daughter of someone famous sucks sometimes.

I talk about Mama and all the plays we've been to, and our secret burger runs. I tell her about how Krista finally stopped texting me altogether after days of my ignoring her, how quickly she managed to find a new best friend, and how much that hurt. And I tell her about Papa, how so far he's the only person I can't see when I touch him, but I wouldn't want to anyway.

When my hour is over, we schedule a follow-up appointment for next week. Leaving Dr. Walsh's office I feel lighter somehow, actually relaxed. Maybe she can help me. Maybe there *is* hope for me after all.

AFTER CLOSING THE DOOR to Dr. Walsh's office I step into the waiting room, a claustrophobic space not much bigger than my walk-in closet at home. A half-dozen, brown, faux-leather chairs sit against the walls, with an oval glass coffee table in the center, covered with old magazines. A massive fish tank overwhelms the far wall. In it, the entire cast of *Finding Nemo* swim around a forest of pink plastic coral. My mind is not on the fish, but on the fact that Jordan is probably outside, waiting impatiently for me.

All of a sudden my right foot catches on something, and I tumble forward, my face careening toward the carpet. But my fall is cut short. I'm suspended midair above the floor by something pressing into my chest. I look down and see five fingers spread out across the front of my hoodie. Five slim, strong fingers. And then it hits me—some guy's got his hand between my breasts!

I roll away, and as my shoulder hits the floor, I see a pair of orange and lime green checkered Vans at the end of a pair of denim clad legs—the culprits responsible for my unladylike entrance. I scramble awkwardly to my feet, preparing to give the owner of those Vans a piece of my mind.

"I am so sorry about that," he stammers.

The guy is a little older than me, maybe eighteen, with a head of moppy, brown curls—the same color as his eyes, which I admit are rather striking.

"Are you all right, Mira?" he asks.

"I'm fine. Fine," I say, twisting away from him. Then I stop and turn back. "Do I know you?"

Three other patients witness our awkward collision: an old man wearing a U.S. Navy baseball cap, and two middle-aged women, one with blue hair and one without any hair at all.

"This is really embarrassing," the guy who tripped me says, lowering his eyes to the floor.

"For who?" I ask quietly to avoid even more unwanted attention. "I'm the one who got groped in public."

For a second, he raises his gaze and looks at me like he doesn't know what I'm talking about. Then, realization hits, and every drop of blood in his veins races to his cheeks.

His words come quick. "I am so, so sorry. I was trying to break your fall. I didn't mean to—I really am sorry."

"You said that."

"But I am!" He clears his throat—loudly. "I'm David."

Pausing, he waits for me to respond. He does look a little familiar, but I can't place him.

"David Valdez?" he adds hopefully. "I used to go to your school. Graduated last year."

CONTACT

A vague memory coalesces in my mind. I think he was a senior, though I only saw him at a distance from time to time. As a tenth grader last year I was too involved in my own world to pay much attention to the 'untouchables'.

"Yeah. I remember you." I smile back to be polite, then glance at my watch, certain Jordan's outside looking at his, too. I just want out of here, but the guy, David, stands between me and my escape.

"Anyway, I'm really sorry about tripping you," he adds, as the color begins to fade from his skin. "I shouldn't have been on the floor."

"What *were* you doing on the floor?"

"Looking for Charlie."

"Who's Charlie?"

Lifting his hand to eye level, something gray and glossy looks up at me and blinks. I let out a shriek and leap backward. My legs collide with the coffee table, and once again I lose my war with gravity. Toppling over, I land butt first on the floor.

When I open my eyes, I see the huge gray lizard perched on the guy's arm peering at me from between my legs, which are sticking straight up like two Florida palm trees. And that guy—*that guy*—stands over me with his hand out, presumably trying to help me up. Only he's got this indecisive look in eyes, like he'd rather I didn't take him up on the offer. He probably thinks with my grasp of balance I could take him *and* his lizard out.

The others in the room steal furtive glances as I somehow manage to untangle myself. Ignoring David's hand, I get to my feet for the second time in the last two minutes.

34

David starts to apologize, but I hold up my hand to stop him. "It's good," I tell him. "It's all good." Then, without another word, I throw open the office door, step out into the hall, and shut it firmly behind me.

So far this day is *not* going well.

# 7

"BLUE OR RED?"

In one hand, Mama holds up a blue, satin, floor-length dress, a sleeveless number with a simple bow at the shoulder. In the other hand, she holds up a burgundy, crushed-velvet dress, knee length, form hugging, and strapless.

"How about purple flannel?" I flop down on my bed, bunching my favorite PJs under my head for a pillow. "I don't want to go to some stupid fundraiser."

"I don't know," Mama says, tilting her towel-turbaned head to one side. "I kind of like the blue. It brings out your eyes."

"Red." Papa passes by my bedroom door with a cursory glance. "Definitely the red."

"Papa!" I toss my pillow in his direction. "Dr. Walsh said I should be resting."

"Getting out of the house will be good for you," Papa shouts from down the hall.

I wait for the sound of the bathroom door closing before I speak to Mama in a quiet tone.

"I've only been home for a couple of days, and Dr. Walsh *did* tell me to rest."

"Rest, not hibernate," she corrects with that comical look of hers. "This evening is very important to your father. If you don't come, it will just confirm the media rumors."

"What rumors? You mean the ones about me trying to kill myself?" I pull up my sleeve, revealing my still bandaged arm.

Mama grimaces and turns away, closely examining the stitching on the dresses. It's too painful for her, I realize. I've upset her. I push my sleeve back down to my wrist.

I sigh, defeated. "Okay. I'll go if you really want me to."

Mama smiles up at me, gratitude beaming from her face. "You can borrow my cocktail gloves." She drapes the velvet dress over my arm and brushes the ends of my hair with her fingertips. "It's just for a few hours, Mira. Just put it on. Make your father happy."

As she heads out of my room, she pauses, as usual, in front of the photo-collage hanging beside my bedroom door. It's got more than a dozen pictures of me when I was little. Christmas, birthdays, any event big or small that Mama thought warranted a permanent record. Mama gazes at it wistfully, then wipes a smudge from the glass with her thumb and exits the room.

Later, standing in front of my full-length mirror with hair straightener in hand, I wonder how Mama managed to talk me into going to this fundraiser. Out in public is the last place I want to be right now, especially in a velvet gown that leaves too much of my skin exposed.

I pop a pair of diamond studs into my earlobes and reach for the matching choker. Mama's white silk gloves are already on, making it difficult for me to get the clasp open. I hurry down the hall to ask Mama to help.

"That will do nicely." Papa nods, sending me a smile of appreciation when I enter the room. I do a model's spin for him, and he turns to his mirror to adjust his tie.

"The gloves are perfect," Mama says with a grin. "And I've got a shawl to drape over your shoulders. That way if anyone should inadvertently bump into you—"

Papa groans. "You're not serious, are you?" His expression shifts from pleased to irritated in a fraction of a second.

"Beto, you know how she feels about being touched."

"Yes, but it's all a bunch of—"

"Beto!"

"Bull," Papa concludes. "I thought you're seeing a psychiatrist. Hasn't that cleared things up?"

Mama shoots me an apologetic look. When Papa sees it, he fumes even more.

"Mama," I speak quickly, trying to divert the topic of conversation onto some other path. "Would you mind helping me with this choker?"

She takes the diamond-studded chain in her hand and links it at the back of my neck. She's so careful not to touch my skin, and I silently thank her for that.

"I sure hope the new planner I hired gets everything right. It's a good thing you called me when you did the other day," Mama says, her voice cheerful. She's in good humor tonight. "That florist at the convention center didn't know squat."

38

"Uh-huh," answers Papa, distracted with trying to straighten his bowtie in the mirror.

"I wish I could have called that one office assistant you had years ago. Her parents were florists, if I remember right. She always had such lovely arrangements on her desk. What was her name? Jackie, wasn't it?"

"What? I don't remember."

"You mean to tell me that you don't remember your own office assistant?"

"Why should I?" Papa huffs. "I had several during my years at Rawley."

"Jackie Beitner. That was her name, I think. You don't remember Jackie? You hired her through the local temp agency. I know it was a long time ago, but even I remember Jackie. She was breathtaking."

There is a slight pause before Papa responds, "I may recall… Yes, the young blonde from Bakersfield? Parents were florists, huh?"

Mama laughs. She steps over to Papa and fixes his tie. "Do you think there was any chance she might have been involved?"

He leans back, a look of confusion settling on his face. "Involved?"

"In the Guadium trials."

"What? Why would you ask that?"

"Mira, could you grab your father's gold cufflinks from the dresser there?" Mama says to me, sending me across the room.

"She did work there when all that secret testing was supposedly taking place," Mama continues. "And do you remember the Christmas party that year? I remember seeing her chatting with Gregory Stark on the balcony. Of course, I didn't think anything of it at the time. But with everything that's been in the press lately—"

"That's a little far-fetched, Ana, don't you think?" interrupts Papa. "She only worked for us a short time, if I'm not mistaken. Besides, you saw the list of trial participants when they released it to the public last week. Her name wasn't on it."

I drop the cufflinks into Mama's hand, and she fastens them to Papa's sleeves.

"You read too much into things, Ana," his voice sounds like a teacher telling his student to relax. "In any case, I've got enough on my mind without worrying about who may or may not have had a conversation at a party more years ago than I can even remember."

"You're right, of course," Mama agrees. "I'm sorry, Beto. Let's just concentrate on tonight and having a wonderful time."

Papa turns and gives Mama a quick kiss, then another.

"I think I'll go finish getting ready in my room," I say, not wanting to stick around in case things get any kissier. As I turn to leave, I nearly crash into Jordan coming through the door.

"Wow!" His eyes shine.

I do a little curtsey for his benefit.

"You're a knockout, Sunshine."

"You're not half bad yourself," I tell him. And he's not, although in his tails and gloves I can't decide if he looks like Fred Astaire or a butler.

Papa waves him over, and the two of them start talking about tonight's event. I hear several names of important people tossed out, and Jordan advises Papa how to approach each one so as to make the best possible impression. That's my cue to leave. I still need to find my heels, which are buried somewhere in the back of my closet. It's been a while since I've needed them, and I'm hoping they're still in decent shape. I'd ask for Mama's, but she wears a half size larger.

THE FUNDRAISER TURNS OUT to be a huge success. Papa struts around like a political peacock, hobnobbing with all the tycoons and government officials who are more than eager to empty their wallets for him. If it weren't for the stiff, black-suited security guards shadowing his every move, he would have looked like any ordinary guest having a good time.

Mama stands dutifully beside him, her hand elegantly clasping a flute of champagne. I choose to remain cloistered behind a large round table with forest-green linens and a copious flower arrangement, a perfect hideaway for someone determined not to make contact in a room packed with several hundred humans—a can of sardines dressed in silk gowns and cumberbuns.

I sit for a while, enjoying the music. I wonder why Papa doesn't ask Mama to dance, but even from where I'm sitting I can see that his attention has been diverted by Senator Morgan, a stodgy-looking man with a halo of fuzzy white hair and a face webbed with purple veins. Stepping away from them, Mama heads to the bar for a refill.

"Peek-a-boo." Jordan slips into the seat across the table. "Having fun?"

I give him a sideways "yeah right" glance.

"I didn't think so," he says, laughing. "Anything I can do to help?"

"Take me home?"

"Your dad would hang me. How about a dance? The band's not bad."

I shake my head. "No, thanks."

"C'mon, Mira. Live a little."

Funny. That's what I was trying *not* to do. I consider Jordan's offer, but as luck would have it, nature calls just at that moment. I guess the four empty plastic cups on the table—the ones once filled with cherry cola—have finally hit me.

"Maybe later?" I try to sound like I mean it. Jordan pretends to pout. "Why don't you dance with one of those foreign heiresses over by the door?"

"You know your father expects me to keep an eye on you tonight," he says, finishing off the glass of wine in his hand. "Like it or not, Sunshine, I'm yours for the entire evening."

The pressure mounts. I have no choice but to dodge the social gauntlet and get to the ladies room pronto. "Listen, Jordan, I've gotta—you know—go."

He starts to get up from the table.

"Alone," I add, over-emphasizing the word. The bathrooms are just on the other side of the room. I slide out from behind the table, taking the flower arrangement with me. The last thing I need is for everyone to notice the candidate's daughter and start introducing themselves. Just the thought of having to shake a bunch of rich old geezers' hands makes me ill, let alone the possibility of one of them brushing his wrinkled fingers across my arm. I can't even begin to imagine what thoughts and emotions would come barreling into my brain. *Ugh!*

Making sure my shawl is wound tightly around me, I carry the arrangement high enough to obscure my identity and low enough to see through the sparse greenery near the top. It feels a little like prowling through African grasslands, though my field of vision is rather limited, blocked by a sprawling fern on one side and a sprig of baby's breath on the other. I keep my back against the wall and make my way toward the restrooms as quickly as I can manage in my heels—not *my* heels, Mama's. I couldn't find mine after all. So I'm tottering along trying to keep my ankles from snapping, when all of a sudden something whacks me in the hip and knocks me off balance. The flower arrangement catapults out of my hands, and I hit the floor face-first.

The silence in the room is palpable. Maybe if I lay here sprawled out on the wood parquet someone will call an ambulance, and they'll wheel me away on a gurney covered from head to toe with a white sheet... No such luck.

"I am *so* sorry!" The apology comes from above me. "Are you okay?"

I glance up to identify the culprit. Moppy, brown hair. Dazzling eyes. It's him! The guy from Dr. Walsh's office! What was his name?

David. No. This cannot be happening.

"We seem to be making a habit of this." He smiles, recognizing the girl who keeps falling at his feet.

"What?"

43

"When you stepped on my foot with your heel, I sort of fell against you."

"I stepped on *you*?"

Could this be any more embarrassing?

"Yeah. Those flowers. Probably couldn't see me."

"What are you doing here?"

"I work here," he replies cautiously. "I'm a special events server."

I realize now that he's wearing a white waistcoat, bowtie, and the same eye-strain producing Vans from the other day. A tray of scattered hors d'oeuvres lay near the now demolished flower arrangement. Since I'm already on the floor, I start gathering up the mushroom puffs, as David squats down beside me.

"Let me do that."

Together we scoop up the rest of the puffs and the scraps of greenery. David deposits all of it into the nearest trash bin, and then offers me a hand. I silently thank Mama again for the gloves while I do my best to get on my feet with as little ineptness as possible.

Though the conversations throughout the room have resumed, Jordan watches me like a hawk from the table. His expression asks if I need any help. I appreciate that he hasn't leapt to my aid, which would have drawn even more unwanted attention my way. Sending him a smile, I wave to let him know I'm fine and I'll be back soon. Then, I turn to David.

"Right. Okay. Well, it was nice to see you again— David—and I apologize for—"

"I wasn't there for me."

"Excuse me?"

"At the psychiatrist's office the other day? I drove my uncle there for an appointment."

"Okay."

"I just didn't want you to think…"

"Of course."

"Not that there's anything wrong with—I mean, *you* were there. I mean—" Looking away, he combs his fingers through his dark curls. "I'm sorry," he adds. "I'm not very good at expressing myself."

I give him a polite smile. "I'd like to stay and chat, but—" I nonchalantly glance toward the ladies room. My bladder is about to explode, and if I wait one more minute I just might have another embarrassing moment.

"Right," David says. "Sorry."

"You say that a lot." I offer a little laugh, knowing that the majority of our dialogue has been based on apologies.

As I turn to go, David's eyes remain fixed on mine. It's a little awkward—but nice, too. He gives a little wave, tucks his tray under his arm, and turns toward the kitchen as I head straight for the bathroom.

Relieved at last, I exit the restroom while tugging my left glove back up to my elbow. Not far from where I am, Mama and Papa stand beside each other as numerous cameras snap poses of them for the press. The pics will likely show up in every major paper before dawn. But something doesn't seem right. Papa's arm is wound tightly around Mama's waist, as she lists to one side like a sinking ship. Each time she starts to collapse, he props her back up for another round of pics. Then I realize—Mama's smashed.

45

I've never seen Mama drunk before.

When the cameras start to disperse, Mama pulls away from Papa and heads back toward the bar. She lifts a glass from the counter, but Papa takes it from her and sets it down again.

"Ana, don't you think you've had enough?"

She doesn't say anything, but gives him a playful little smirk. Picking up the glass, she swallows it down. This isn't at all like her.

Papa frowns. Then he straightens his tie and half turns toward the room. His voice is louder than it needs to be, loud enough so that several people turn to look.

"Suit yourself, Ana. Just be sure to take enough insulin tonight to cover all that champagne."

Marching away, he leaves Mama alone with her empty glass. Jordan's already there with her, holding her elbow to keep her steady. He's too concerned about Mama to notice me.

I'm about to join them when I feel a tentative tap on my shoulder. I prepare for the tsunami of memories and feelings that are sure to follow, but nothing comes. Mama's shawl is a thin but adequate shield between David's skin and mine.

"Listen Mira," he says, his eyes locking on mine. "This party's about over. What do you say we grab a cup of cocoa?"

# 8

"I CAN'T LEAVE," I TELL DAVID, keeping Mama in my line of sight. "My father would kill me." But I have to admit, the offer is tempting. I've hardly had a moment alone since I've been home from the hospital.

"We won't go far," David urges. "There's a Starbucks just outside at the corner."

Across the room, Papa's attention is on Mama. Even Jordan has temporarily forgotten about me as he helps Mama to a chair. I watch the security team for a second. At the moment, all eyes are on them. Maybe a few minutes away wouldn't hurt.

"Is there a back way out of here?"

David smiles wide. "Come on."

I follow David through the kitchen and down the back stairs. A minute later we're in Starbucks ordering two hot chocolates with whipped cream. Taking a table in the back near the window, we jump right into conversation, knowing that there's only twenty minutes to closing.

"So, you're Alberto Ortiz's daughter? That's totally intimidating." David laughs, undoing his bowtie and stuffing it into his pants pocket.

I swirl the whipped cream into my drink with a straw, and the white froth perfectly matches my gloves. "Yeah, right. I believe my bumbling has already proven that there's nothing intimidating about me."

"By your bumbling, you must be referring to your falling all over me."

He cringes at his own comment, as I burst into laughter.

"That sounded very wrong," he says with a groan.

The TV hanging over the counter is way too loud, so I lean over the table a little to hear David better. "But you knew who I was before, didn't you?"

"Not really," he says. "I mean, I saw you at school sometimes, and I knew your name, but I didn't make the connection until now."

"I see. So, if we went to the same school you must live in Flintridge."

"Actually, I live with my Tio Ramón in North Hollywood. I got special permission to go to school in Flintridge because he's the custodian there."

"And you work as an events server on the side?"

"Just for the summer. I'm socking away every penny to pay for college."

"Really? What do you want to study?"

David drops his head, seemingly embarrassed. "Government," he answers quietly. "I want to go into politics."

"Now you're just trying to impress me," I tell him. His smile vanishes and his eyes get wide. Now I *am* intimidating him. I fish for something to say to set him at ease. "I thought for sure you must be studying herpetology."

He laughs at my allusion to our first meeting. "The study of reptiles and amphibians?"

"Charlie *is* a reptile, isn't he?"

Leaning back in his chair, David's face relaxes into a comfortable grin. "A bearded dragon, actually, and Charlie is a *her*. I take her with me sometimes to keep me company. She jumped off my shoulder just as you came into the room that day. I made a nose dive for her, but you—well, the rest is—"

"The rest is history I'd rather forget."

"Really?" asks David, a twinge of disappointment in his voice. "I'm kind of glad it happened." When he smiles, those dimples of his send pleasant chills through my body.

"So, what about you?" he continues. "Other than the fact you're the future first daughter of California, I know nothing about you."

"What do you want to know?"

"Tell me one thing that no one else knows." Unwrapping the straw, he plunges it into his drink.

Something no one else knows. For a second I actually consider telling him about my condition, but I don't want him to realize how weird I really am—at least not yet.

"I was adopted," I tell him. "But I guess my parents know about that, and a couple of other people, so that doesn't really count."

"Adopted? I would have never guessed. You look so much like your dad."

David takes a long, hard pull on his straw. A moment later he's gasping, his tongue hanging out of his mouth.

"Gawd!" he says, his words distorted. "I burned my tongue!"

Rushing to the counter, I ask for some ice water. While the cashier fills a Styrofoam cup, I glance up at the TV to see a local anchor covering a story about a murder trial. As soon as I get the cup, I promptly return and hand it to David. He fills his mouth with the water, swishes it around, and swallows.

"Better?" I ask, trying to restrain myself from laughing. This guy is something else. Handsome as heck, but naïve and sweet and…

David nods, shrugs, and then laughs again. "I'm making a great first—I mean, second impression, aren't I?"

Is he for real? Could *any* guy be this nice?

"Hold on." I raise my hand to point out a spot of white at the corner of his mouth. He flinches, jerking his head back. We both freeze.

"I'm sorry." I say, feeling suddenly awkward. "You have some whipped cream…"

David licks off the cream, groans, and drops his head onto his arms. Then raising his eyes, he looks at me with a pained expression. "Could we just start over?"

"Sure we can." I try not to giggle like a relieved schoolgirl. "As long as we erase my tripping over you at the doctor's office, stabbing you with my stiletto heels, and flinging mushroom puffs and mums all over the place."

"Done. But only if…"

"If what?"

"If you let me take you out tomorrow night."

I hesitate. This isn't quite what I had planned when I got all gussied up tonight for an event I didn't even want to attend. Grabbing a cup of cocoa is one thing, a date is quite another.

"I just recently got out of relationship." The words come out so fast, I sound almost robotic.

"Oh." Lifting his cup, David takes a cautious sip.

His single word response catches me off-guard. What did I expect? For him to protest? To insist? To beg and plead? Was he really giving up on me so easily? I had recently broken up with my boyfriend. At least … he would have broken up with me if I'd given him the chance. So would a date be so terrible?

The sound from the TV is now so loud I can hardly hear myself think. The cashier must have turned up the volume. I'm about to get up and ask him to turn it down a little, but the face staring back at me from the screen stops me in my tracks.

"Hey, isn't that your dad?" asks David.

I nod and listen.

"Alberto Ortiz, former Rawley Pharmaceutical CEO and frontrunner in the race for the governor's mansion, denies any knowledge of wrongdoing on the part of Rawley researcher, Gregory Stark. Three weeks ago documents were turned over to law enforcement stating that Stark allegedly performed human trials of the 'wonder drug', Gaudium, prior to FDA approval. Unfortunately, Stark is unavailable for questioning. He has been dead for sixteen years."

The TV switches off and the Starbucks cashier announces that it's closing time. David and I empty our cups and toss them into the garbage on the way out. It's barely midnight, but from the trail of well-dressed guests streaming out of the convention center, it looks like the fundraiser is officially over.

We laugh as we step out of the shop, but our laughter is cut short by the sound of a sharp metallic *click*. David sucks in a nervous breath and freezes in place. His eyes widen in fear, and for good reason. Someone's got a gun pressed against his temple.

# 9

I IMMEDIATELY RECOGNIZE THE GUN as Jordan's Colt pistol, and take a deep breath.

"You move, you're dead," says Jordan.

"What are you doing?" I've never seen Jordan draw his gun before, let alone point it at anyone. "Put that thing down!"

Jordan ignores me, roughly shoving David's head with the gun barrel. "Who are you?" he shouts. "Put your hands where I can see them!"

David obliges, raising his hands in the air immediately. This is crazy. What does Jordan think he's doing?

"Jordan, stop!" I yell. "You're scaring him!"

"Where have you been?" asks Jordan, finally acknowledging me.

"Here!" I yell back, trying to steady my voice. I'm starting to feel scared. "We've been right *here*. We had hot chocolate, for God's sake, not holding up a bank!"

"You're in serious trouble, Mira." Jordan's voice is loud and angry. "Luckily one of the kitchen staff alerted us when you turned up missing. Jesus! What the hell were you thinking?"

I've never seen Jordan like this before, his eyes wild with rage. But his hand—the one holding the gun—is frighteningly steady.

"I-I guess I wasn't thinking," I'm trying to find the words that will calm Jordan and allow David to run. God knows, by now he should want to run as far away from me as he can.

"And you," Jordan continues his tirade, aiming his words at David, "I should shoot you right here where you stand. Kidnapping is a very serious charge."

Shoot David? Would he *really* do that?

"I didn't kidnap her, sir," says David, his voice surprisingly calm.

Four members of Papa's security detail exit the convention center. One spots us and begins speaking into the mic on his lapel.

"It was my fault," I stress. "I needed to get out of there, Jordan. I'm sorry I snuck away. I was only going to be gone for a few minutes. I swear! I just lost track of time. Please put the gun down. *Please.*"

The security team jogs toward us, guns drawn. Jordan looks at them and then at the few spectators that have gathered to gape at us.

Finally lowering his pistol, Jordan tucks it beneath his jacket. "It was nothing, boys," he shouts out to the team, stepping away from David. They secure their weapons and turn their attention to dispersing the crowd.

Just then Papa's Mercedes pulls up to the sidewalk. The back window rolls down and Papa's angry face appears. "Get in the car," he demands.

Jordan climbs into the car beside the driver, slamming the door shut. I turn to David with an apologetic expression. "Thanks for the hot chocolate." I search my brain trying desperately to say anything that will make sense. "I'm so sorry about this."

To my surprise, David smiles and shrugs his shoulders. "No problem. It's not every day I get mistaken for a criminal mastermind."

"It's not funny, David."

"Maybe not, but it's over now."

"Yeah," I say. It is over, isn't it? I barely know this guy and I've already blown it. I turn toward the car.

"Hey," David adds, "what about that date?"

Our date? *Is he serious?* After all this?

I really am shocked. "Sure. Okay."

Papa honks the horn, or at least he's instructed his chauffeur to do the job.

"Six o'clock tomorrow night?" asks David expectantly. "I'll come by your house and pick you up."

He asks for my number, and I quickly recite it while he inputs it into his phone.

"The media's going to show up any second," Papa states in an annoyed voice from inside the car. "And your mother's not feeling well. Mira, get in the car. Now."

"Meet me at the park on Foothill Boulevard instead," I tell David in a quick whisper.

"You'll be there?"

"I'll be there."

Opening the back door, I slide into the car beside my mother. Her head rests against Papa's shoulder and her skin looks a tad bit green. Jordan shoots me a reproving glare from the front seat before Papa slaps the driver's headrest and the car lurches forward.

I don't dare look back.

"Was *that* really necessary?" I ask once we're on our way. My question is directed at Jordan, but Papa answers.

"How could you be so irresponsible?" His voice comes out in a forced hiss. "Do you have any idea of the commotion you caused? Somehow I managed to keep the guests from finding out that the future governor's daughter had outwitted security and run off to God knows where."

Papa's eyes dart angrily to the back of Jordan's head.

"Don't blame Jordan," I snap. "The last place I wanted to be tonight was surrounded by a bunch of people I don't even know. I just needed to get away for a few minutes."

Clamping his mouth shut, I can see the muscles tense along Papa's jaw. He takes a deep breath, letting it out slowly. He's calming himself down, trying to act dignified.

"I called your cell phone several times," he says in a restrained tone. "You could have just told me where you were going."

"And have half your security team hovering over my shoulder? Your little surprise attack back there was embarrassing enough, thanks."

"If I'd been able to reach you, maybe we could have avoided a scene."

"I'm sorry. I left my phone at home." Where would I have carried a cell on an evening dress with no pockets?

"That's a bad habit, Mira. There's a reason I bought you that phone."

Yeah, so he can track me day and night. Stupid parental controls. GPS sucks.

"It was all good," I tell him. "We just got something to drink and were on our way back."

"Who the hell is he anyway?" Papa asks.

"His name is David. He was a server at your party."

"That's just great. You ran off with the hired help."

"That's not fair, Papa, and you know it. He's actually very nice."

"Fine, if you're interested in that sort of thing."

"He plans to go into politics."

Papa casts me a derisive glance. The car radio is playing and a news report comes on, but Papa tells the driver to shut it off.

We drive for a few minutes in silence. Mama's eyes are closed. I'm jealous. She's the lucky one, she's fallen asleep. Papa looks down at her. He tugs off one of his evening gloves and touches her hair, gently shifting it away from her face.

"I was worried about you," he says, his voice so low that I doubt Jordan or the driver can hear him. He looks up just long enough for me to catch the apologetic expression on his face before turning back to Mama.

The city is quiet, just the lights from the shops and gas stations, and headlights from the occasional car can be seen. I let the events of the day play over in my mind, taking care to avoid the part about stepping on David's foot and the evening's disastrous ending. Instead, I think of David's eyes. Deep, warm brown. The kind of eyes I could get lost in and never want to be found. I think of his hands. Strong hands with long, lean fingers and broad palms. I felt them when he stopped me from falling at Dr. Walsh's office, and again when he helped me up from the floor at the fundraiser.

I glance at Papa. He's got the evening glove clutched in his fist and he's slapping it against his knee.

"You really are worried, aren't you?" I ask.

"Hmm?" The slapping stops. "About the inquiry? Heavens no."

It's not what I meant, but I don't tell him so.

"Like I told the press," he continues, "what that Stark did on his own time has nothing to do with me. The matter will soon be forgotten."

He offers me a smile, but quickly turns away, staring out the window. I can see his reflection. He looks apprehensive, and soon he is lost in thought again. Somehow it doesn't seem right to intrude, so I turn to my own window. And yet I cannot shake the feeling that no matter how adamantly Papa insists everything will be fine, deep down he knows it won't be.

# 10

As Monday dawns, a shard of sunlight slices across my eyes. But I don't mind. Today waking up doesn't seem so bad. I stretch and swing my feet out of bed. As wonderful as I feel right now, I know this is going to be the longest day in history. My clock says it's barely eight a.m., which means I've got ten whole hours to go until I see David again. I'm sure I can find some way to pass the time. But first—breakfast.

Throwing on my robe, I head for my bedroom door, but before I reach it, my cell vibrates on my nightstand. It's a text from Papa. It was sent hours ago. I must have been too deep asleep to hear it:

CHECK ON YOUR MOTHER

I delete the text and drop the phone into my robe pocket. "Can't I at least go pee first?"

After last night's shindig and Mama's condition on the way home, I doubt she's going to appreciate my waking her up and pricking her with a metal barb. Her sugar levels will probably be soaring. Too much alcohol will do that to a diabetic.

I use the restroom and wash my hands. Then I enter my parents' room to see Mama lying on her stomach in the bed, her feet peeking out from beneath her yellow sham. Her face is half buried in a pillow. I watch her breathe for a moment. She's gone, really gone.

"Mama?" I speak gently. No sense in startling her. Her insulin bottle and a used syringe lay nearby along with her other prescriptions. At least she took Papa's advice last night and gave herself a little extra. Maybe her levels won't be through the roof after all.

"Mama," I say more firmly. "It's time to test."

She doesn't stir. After donning a pair of surgical gloves, I prep the monitor and insert the strip. I lift the index finger of her limp left hand, prick the pad of her finger, and a small bead of red appears. Touching the blood to the end of the test strip, I watch the numbers count down.

Three-two-one...

I read the monitor. This can't be right. The number is low, way too low. Quickly I prepare the monitor for another reading, but the result is the same.

Oh my God.

Juice! She needs juice! I grab a box from the shelf. My hands shake as I insert the straw. What the heck am I thinking? She's unconscious, damn it! How is she going to drink this?

Glucose.

I drop the box not caring where it lands. Hurrying to the bathroom, I rummage through my parents' mess of a medicine cabinet and find a nearly empty canister of glucose tablets. I run back to Mama and place one of the thick, chalky discs under her tongue.

"Mama, wake up." I pat her hand and rub her arm, and my gloved hands slide clumsily across her skin. Mama doesn't move.

I fish in my pocket for my phone. My fingers tremble as I dial my father's cell number which, of course, goes to voicemail. "Papa, she's not waking up. I gave her glucose, but—I don't know what to do! God, please get this."

I press END, then dial 9-1-1.

Is this real? It couldn't possibly be. Why does Papa have to be gone *today*? Why won't he answer his phone?

The chaos happens so fast—the sirens, the paramedics, the ambulance. I climb into the back with Mama and hold her hand, but I'm crying so hard I can't think straight.

We arrive at the hospital, and the ambulance doors swing open. Looming above us, the skeletal frame of the half-finished wing glares at me like a disapproving deity. Mama's whisked away, vanishing through the doors to the ER.

A nurse with a plump, kind face leads me to the check-in counter. "What's your name, honey?"

Another nurse, chomping on a wad of gum, gestures with a pen. "Louise, that's the Ortiz girl. Hey, sweetie, is that your mom they just brought in?"

I nod, unable to find my voice.

"Christ," Louise mutters.

"You know what that means," says Gum Chewer, rolling her eyes. "The media's gonna be here any minute."

The automatic door slides open and Papa rushes in, followed closely by two security guards. Through the glass I see some reporters gathering. It feels like we've turned back time. It's last week all over again. Only this time I don't care that the media's here.

Papa hurries over, his face puckered with worry. "I got your message and tried to call you back."

Noticing that I'm still wearing my bathrobe, I pat the empty pockets. Once again I am without my phone. I must have left it in Mama's room.

"I tried the house," Papa continues, "but Helen said you'd just left with the ambulance, so I came straight over. Are you all right?"

I shake my head. The tears won't stop coming. "She won't wake up," I say, choking on the words. "Why won't she wake up?"

Louise the nurse spots Papa and ushers him away from me. She's taking him to see Mama. Gum Chewer leads me to a private waiting room, sits me in a chair, and turns on the overhead TV, like I could pay attention to some stupid show right now. A moment later ... I'm alone.

I don't know how much time passes, but eventually Louise comes in to check on me. She offers me a granola bar, but I can't eat anything.

"There are some magazines here." She picks up a stack and flips through a few. "*People*? *GQ*? *Martha Stewart*? Damn, this one's a year old. Can you believe that?" She lays them down again. "I'm sure someone will be in soon, honey." She smiles warmly. "The moment there's any word, any word at all, I'll let you know."

As the minutes wear on, I finally turn my attention to the TV. Anything's better than sitting here wringing my hands. When the morning news comes on, I turn up the volume. The lead story is about Mama. A reporter appears on screen standing in front of the hospital doors:

"Ana Ortiz, the wife of Alberto Ortiz, has been taken to the hospital in what is believed to be critical condition. Sources say Mrs. Ortiz may be in a coma."

Someone should get fired for leaking this to the press.

The report is followed by a recap of last night's story— Papa's investigation. I shake my head... I wish they would just leave us alone.

I get the feeling I'm being watched, that odd sixth sense that makes the hairs on the back of your neck stand up washes over me. I turn around and find Papa observing me from the doorway.

"Is it true?" I ask, though I don't need to. I can see the answer clearly on his face. "The news says Mama's in a coma."

Papa stares at the wall behind me. He looks exhausted, wrung out. Just then a doctor comes in. He's in green scrubs and is pulling off a pair of surgical gloves. Mine are still on. I'd forgotten all about them. I peel them off behind my back and stuff them in my pocket.

"Your daughter?" asks the doctor. My father nods.

"I'm Dr. Zimmerman. You did the right thing calling 9-1-1."

"Will my mother be all right?"

"She's in a coma. Her blood sugar dropped dangerously low."

"But she'll wake up."

"It is possible, in theory. But—"

"But?"

"When the sugar level in the blood drops that low sometimes damage occurs, irreversible damage."

"But I don't understand. Mama's levels drop all the time. She always wakes up. She says it makes her feel sick."

The doctor glances at Papa and then back at me. "Your mother takes Trazodone, a mild tranquilizer. There was quite a bit of it in her bloodstream. Not enough to hurt her, but enough to put her into a deep sleep. That, combined with the extra insulin she took before she went to bed last night, well … she just couldn't wake up when she needed to."

Louise comes in and turns off the TV. Papa sits down and buries his face in his hands. I should say something, but I decide it's best to let him alone—at least for now. I look up at Dr. Zimmerman. He's younger than Papa, with eyebrows and freckles that match his auburn hair.

"I want to see her," I tell him.

He pauses, his face full of concern, and then looks toward Papa for approval, but Papa is too absorbed in himself at the moment to notice. Dr. Zimmerman fingers the end of his stethoscope. "Of course," he says, finally. "Come with me."

I follow him out of the waiting room through a wide automatic door and down a hall with a yellow stripe painted down the middle of the floor. We pass several glass-fronted rooms and the nurses' station. Dr. Zimmerman says something to one of the nurses about my presence, and then takes me to patient holding room eight.

Mama is on the bed covered with a thin white sheet up to her chest. The side rails are up, and she's got an IV going. Such a familiar sight. I was here in this ER only a week ago, lying in a bed and hooked up to an IV just like this. I lower one side of the rail and sit down on the orange plastic chair beside Mama's bed.

How did this happen? How did I *let* this happen? My brain is spinning with questions. I watch Mama's face, peaceful like she's sleeping.

"Mama?" I say quietly. I lean a little closer. "Mama, can you hear me?"

My throat feels tight. I don't fight the tears when they come, or the anger. I blame myself, though I don't know what I've done to cause this. If I'd gone in to check on her sooner … if I had called 9-1-1 before giving her the glucose … if I hadn't left the fundraiser so Papa could have brought her home sooner…? I don't know. I don't know.

"I'm so sorry. I just—I want—"

A sob explodes out of me and I bury my face in Mama's sheet, letting my tears soak the coarse fabric.

"Mama, I just want to know you're still here." My voice is muffled against the bed. I lift my gaze to look at her. Can she hear me? Deep down does she know I'm here, know what's happening around her?

I stare at my fingers, alien to me, always hiding away in my pockets or gloves. I watch them hover like spirits over Mama's face. Then slowly they come down and make contact.

# 11

PAPA AND I DRIVE HOME in complete silence, each left to our own thoughts. A thin rain begins to fall, and the only sound is the car wipers slapping against the windshield. The signals and brake lights from the cars ahead of us are indistinguishable blurs of color. The sky is a drab shade of gray.

The grandfather clock just chimes six p.m. when we walk in the front door.

Six o'clock. I was supposed to do something at six.

The aroma of cornbread and chili permeates the air. "Smells like Helen's been cooking," Papa says. He pulls off his overcoat and lays it across the dining table. I am already halfway up the stairs.

"I'm not hungry," I tell him, and I mean it even though my stomach rumbles.

"Me neither," he replies, but he glances toward the kitchen with a tell-tale look of hunger in his eyes. He looks back at me. "Are you all right?"

*Am I all right?* Did he really just ask me that? My mother happens to be in a coma, but I'm just dandy. What about you?

"I'm good," I say.

Papa pulls off his black leather gloves one finger at a time. He holds them in one hand and absentmindedly slaps them against his other palm.

"I should know what to say to you," he says finally. "I've run a major corporation and I'm going into politics. I always know what to say, right? This has been a rough day—for both of us."

He pauses, waiting for me to respond. My robe is damp from the rain, and I'm starting to feel the cold against my skin. I want a hot shower. I want to go to bed. The chili smell makes me feel ill.

Papa continues, "Your mother had an insulin reaction in her sleep. You heard what Dr. Zimmerman said. Too much alcohol, too many sleeping pills, too much insulin." He comes to the stairs. He's close enough to touch me, but he doesn't. He tries to smile, but his lips won't obey.

"Mira," he says gently, "you did everything you could. Don't blame yourself."

Don't blame myself. How can I not blame myself? What's more, how can Papa not blame himself? Isn't it natural for people to blame themselves when tragedy strikes?

Papa walks away and slips into the kitchen and I continue up the stairs. In my room, I take off my robe, letting it fall to the floor in a soft, fuzzy, wet heap. Then I crawl into my bed. I spy my cell phone on the nightstand—not where I left it. I'm sure Helen must have found it and brought it in here for me. The screen shows I have a text. Reaching for it, I power it down. I'm not in the mood for messages tonight.

# CONTACT

All I want to do is close my eyes and let Mama's memories fill me up. The initial jolt of her psyche colliding with mine was like the stab of pain you get from an electric shock—only times a hundred. But after the shock subsided, the floodgates of my mind burst open and a deluge of everything Mama entered my skull. The memories came in a jumble, but lying here now I have time to sort them out, to reflect on each one.

I see her as a child, the youngest of five, happy and loved by parents who adored her. Her mother was affectionate and her father was even-tempered and kind. Though I saw no evidence of wealth in Mama's memories, she lacked nothing to make her feel safe and loved at home.

On her fourth birthday, she got a yellow lab pup named Squiggles. She and the pup grew up together. He was her best friend, guardian, and confidant until he died quietly in his sleep when Mama was fifteen. Losing him was the second greatest sorrow she ever experienced. The greatest came not from loss, but from never having what she yearned for the most.

I felt Mama's emptiness and heartache after years of infertility. I experienced the discomfort and disappointment of in vitro fertilization and four miscarriages. And then I felt her immense joy at holding me for the first time, a motherless newborn healing the heart of a childless mother.

I felt her love for Papa, her pride in his successes. But I also felt her pain at being so often overlooked and cast aside when those successes pulled Papa further and further away from her. When I came into the picture she hoped it would

68

change things, but Papa spent more and more time away from home.

There were so many times she tried to protect me, like when she told me Papa missed my eighth birthday party because he was away on a business trip, when he was just working late again. I felt her anger at the fact that he couldn't love me as much as she did.

I saw Mama last night drinking at the bar, coming home half asleep in the car, leaning against Papa and Jordan's shoulders to get upstairs, and feeling the warm, enveloping comfort of sleep as her mind slipped into a dark and painless void.

I lie in my bed and let every bit of Mama occupy my mind. I push my own thoughts and feelings away to make room for her, knowing that once I fall asleep most of it will fade. In the morning all that will remain are vague images and a few scattered details—only remnants of the few moments when Mama and I were one.

A faint chiming penetrates my room from downstairs. It's the grandfather clock again. An hour has already passed. The chimes call me back to my own mind, my own being. I leave Mama somewhere deep inside me.

I count the chimes. When I reach six, I remember.

David. I was supposed to meet David.

Outside my bedroom window, the rain is insistent. He wouldn't have waited in the rain, I tell myself. And if he did...

But I can't worry about that now. I don't really care anyway.

I close my eyes again, abandoning David in the rain. I am with him there, standing in my blue bathrobe soaked through.

# CONTACT

I leave them both—David and me—and drift away deep into my mind where Mama waits.

# 12

BACON. I SMELL BACON.

My mouth starts to water before I'm even fully awake. Not fair. Helen's playing dirty this morning.

With my eyes still closed, awareness seeps in. Mama's been in the hospital almost a week. Papa has left me mercifully alone. Helen did manage to coax me to eat some fruit and yogurt on some days. The remains of other barely touched meals still sit on a tray beside my bed. But today is different. The sweet, oily fragrance of breakfast seeps into my room and tugs me out of my stupor.

As I sit up, the horrible details of that day drip into my consciousness one drop at a time—a leaky faucet of fear and pain. I realize once again that I'm alone. Mama has gone. All I have left is the hazy memory that, for a while at least, she was with me—in me.

I feel so empty.

I don't even bother with my robe or slippers. I drag myself downstairs and into the dining room where a feast has been laid out on the table. Steam rises from a pile of fluffy scrambled eggs, and a tall, frosty glass of orange juice stands beside a glistening china plate. I lift a strip of bacon from a white ceramic platter and insert it into my mouth. Why does bacon have to taste so good?

I sit down. I eat. My stomach begs for more. I feel guilty.

Papa comes in, a newspaper folded beneath his arm. "Morning, Mira. I see you've started without me. Good girl."

He takes the chair across the table from me and fills his plate. He lifts his first forkful of eggs, but then pauses, setting it down again.

"Doesn't seem right, does it?" he says. He stares at his fork for a while, then slowly lifts it again and deposits it into his mouth. He sets the paper on the table beside him, but he doesn't even glance at it. I watch him as he eats.

"It's a relief to see you up finally," he says quietly. "I was beginning to wonder if you'd ever come out of your cave again."

I fill my plate with more eggs, all the while wishing I didn't have to eat. Papa takes more bacon.

"Papa," I say after a while.

"Hmm?"

"Can I ask you something?"

"Of course," he replies. "What's on your mind?"

"I've been thinking about what Dr. Zimmerman said—about Mama. Remember?"

He takes a sip from his glass.

"He said Mama had Trazodone in her blood sample that night."

Papa nods. "You know she uses it from time to time. She keeps the bottle on her nightstand."

I turn my fork between my fingers, swirling what's left of my eggs. My appetite has calmed down a bit. The smell of food has lost its power over me. "Is it possible the blood test was wrong?"

Papa slips a slice of bacon into his mouth and chews, washing it down with more juice. "Blood test? What do you mean, Mira?"

"I mean, could there have been a mistake? An error in the results?"

"No," says Papa. "I doubt it."

"And Mama's insulin. How do they know she took too much?"

Papa sets down his fork, wipes his mouth on a napkin. "Mira, what's this about?"

The sound of shattering glass bursts through the kitchen door followed by Helen's version of swearing. After spending her last summer vacation in Europe, she's taken to using the word *bugger* in lieu of what she calls "offensive American profanity."

Papa cracks a smile. He pushes his chair back from the table. "If you're concerned about the tests," he announces, "you can certainly ask Dr. Zimmerman about them. I'll make sure he knows he can disclose any information to you that you like. Will you be visiting your mother today?"

"Will you come with me?" I ask. I lift another bite of eggs to my lips, but it's cold now, so I drop it back onto my plate.

Papa gets up from the table, the newspaper tucked securely beneath his arm once again. "I wish I could, but I have another day of inquiries to face. Damn tribunal, that's what this is. At least so far they haven't got a stitch of evidence linking me to that rogue researcher, Stark. So hopefully this will all blow over soon, and I can get on with my campaign."

He pauses a moment as a hint of sadness flits across his face. Just then his cell phone buzzes, and he pulls it from his suit pocket. "Jordan? I'm on my way now. I'll meet you at the courthouse." He snaps it shut and slips it back into his pocket. From his other pocket he removes his gloves. He slides the first onto his right hand, flexing his fingers to get the fit just right. He does the same with his left.

"Supposed to rain," he comments nonchalantly, turning to leave. "Give your mother a kiss for me, all right?" But then he stops. His forehead creases in thought. "I mean—tell her I love her. I'll try to stop by later tonight."

And then I'm alone. Just me and enough scrambled eggs to feed a third-world nation. Helen comes in, wiping her hands on a dish towel. She's a short, squat woman who resembles Mrs. Santa Claus, right down to the white hair and wire-rimmed glasses.

"Anything else I can get you, sweetie?" she asks. The tone of her voice is gentle and compassionate. She's done all this for me—for Mama. It's her way of grieving.

"I'm good," I tell her. "This is delicious."

I take another slice of bacon to prove my sincerity. She seems pleased, but there are tears in her eyes.

"I'm just happy to see you up and about today." She smiles, dabbing her cheeks with the corner of her apron. "I'll be up later to get your trays. And if there's anything else you want, just say the word, all right?"

I watch Helen turn and push through the swinging door into the kitchen. Only after she's gone am I struck with the realization that I haven't seen Papa cry. Not a single tear.

# 13

THE SILENCE IN DR. WALSH'S OFFICE is thick between us, like a swirling unseen mist that acts as a barrier, giving us time to collect our thoughts. I missed the last couple of weeks and would have preferred to skip today, too, only Jordan insisted I come.

Walsh has that clipboard again, and she's reading over her notes from last time. After a minute or two she makes eye contact. "I'm so sorry about your mother." Her voice sounds considerate, as if she truly cares. "Has there been any improvement in her condition?"

Sponge Bob smirks up at me. I want to tear his eyes out.

"No," I say. "It's been almost two weeks now with no change."

"How are you coping?"

"I'm—I'm not."

She jots a few words down on her clipboard. "How's your father holding up?"

Something inside of me cracks, something fragile and vulnerable. I fight the urge to scream. Instead I keep it all packed down deep inside me. "He's doing fine," I reply in a voice that sounds cold and judgmental to my own ears.

Dr. Walsh must sense the turmoil because she nods as if in agreement. "He's not hurting as much as you think he should be."

"He's not hurting at all."

She contemplates this for a moment before responding. "He's in the public eye, Mira. He may feel he's got to keep up appearances."

"Oh, he's perfectly tormented when he's in public, Dr. Walsh," I reply. "But in private it's a whole different story. He doesn't care that Mama's in a coma."

"Now, Mira, think about what you're saying. This is your father. He's got a huge burden to carry. Couldn't it be possible you're misreading him?"

My father. Burden. Yes, it makes sense. Of course he's as torn up about Mama as I am. Why wouldn't he be? He's never been outwardly emotional, so he's probably keeping it in. Hurting in his own private way. What was I thinking?

Even the tone of my thoughts is cynical. I can't help it. "I'm sorry," I say. "You're right. I can't even sleep at night. I'm all messed up."

"Of course you are," Dr. Walsh replies. "You need someone to turn to, but your father is so wrapped up in everything he just can't be there for you the way you need him to be right now."

She opens a drawer beneath the table and rifles through it, extracting a small pad of white forms. "Hang on while I have my colleague sign this," she says, scribbling something on the paper. She leaves the office for a couple of minutes.

When she returns, she tears off the prescription and hands it to me.

"What is it?"

"Just some Trazodone to help you sleep."

Trazodone. The same medication Mama took—*takes*. I accept the prescription from Dr. Walsh and slip it into my back pocket. I don't want it, but I don't feel like explaining why right now.

"There's something else I want to discuss," Dr. Walsh continues, returning to her chair. "I've spent some time researching your case."

"My case?"

"The symptoms you described to me in our first session. It seems that what you're experiencing—the flashes of insight, seeing into other people's minds—may not be completely unique. Have you ever heard of Edgar Cayce?"

The name sounds vaguely familiar.

Dr. Walsh goes on, "Mr. Cayce was a clairvoyant who lived in the early twentieth century. He performed thousands of readings over the course of forty years. He would put himself into a trance and answer all sorts of questions, including questions about complete strangers living in other parts of the world."

"Sounds like a bunch of bull to me," I remark.

"Maybe so. Some people claim Edgar Cayce was a prophet. Others think he was a con artist. The truth may lie somewhere in between."

This is unreal. I look at Dr. Walsh, searching for some glimmer of humor in her eyes, something that proves she's joking. But her expression remains serious.

"I'm not a clairvoyant or a prophet," I tell her. "And I'm no con artist. You can believe whatever you want about me. Heck, *I* don't know what to believe about me. All I want is…"

My voice trails off. What *do* I want? Two weeks ago I wanted it all to stop. I wanted to be normal, to be able to touch someone without their whole life being zapped into my brain. But now there's Mama.

Dr. Walsh is writing again, this time on the blank backside of a prescription form.

"The Cayce Institute for Intuitive Studies is located in Virginia, but they've recently established a West Coast office about twenty minutes from here in Glendale. If I could arrange it, would you consider letting them evaluate you?"

"Why?"

"I think your particular—gift—might be right up their alley. With your permission, I'll call in a referral."

"Sure, I guess."

"Good. I'll schedule an appointment for tomorrow morning. If there's any conflict, let me know. In the meantime, tell me about the emotions going on inside of you."

AFTER THE APPOINTMENT IS OVER, I see myself out. Dr. Walsh wanted to know if I was still feeling suicidal. She seemed surprised when I said 'yes', though I've been too worried about Mama to worry about me. In addition to the Trazodone, she also renewed my prescription of Gaudium.

"Maybe you have a higher tolerance to it than most people," she explained, "but one more round should do the trick."

One more dose—as if feeling depressed is a virus like the common cold, and Gaudium is nothing more than a mega-dose of Vitamin C.

I'm thinking about Mama when I step out of Dr. Walsh's office. I don't notice David until he's standing right in front of me, a pained expression on his face.

"You ditched me," he says.

I don't come out of my thoughts easily. It takes me a couple of seconds to realize what he's talking about. "The park." It all comes back to me.

"I waited for more than an hour." He speaks in a clipped, hurt voice. "I even came to your house."

He did? He came to the mansion?

"Your place is like Fort Knox. I couldn't even get to the door before a security guard ushered me away."

He came looking for me. In the pouring rain.

"I texted and called you," he continues, "but you never replied."

"I'm sorry," I say, but the look on his face tells me he's not buying my apology. I don't expect him to.

He slips his hands into his pockets. His arms are stiff. An invisible wall has already risen between us.

"Let me explain—"

"You don't have to explain anything," David says. He starts to turn away like he's cutting off this conversation. He doesn't want to hear any more.

"It's my mom," I say. "It's been all over the news."

"I don't pay attention to the news. Too busy," he says.

For some reason his indifference hurts deeply. "Well, if you had paid attention you'd know why I couldn't meet you that night." I push past him out the door into the parking lot. It's hot and humid. Sweat gathers on my skin under my hoodie. Jordan's car isn't here yet. When David follows me outside, I have half a mind to walk home just to get away from him.

"So, are you going to tell me?"

I ignore him as best as I can, but he steps in front of me. Does this guy ever stop?

"Okay, look, I didn't mean to be rude." He sighs. "If you didn't want to meet me, just say so and I'll leave you alone. But I have a right to know."

A city bus passes by, its gears grinding and spewing black exhaust. Maybe I'll flag it down and get on it.

"It just so happens that my mother is in the hospital. She's in a coma." My tone is purposely sharp. "I spent that entire day in emergency with her. So sorry I missed our little rendezvous, but I had more pressing matters to attend to. Now, if you don't mind, my ride will be here any second."

The color in David's face drains away. The anger in his expression vanishes and in its place is something much softer—empathy. He doesn't say anything for at least a minute. Seeing his reaction to the news about Mama shoots pangs of guilt through me. I was too hard on him. Why should he have known? And of course he'd be mad when I didn't show up after I'd promised to.

"I'm sorry." His voice is sincere. "I'm sorry about your mom and the fact that I was such a jerk. I just—" His hands

81

slide out of his pockets, and he folds his arms over his chest. "I just wanted to see you again."

Down the street I spot the Benz. In another thirty seconds, Jordan will be here.

"I'm willing to try this again if you are," I tell David. "If you happen to come by the park tonight around six you just might find me there."

The car pulls up to the curb. I open the door and slip into the backseat. Jordan casts me a curious glance in the rearview mirror, but I ignore it. As we drive away, I turn and look back at David. He's still standing where I left him, hands back in his pockets ... and a wide grin on his face.

# 14

AT SIX O'CLOCK, I HEAD OUT for the park. Papa isn't home yet. I didn't expect him to be, and yet I can't help but feel disappointed. During the past week he's only visited Mama once while I've gone every day, sometimes staying for hours. I know he's busy, and Dr. Walsh suggested that maybe this is all too much for him, that he's carrying his burden in his own way. Maybe distancing himself from Mama is the only way he can bear it.

I arrive at the park at a few minutes past six. It isn't very big, just a little bit of grass, two picnic tables, and some trees. The kids' play area is toward the back. I can see in a second that I'm alone. What did I expect after I bailed on him the last time? I told him I'd be here. He said nothing about taking me up on it.

The thought crosses my mind that I should just turn right around and go back home, but then I hear David's voice. "You're late!"

I look up and see him standing on the yellow roof of the play gym. His legs are spread wide for balance, but his feet keep slipping on the dome-shaped metal.

"What are you doing up there?" I holler. "You're going to break your neck!"

"I was keeping watch," he says, grinning. "Come on up. The view's spectacular."

"No thanks."

His arms flail awkwardly, like an injured duck coming in for a landing. He's making me nervous. "Get down here, David, before you kill yourself."

Too late. One foot slides too far forward and David loses his balance. It all happens so fast I don't even have time to scream. Suddenly he's vanished from the roof, and I hear a dull thud behind the gym.

"David!"

I run fast, discovering him sprawled face-first in the sand, groaning. I squat down beside him, wondering if I'm about to take my third ride in an ambulance in as many weeks. David rolls onto his back. Sand covers his face. It's in his eyes, nose, and on his lips. He spits out a wet, gray wad of it. "Yuck."

"Are you all right?" I ask, trying not to laugh. "Is anything broken?"

He sits up and spits again. "Just my pride, not that I ever had any to start with around you." David stands up and brushes himself off. He wipes some of the sand off his face, and then shakes it out of his hair, like a wet dog would shake the water out of its coat. I can't help but burst out laughing.

84

He makes a playful grab for me, but I'm faster. I twist away, just out of reach. He doesn't try again, but grins at me from ear to ear.

"I don't know about you," he says, "but after all that, I'm hungry. How about we get something to eat?"

"Okay. What do you have in mind?"

"We could head to my place. I made some mean chile rellenos for dinner last night—"

"Do you live far?"

"Just through the Lowell pass off Laurel Canyon, actually. Can't miss my house. It's the one that looks like a rainforest."

I love chile rellenos, but I wonder what Papa would say if he found out I'd been at a stranger's house—let alone a boy's—without proper security. David seems to sense my hesitation.

"Or we could just stay in town," he says. "Ever been to Bergie's?"

I shake my head.

"No? You've got to be kidding. *Bergie's?*" David grabs his stomach and groans like he's been mortally wounded.

"What's Bergie's?"

"Only the best sandwich shop in Flintridge. How long have you lived here?" His eyes sparkle at me, playfully doubting my integrity.

I look at the cars parked along the street, guessing which one might be his, but he's already walking away.

"Aren't we driving there?"

"What for?" he asks. "It's just down the street, and it's a perfect day for a walk."

85

I have never heard of Bergie's. Papa doesn't normally let me roam around town by myself, and when we do go out, it's usually to four-star restaurants. I'm sure if Papa knew I was walking into town with David, a server from one of his big shindigs, he'd probably burst a jugular. But I don't care.

After a quick stroll up Foothill Boulevard we reach the sandwich shop. I know now why I've never heard of it. It's nothing but a little hole in the wall wedged in between a vintage record shop and a hair salon. If someone didn't know it was there, they'd walk right past and never even see it. Only the long line of hungry patrons waiting on the sidewalk alludes to the fact that something phenomenal is in our midst.

"There aren't many tables here," David explains. "Most people order ahead for pick-up. Those who don't have to wait their turn, but it's worth the wait."

"Obviously," I reply, noting the collection of businessmen, teens, and women toting babies or shopping bags.

We find a shady spot beside the door where he tells me to wait while he slips inside. Some of the people in line scowl at me, and I realize they're probably jealous that they didn't think to call in their order. A few minutes later, David returns with two Styrofoam boxes in one hand and a couple of sodas in the other. We head back to the park where we settle on the floor of the wooden gazebo where local bands perform at night all summer long. David twists the caps off both sodas and hands me mine. Then he holds up one of the boxes.

"Ta dah!" he says, flipping open the lid. Lying in the box is the thickest Reuben sandwich I've ever seen. Corned beef piled at least two inches high on toasted rye. Sauerkraut.

Thousand Island dressing. Melted Swiss. And a dill pickle spear on the side.

I stare at the monster sandwich, and then at David. "How did you know?" I ask, reaching for the meal that's making my mouth water. It's heavy in my hand and dripping with juice and sauce. Taking a big bite, I roll my eyes from pure satisfaction. David couldn't have looked more pleased if he had made the sandwich himself.

"That interview you gave last year for the local paper. You know, when your dad announced he was running for governor? The writer asked a lot of 'What's your favorite...' questions. And you said your favorite sandwich was a Reuben."

"You remembered all that?"

"Well, not really," he says, blushing. "My uncle is sort of a fan of your dad's. He's cut out a bunch of articles and stuff."

I take another bite of the sandwich. It's so good I can't stand it. "What about you?" I ask between swallows. "What kind of sandwich did you order?"

He lifts the lid to his box and reveals a croissant. "Vegetarian," he says, opening the croissant to prove it. Sure enough there's nothing but tomatoes, cucumbers, and avocado inside. I start to laugh, but my mouth is full. So I'm half laughing, half trying not to spray David.

"What?" he asks defensively.

"Your sandwich," I answer, giggling.

"What's wrong with it?"

"Vegetarian? You don't seem the type."

For the next half hour we eat, we talk, we laugh. It's the most fun I've had in a long time. I feel so relaxed with David that I don't even notice when our food is gone. It's David who finally points out that we finished eating a while ago. I feel almost disappointed that it's over and that I'll have to head home soon. David seems to sense the change in my demeanor.

"Hey, you mind if we stop by the record shop before I take you home?" he asks. "There's something I want to show you."

I don't have anything better to do, so I agree.

The shop is small and smells of dust and cedar, probably from the incense sticks burning on the sales counter. Two ceiling fans turn overhead like propellers, sending a pleasant breeze through the otherwise sweltering store. Nearly every inch of floor space is occupied by wooden bins, each containing a stack of square cardboard album covers. David flips through one stack.

"You ever see some of these?" he asks. "Look. Madonna. Fleetwood Mac. Cher."

"Don't you have an iPod like everyone else?"

He glares at me for a second, but in good humor. "Sure I do, but it's not the same. Analog reigns if you want to really *feel* the music."

I look at him strangely.

"Besides, vinyl has made a comeback," David adds, moving to the next bin and leafing through it. "C'mon. Your dad doesn't own an old stereo? In a house like yours, there's got to be one hiding somewhere."

"Papa's got a portable player in his office. Looks like a box with a handle on it. He played some records for me a few times when I was little, but it hasn't been used in years."

David moves across the aisle to another bin. I walk slowly down the opposite aisle, letting my fingers glide across the top of the smooth, polished wood.

"Ah, here it is." David pulls out an album still in its original plastic. "I read something else in that interview of yours. I spotted this the other day and thought you'd like it."

I take the record from him and for a moment I can't believe what I'm seeing.

"You do like Broadway musicals, right?" he asks.

I nod.

"Then you've heard of *Les Misérables*?"

"Of course I have. It's my favorite."

"I know. It's everyone's favorite. But this is special. Look."

The cover is in black and white. Across the top is the title, below is a sketch of a young girl holding a stick broom. The girl's face is the iconic image for the play. I look closer and gasp in surprise.

"It's the original French conceptual album," says David, "the inspiration for the English version."

I'd heard about this, but until now I'd never thought to listen to it. But what's even more astounding is that David took the time to share it with me. "This is amazing," I tell him. "I don't know what to say."

"You don't have this on your iPod?"

"No, I don't."

"Well, even if you did, you should hear it on LP. It's a different experience altogether. Here, I'll take that."

I hand the album to David, but instead of putting it back in the bin, he carries it to the counter. "I'd like to purchase this distinctive contribution to theatrical history," he states in the worst fake French accent I've ever heard.

I start to protest. "David, you don't have to—" But he holds up his hand to silence me. The cashier rings it up and David pays with an ATM card.

"Jolly ho, my good man," he says, accepting the bag with the record inside.

"I think that's British," I tell him.

"Righty-O, then." He shrugs and hands me the package. When I reach out for it, he steps close and leans forward. At first I think he wants to tell me something, but his face keeps getting closer.

He wants to kiss me? *Now?*

I don't have time to think. A second more and his lips will be on mine. His eyes are closed now. He can't see me pulling away. I step back, but he keeps coming. Then he takes a step forward and—Wham!

Who the heck installs electrical outlets on the floor? David trips on it and goes down—hard. On the way, he reaches for something to hold in order to break his fall. He grabs the edge of one of the record bins. It doesn't work. David hits the ground, and the wooden bin topples on him, spewing records across the floor like square Frisbees. It's all over in a half a second.

"David! Are you okay?" I bend down and dig through the pile. I pick up an Elvis Presley album to see David looking up at me. But the expression on his face leaves me feeling cold. I expect embarrassment, annoyance, even anger. But instead he looks wounded—right through the heart.

Once we've helped pick up the mess, David walks out of the store a little faster than his normal pace. I try to keep up, but his legs are longer than mine and I quickly fall behind.

"Hey!" I call out. "David, wait!"

He stops abruptly and lets me catch up. "C'mon," I say, a little out of breath, "I know you're mad but—"

"I'm such an idiot," he says, cutting me off.

"What? You're not an idiot. It was my fault. I'm sorry—"

"Sorry for what?" He turns to face me. "Mira, I'm the one who's sorry. I shouldn't have done that. I didn't give you any warning. I mean, I wasn't expecting you to make out with me or anything. I was just going to give you a little kiss, and I shouldn't have, I know. It's just that … well … you're so damn pretty."

The compliment throws me off-kilter for a second. It's kind of corny, I know, but nice, too. David begins walking again, slower this time. I walk beside him in silence, just trying to grapple with everything that's happened.

It's about a mile to the mansion, and we don't say anything the whole way. We stop when we reach the gate. "I'd better say goodbye here," I tell him. "Listen, David, I really am sorry."

He stares into my eyes like he's trying to read my soul. The way he looks at me makes me feel all warm inside.

"Mira, I won't lie to you. I do want to kiss you. It's all I've been thinking about since I saw you at your father's fundraiser two weeks ago. I know it's stupid—"

"It's not stupid," I say, my eyes fixed on his. I can't look away. It's as though some invisible magnetic force is drawing

91

me to him. I feel excited and frightened all at the same time. And then reality hits me. I break away from his gaze.

"It's not that I don't want you to kiss me—"

"Then you do want me to?"

His expression turns hopeful, and seeing him this way crushes me.

"I can't, David."

"But why not?"

"It's complicated, okay?"

The hope in his eyes vanishes, and the wounded expression from the record store returns. He nods as if he understands, but says nothing. Instead he holds out the paper bag with the record.

"Thank you," I say, taking it from him.

"Can I see you again?"

"Sure," I tell him immediately.

"Tomorrow?"

I can barely hide my groan. "I have an appointment, actually."

"I'll take you."

"To my appointment? But you don't even know what it's for or where it is."

"Does it matter?" He shrugs indifferently. "Anyway, I've got the day off."

I start to decline his invitation, but how else would I get there? Then I think of how uncomfortable it would be having Jordan along as an escort. Not to mention what he would tell my father.

"All right. Thanks. Can you pick me up at nine?"

"Sure."

As David walks away, he glances back at me over his shoulder and gives a little wave. I find myself wishing more than anything that I *could* kiss him.

# 15

"MIRA, IS THAT YOU?"

I step through the front door to the mansion and spot Papa sitting at the dining table. He must have just got home, because he's still wearing his gloves.

"Where have you been?" he asks.

"Out walking," I tell him. He glances at the package under my arm. "I found this record shop and picked something up."

"Records?" Papa sounds amused. "I didn't know anyone still listened to them."

"You have that old record player still, don't you? I think I saw it in your office once."

"It's there in one of the cabinets. You're welcome to it."

I tell him thanks and start for the kitchen. Papa's home office is at the back of the house, and the quickest way there is through the kitchen. As I walk past him, I happen to glance at the papers lying between his hands, papers with the hospital's logo on them—and Mama's name printed in bold letters at the top.

"What are those?" I ask.

Papa shifts a hand over them, spreading out his fingers. "Nothing," he says. "You saw your mother again today?"

"This morning before my therapy appointment."

"Any change?"

"No. Not yet." I slip my hands into my hoodie pocket. I don't even realize I've done it until my fingers find each other. "Did you make it over there today?"

Papa's stare remains on the papers in front of him. "Hmm? What was that?" he asks, distracted.

"I asked if you'd gone to the hospital today."

"Yes, I was there."

"But did you see Mama?"

He doesn't answer. His eyes are still fixed on those papers. "What's the point, Mira?" he says finally.

"What do you mean?"

"I mean you've gone just about every day. Why?"

"Mama needs me," I say.

Papa glances up at me. He looks tired. Worn out. "She's in a coma, Mira."

It's the way he says it that irritates me, the resignation in his voice. I try to bite my tongue, but I can't keep silent. "Maybe she didn't have to be," I tell him.

His expression changes. I can see the patronizing doubt in his eyes. "What are you talking about?"

"The Trazodone."

"What about the Trazodone? Didn't you confirm the test results with Dr. Zimmerman?" Papa rolls his eyes. "Oh, that's right. You don't believe the blood tests. You think she didn't take a sedative that night."

"She didn't. And she didn't give herself the insulin either."

"Mira, how could you possibly know that?"

I don't answer him. He never did understand me. Why should now be any different?

"I see," continues Papa. "You can read your mother's thoughts, is that it? Her memory reveals that she didn't take any sleeping pills or insulin, and yet the blood tests confirm, without any doubt, that she did."

He takes a deep breath and lets it out slowly. After a minute or so, he speaks again. His voice is subdued, as if the words are difficult to say. "Dr. Zimmerman says she will probably never recover."

His words hit me like a boxer's fist. Of course I already knew it. I, more than anyone, know how much damage Mama suffered that night. But maybe somewhere deep inside, I was hoping for a miracle.

Papa stares at his hands. If I didn't know him better, I'd swear his eyes were tearing up. After a moment, he looks up at me, but his eyes are dry. "Mira, we need to discuss our options."

"What options?"

"It's just a matter of time before she—before your mother's body stops functioning. Why prolong the inevitable?"

"What are you talking about?" I point at the papers beneath Papa's hand. "What are those? They have Mama's name on them."

He hesitates, then lifts the top sheet and hands it to me. I see now what they are, but I can hardly believe it. "Termination of Life Support? No! You can't!"

He rises from the chair and faces me, his expression pleading. "This has taken its toll on you, Mira. It's the humane thing to do."

The space between us feels like miles. I see the sadness in his eyes and think of what Dr. Walsh said, that deep down he's hurting as much as I am. But to terminate life support? If he really cared about Mama, or about me, he could never do something like that. Could he?

I hold out the paper to him. "You've already signed it."

He takes it, laying it carefully on top of the others, and then rests his hand there.

"Don't," I say. Grief and anger swell in my throat, constricting my vocal chords. "Don't kill Mama."

Papa stares at me like I am a stranger to him, unrecognizable. I can see that I've hurt him, but I don't care.

His reply is muted and resigned. "She's already gone."

I'm shaking. He continues talking to me, but his eyes refuse to meet mine. His voice becomes steady, practiced, like one of his political speeches. Whatever trace of emotion was there before has vanished.

"I know it's hard to accept," he says, "but we must—"

"Please, Papa."

"—move on, Mira. Don't you see?"

"Papa, listen to me."

"Be adult about this."

"No—"

"It's time to let go."

"No!"

My outburst takes Papa by surprise. His body stiffens in response, his fists clenching at his sides. But I'm not frightened.

"She's still in there! I know you don't believe me, but it's true. I've felt her, seen her—her mind, I mean."

"Mira—"

"Please, Papa. You have to believe me." Tears spring from my eyes. I try to fight them, but the battle is already lost. "Just give her more time, *please*. She wants to live."

"That's enough, Mira!"

Papa's fist comes down on the table so hard that the flower vase in the center wobbles precariously until it finally settles back into place. We both notice him in the same moment—Jordan standing in the entryway. How long has he been there? He glances at the papers on the table, but says nothing. He just turns and walks into the living room.

Jordan's brief presence somehow quells the tension between Papa and me.

"I'm sorry," Papa says, rubbing his temples with his thumbs. "You're right, of course. All this pressure—your mother—the investigation—those relentless reporters—it's all just getting to me, I suppose." He looks at me with an apologetic expression. "I'll just file these in my office for now. There's no rush. I won't do anything until you're ready."

He takes a few steps away from me toward the entryway, but then he stops. "Maybe all we need is a good night's rest and a day off. Hmm? Why don't you and I take a drive up the coast tomorrow, like we used to do when you were little? I could clear my schedule."

I remember those drives, though they were not always pleasant. What I remember most is Mama and Papa bickering in the front seat.

Composing myself, I pick up a linen napkin from one of the place settings on the table and wipe the moisture from my cheeks. "I can't," I tell him. "I've got other plans."

"Plans? With who?"

I have to think for a second. I can't tell him about the Institute. He'd pepper me with questions and insist on sending Jordan to accompany me.

"A friend from school," I say, which isn't a lie. "We're going shopping." Which is. "Of course, if you want me to cancel—"

"No, don't cancel your excursion on my account, but maybe I should send Jordan with you."

I give him the 'you've-got-to-be-kidding' glare.

"All right, but at least promise me you'll take your phone with you. I can't stand not being able to contact you when I need to."

"I promise," I tell him.

"And let's plan to do something together this weekend. I think you and I both would benefit from a little R&R."

Papa turns away and joins Jordan in the living room. They start talking in voices too low for me to understand. I head for the kitchen, which is empty this time of night. Its stainless steel appliances gleam, and the marble tile on the floor shines. It's hard to believe that anyone actually cooks in here.

Once through the kitchen, I continue down the hall to my father's office. I don't know why he calls it that. He hardly ever uses it anymore, not since he resigned from Rawley. Now he spends most of his time at campaign headquarters.

I flip on the light switch, and the single overhead lamp illuminates the spacious room. Dark wood paneling covers three of the walls, and the fourth is nothing but floor to ceiling book shelves and cabinets. In the center of the room sits Papa's desk, formidable black mahogany carved with Aztec-like designs. A statue of a bald eagle in flight is perched on one corner while an antique Tiffany lamp sits on the other.

It's been at least a year or more since I've been in here, and even then it was just to fetch a book from the shelf that my father asked me to find. But even so, it isn't difficult to locate what I've come for.

I wipe the layer of dust off the record player cover with a paper towel from the kitchen. Then I set it on Papa's desk and plug it into the wall. I don't know where his old records are anymore. Probably hidden away and forgotten in a box or drawer somewhere. Slipping the black vinyl disc from the cover and setting it on the turntable, I lower the needle into place and turn it on. As the LP starts to spin, I hear a few faint crackles. The sound is odd, as if I'm calling the artists from their graves to bring back the beauty that's been gone for too long.

Then... the opening prelude to *Les Misérables* begins. Not the brisk, powerful theme I'm used to hearing, but a slow, lilting melody. The richness and depth of the notes thrill me. I close my eyes and imagine myself sitting in the front row beside the orchestra pit. When the voices begin, the poetry of the French lyrics melt into my soul, and I realize that David was right. This is an entirely different experience than anything I've ever known before.

Suddenly it hits me all at once—the music, Mama, those forms. I crumple to the floor beside Papa's desk and let the tears fall until long after the artists have returned to their graves.

# 16

AT EIGHT A.M. MY CELL PHONE alarm wakes me from a deep sleep. I shower, dress, and snatch a yogurt from the kitchen before heading outside to wait for David. He arrives in a bright-orange sports car with black racing stripes. Hopping out, he opens the passenger side door.

"Nice wheels," I tell him, dropping into the black leather bucket seat.

"Thanks. '77 Celica GT. You don't see many of these around anymore."

Once he's in beside me, he revs the engine and puts it into gear.

"David, are you sure about this?" I ask, suddenly doubting myself. "Taking me to this appointment, I mean. If you have something better to do, I can get there on my own."

He grins at me in a way that melts me from the inside out. "I can't think of anything I'd rather do than spend a couple hours with you. Ready?"

The car jumps forward, quickly gaining momentum. The car is an old stick-shift model. Even the windows are manual.

I roll mine down and let the wind whip through my hair. David does the same.

"The car," he shouts over the wind and engine noise, "is my uncle's, but he lets me drive it since he can't anymore." Pride is evident on David's face. Here, in this car, he seems confident and relaxed. I like seeing him this way.

We jump on the 2 south and then take the 134 west toward Glendale. I printed a map off Google, but David insists on using the GPS app on his phone to locate the clinic instead. We arrive about twenty minutes later, park in back, and walk around to the front door. Inside, we're greeted by an elderly receptionist with cotton-candy hair and bright-red lipstick.

"Do you have an appointment?" she asks, glaring at us over the rims of her bifocals as if we've somehow disturbed her bright and shiny day. "Or are you here for the tour?"

"An appointment, I think."

The woman looks over her desk calendar and suddenly she's all smiles. "Miss Ortiz, is that right?"

"That must be me." I laugh nervously, but she doesn't seem to notice.

She hands me a clipboard with a blank Patient Information form and a pen clipped to it. "Fill this out," she says.

I stand at the desk and scrawl the answers to the questions: name, address, phone number, reason for visit. I'm not exactly sure what to say for the last one, so I leave it blank. When I'm finished, the receptionist asks David to wait in the lobby. She escorts me to a roomy office in the back where she introduces me to Dr. Frank Felton, a lean man in his late thirties sporting a scraggly goatee and a pair of black gages.

"Nice to meet you, Mira," he says, standing behind his desk. He extends his hand, but then quickly retracts it. Dr. Walsh must have filled him in on the details beforehand. "Why don't you take a seat?"

I sit in a chair in front of his desk and note the chaos. Papers are sprawled everywhere, a coffee mug filled with pencils, and an open one pound bag of peanut M&Ms. So different than my father's uncluttered desk at home. I feel immediately at ease here.

"So, your therapist set up this interview for you. Trisha Walsh and I go way back. We went to the same high school. Did she tell you that?"

"No, she didn't." She didn't have to tell me. I recognized him the moment I came in.

"Yeah, well… I'm glad she thought to contact me about your gift."

"It's not a gift."

Dr. Felton leans back in his chair and taps his fingertips together. "Okay. What would you call it then?"

"A curse. I can't touch anyone without being deluged with all their mental crap. I hate it."

"And you have no idea how this so-called curse developed?"

"I think I've always had it to some extent," I reply. "I remember as a child I would get impressions or insights into how people were feeling or what they were thinking. It wasn't a big deal, and it didn't bother me then. I didn't even know I was doing anything out of the ordinary. It's only been the last few months that it's morphed into what it is now."

"Was there any catalyst that may have triggered its development? A physical or psychological trauma of some kind? An illness?"

"Not that I'm aware of. In fact, I've been pretty healthy. Except for my two recent visits to the ER, the only time I saw a doctor in the past decade was when I got immunized."

"Right. The new Guadium law. Wish they had that when I was your age," he says, smiling. "Would have made adolescence a hell of a lot easier for me. So, you received your Gaudium injection on your birthday then?"

I nod. "Just like everyone else. But I guess it didn't take, or maybe it was a bad batch. Because when all this hit, I couldn't handle it."

"You became depressed." Dr. Felton selects a pen from the container on his desk and tests it on the corner of his notebook. Then he scrawls something inside. "Trisha—I mean, Dr. Walsh, said you've attempted suicide twice despite being immunized and being given oral Gaudium as well," he continues, setting his pen down again.

At the mention of suicide, I tense up. Exactly how much did Dr. Walsh tell him about me?

"You know, I think I've changed my mind about this," I say, getting to my feet. "I shouldn't have come."

Dr. Felton holds his hands up, defensively. "Whoa, whoa," he says. "Did I say something wrong? If I did, Mira, I apologize. Don't leave. Please."

I glance between him and the door, then cautiously sit back down.

"It must be intense," he says, tapping his lips with the side of his forefinger, "seeing inside another person's head."

"Intense is a major understatement."

"Can you describe it for me?"

Describe it. I've been trying to do that since day one, to put it into words, but somehow words always fall short.

"It's like a brainwashing movie, sort of. You know, the ones that flash all those images on the screen so fast you can't really see all the details, but you get the general idea of what you've seen. Only for me it's not just images. It's emotions, dreams, memories. And all the details are there, everything, except it all comes at me so fast and in no particular order— like a random info dump. Every time it happens, all those other thoughts crowd into my brain threatening to push *my* thoughts and *my* memories out. I lose myself for just an instant, and in that instant it's like I'm someone else. When I wake up the next morning I'm me again, only changed a little. Those thoughts and feelings have become part of me. But I don't want them. I don't want any of them."

Dr. Felton considers this for a few moments, then he swivels his chair around, takes a book from his bookshelf, and turns back to face me. He opens the book up to a black and white photo of a man and pushes the book toward me. "That's Edgar Cayce," he explains. "Dr. Walsh told you about him?"

"A little."

"He made a lot of predictions, which are very interesting, but he also did readings. Do you know what a reading is?"

"Telling someone something personal that only they would know?"

He nods. "Something like that, yes. Edgar Cayce defied all logic. He would lie down on a couch and put himself into a trance. In that state he would answer questions about people and things he couldn't possibly know unless he had some sort of extraordinary gift. Sometimes visitors would need to touch Cayce to help him get the ball rolling, so to speak. And Cayce isn't the only one. There have been dozens of documented cases like his, though he is the best known. My point is, Mira, that what you're experiencing is not necessarily unique."

He stops talking, letting me absorb everything he's just said, which seems to be that what I am, what I experience, has happened to other people. But has it really? I looked up a little about Edgar Cayce on the internet before coming here, and a lot of what I read sounded bogus. It reminded me of those palm readers at the fair. Plunk down a fiver and she'll tell you your fortune, usually vague stuff that could apply to anyone. Throw out enough of that garbage, and something is bound to come true.

I know one thing. I'm no fortune teller. I don't see the future, and I don't make wild guesses about people's lives based on some vague impressions.

Dr. Felton must sense my skepticism because he closes the book and starts shuffling through the papers on his desk. Finding what he's looking for, he slides a printed form toward me.

"This is a preliminary release form," he tells me. "It gives us permission to study you. Of course, we'll need parental consent for you to join the program officially."

He hands me a black ballpoint, but I don't pick it up. "I'm not sure I want to be studied."

"I understand," says Dr. Felton, though I doubt he does. "But I would like to know the extent of your abilities. It seems possible that you were born with a latent power. I suspect that something occurred to bring it out, to fully emerge. Perhaps that initial exposure to Gaudium. I realize that providing a reading may be uncomfortable for you, but it would give me a more accurate idea of what we're dealing with here."

I knew this would likely be asked of me when I walked through the door. I mean, that's why I came, isn't it? Dr. Walsh seemed to think this guy could help me, or at least point me in the right direction. Even so, the prospect of exposing myself to the psyche of anyone, let alone a stranger, sets me on edge. Despite my own resistance, however, I agree and sign the form.

Dr. Felton's face lights up like a little boy who's seen Santa for the very first time. He can hardly contain his eagerness. He turns around again, reaching for something on a shelf behind him. When he turns back, he's got a thick, wooden board in his hands about two inches deep and a foot square. He puts this down on the desk between us, then slides open a small drawer and starts to remove plastic blocks of varying shapes and sizes.

"It seems primitive, I know," he says, apologetically, "but the Zener test is a classic method of evaluating clairvoyant abilities."

"Zener test?" I recall reading something about that online. "I thought that had to do with cards with pictures on them."

"Cards. Sure. But kids prefer these." He pauses, holding a block above the board, and looks at me as if he just realized the absurdity of his words.

"I am sixteen," I say, and I can't help but crack a grin.

"Right. Sorry."

He separates the blocks with a cardboard divider so half are on his side and half on mine.

"I'll begin by evaluating your extra sensory perception," he explains. "I'll arrange my blocks in a pattern. The objective is for you to arrange yours to match mine."

"Except I told you before, I'm not a mind-reader. At least not like this."

"Bear with me here." He seems excited, and he uses his hands to punctuate his words. "We'll do this the traditional way first to establish a baseline. Then we'll do it again using your … um … ability. Ready?"

Even though playing with blocks seems rather childish to me, I wait patiently while Dr. Felton arranges the blocks on his side of the divider.

"Okay," he announces when he's done. He glances at me with a look of expectation and challenge on his face that reminds me of the countless games of Battleship I'd played with Mama over the years. Even though we had a virtual version of it on our game system, Mama always insisted on using the same old plastic set she'd had since she was a kid. It was missing one of the submarines and was short a few pegs, but I loved watching her face while she placed her ships in strategic patterns on her board. She looked most like a kid at those times, full of anticipation and gleeful triumph.

"Your turn," says Dr. Felton. "Concentrate and try to recreate my pattern. Take your time."

In front of me are six different colored blocks: red, green, yellow, orange, blue and purple—each one a different shape. I study them for a few moments, wondering how anyone could actually take this seriously, but for Dr. Felton's sake I decide to give it my best shot. Focusing all my attention on whatever invisible brain waves might be floating between him and me, I push the blocks into place with my finger.

"Done," I say.

With only a brief hesitation, Dr. Felton lifts the divider. He rubs the side of his jaw with his thumb, nodding thoughtfully, but I can see the disappointment on his face.

"It's okay. It's okay," he says, probably more for his benefit than mine. "You got one right."

"Yeah, but the odds of getting one right for even normal people are probably pretty high. It's called a coincidence."

"True. True." He smiles at me and replaces the divider. "So we can assume then that you are normal."

Anything but…

"Now let's try it again, but this time during a reading." He smiles again, like there's some private joke between us. Then he looks down at the board, his eyebrows knit together with serious intent. I hear the scraping sound of blocks being pushed around the surface of the board. There are a couple of pauses when he seems to change his mind. Then he sits back and examines the board with a satisfied finality.

"All right," he says. "Are you ready?"

"As ready as I'll ever be," I answer.

"How do we, um…?"

"Just hold out your hand," I tell him.

He rolls up his right sleeve, which is completely unnecessary, and then he lays his hand palm up on his desk. I hesitantly place my hand next to his, not ready to touch quite yet. I have to work up the nerve.

"Does it hurt?" he asks.

"It hurts like hell," I answer.

I take a few deep breaths, then tip my hand just enough to brush against his skin.

His mind erupts into mine like a nuclear blast, shrapnel memories slicing through my brain in a single instant. A young boy wearing leg braces dealing with the brunt of ridicule by his peers. A disappointed father who longed for a sports hero but got a science geek son instead. And lots of happy memories, too: birthday parties and trips to the zoo, his love for his mother who adored him. But things turned dark later on in medical school. I witness a string of heartbreaks, failed romances, struggles to keep up in his studies, the road to neurology, and a strange unexpected detour that led him here.

The images spin around in my head so fast that trying to focus on a single one is a little like trying to jump onto a speeding train. I concentrate, searching for his most recent thoughts—the ones with the blocks. When I've found what I need, I withdraw my hand and set it in my lap. Dr. Felton leaves his where it lies.

"Well?" he asks. "What did you see?"

I study Dr. Felton's face for a moment, this man who has had his share of disappointments in life, but has somehow managed to stay positive. A man full of insecurities—and hope. How do I tell him that he has nothing to offer me? That I've seen all his studies, all his knowledge, and none of it comes even close to what I am. Edgar Cayce was a fascinating man, perhaps, but I am nothing like Edgar Cayce. I'm a singularity. A freak.

I get up from my chair. Dr. Felton rises, too, looking surprised and disappointed.

"There's nothing you can do for me, Dr. Felton. But thanks for your time."

I look at the blocks in front of me, and then rearrange them quickly. I lift the divider, revealing a perfect set of matching blocks. Then I head for the door.

"How do you know there's nothing I can do?" He comes around his desk to stand in front of me, his eyes fixed expectantly on mine. "Mira, tell me what you saw."

I hold his gaze despite the fact that my instinct is to run away and hide. And I'd probably be doing that right now if Dr. Felton wasn't standing in my way. The muscles in my jaw tighten, and I take a deep breath. Then I give him what he wants.

"You were teased as a kid, but you got over it. You have a very strained relationship with your football-obsessed dad. You want a family of your own, but the last girl you dated hated kids so you dumped her. You like Reese's Peanut Butter Cups, Mint Chocolate Chip ice cream, live theater, and flannel bed sheets."

Dr. Felton's mouth drops open, which is pretty comical, actually. I grab the doorknob, twist and pull. Stunned into silence, he steps away from the door to let me through.

"Oh, and one more thing," I add for good measure. "You shouldn't have cheated on that biology final. You didn't give yourself enough credit. You would have passed on your own."

With that said I step out into the hall and close the door behind me.

# 17

I DON'T GET FAR DOWN THE HALL before I hear Dr. Felton's door open again, followed by hurried footsteps. He reaches me in a few short strides. The reception area is just a few yards away. I can see the front door from here and want more than anything to get through it.

"Wait, Mira." Dr. Felton takes me by the arm, my hoodie shielding me, and turns me around. "I know you think I can't help you," he says in a hushed voice, presumably so that no one else can hear. "I don't know what you saw in me that made you believe that, and I admit this is without precedence, but that's all the more reason why you should work with me. I have resources, contacts, computer programs, testing equipment. I want to know, as much as you do, how this happened to you."

"There's no test on earth capable of answering that question," I tell him.

"Then we'll construct one that *is* capable. Just work with me, all right? I'll take a few days to get some preliminary guidelines down, make some inquiries. Then you'll come back and we'll take it from there. Give me a chance, Mira."

Apparently he wasn't quiet enough, because David has now appeared at the end of the hall, watching us. I realize what he's looking at—Dr. Felton's hand on my arm. His eyes flick to mine. Am I safe, he's wondering? Do I need help?

Dr. Felton releases me. "Think about what I've said. Just call me when you're ready."

I continue down the hall toward the exit. As I pass through it, I feel a sense of relief. David and I walk back to his car in silence. He's been a good sport so far, not asking any questions. But I can see the curiosity on his face. I wait until we're back on the freeway heading home before I speak.

"This trip was for nothing," I tell him. "I'm sorry I wasted your time, David."

"You didn't," he replies, adjusting the rearview mirror. "Time with you is always time well spent."

I smile at the compliment, but I can't help but feel the disappointment weighing down on me. I had hoped, truly hoped, for more.

"There's nothing for me back there."

"Really?" David raises an eyebrow. "That guy seemed pretty sure there was. Are you going to call him back?"

Am I? I guess I'll see what Dr. Walsh thinks about everything after our appointment next week. I'm sure she'll have some thoughts on the subject. But for the moment, I really don't know.

I roll my window down and hold my hand out, resisting the air pushing against it. I used to do that as a little girl. I enjoyed the challenge of arm wrestling with an invisible opponent.

"So," David says, "where to now?"

I consider the question and get the feeling that no matter how I answer, David would take me there. But I can't think of anything.

"I don't know," I tell him. "Where do you want to go?"

"Me?"

"Sure. If you could go anywhere in the world right now, where would it be?"

He doesn't answer right away. Instead he cracks an embarrassed smile and laughs a little.

"What?" I ask, my curiosity piqued. "It can't be so bad."

"It's not. I just … it doesn't matter where I'd go."

"Oh, c'mon. Tell me."

He glances over at me, and those eyes of his catch me off guard. So open. So sincere.

"I'll tell you someday," he says. "I promise."

And somehow that's enough. I believe him.

We continue on with the radio blaring and our windows rolled down. We sing along to every song whether we know the lyrics or not, and when we stop for gas, David buys a stash of candy bars and energy drinks—enough for a week-long road trip. By the time we get back to Flintridge, we're totally pumped up on sugar and caffeine.

"I'm going to be sick tonight." I giggle. My seat is completely reclined and my feet stick out of my window.

"I know where to go," David says.

I close my eyes and feel the motion of his turns, the stop and go at the traffic signals, and the vibration of the engine.

The wind blowing against my feet and legs, the cyclone of air swirling around inside the car … it's an amazing feeling of being totally free and completely spontaneous.

A little while later, the car comes to a slow stop. The engine idles for a second and then shuts off.

"We're here."

I open my eyes and sit up. I'm surprised to see our park in front of me, just a short distance from the mansion. We could have gone anywhere, and yet David brought me here.

"Hold this for me?" he asks, handing me his cell phone. I slip it into my hoodie pocket, and then suddenly he's out of the car and doing cartwheels across the grass. He manages to complete three of them before collapsing in a dizzy, laughing heap. Then he rolls onto his stomach and starts kicking his feet and scooping his arms in wide circles like he's swimming.

"Come on in," he shouts. "The water's fine!"

I join him on the grass. He rolls onto his back and moves his arms and legs up and down.

"Snow angels," he tells me. "Try it."

I groan with embarrassment.

"No, really," he says. "You asked me where I wanted to go. Well, *here* could be anywhere. Right now I'm in Big Bear lying on a fresh patch of snow making snow angels."

I tentatively lay back and let the smell of freshly mowed grass fill my senses. Helen's going to kill me when she sees the grass stains, but I try it anyway. I move my arms up and down, my legs in and out. The sun shines down on us through the tree branches above, and I have to admit it feels great.

"What about you?" asks David. "Where are you right now?"

"Disneyland," I answer quickly. "Tom Sawyer's Island playing hide and seek in the caves."

I get up and run over to the play gym. In three seconds flat I've scaled the kiddy slide and slipped into the little tunnel beside it. David's face pops into view.

"Boo!" he shouts. I scramble out of the tunnel and follow him onto the bridge. He sways the metal slats back and forth. "Pirates of the Caribbean! That crazy rope bridge! Hang on or you'll fall into the gorge!"

I scream at the top of my lungs, and then take a flying leap off the side of the bridge. I land on my knees in the sand and pretend to keep falling, falling … falling.

"I'll save you!" shouts David, jumping down beside me. He scoops me up in his arms and runs through the sand. "I'm a bird! I'm a plane! I'm … Superman!"

He trips and we both fall back down in the sand, laughing our heads off. When our laughter quiets, we lie on our backs just gazing up at the blue sky. For a few moments, at least, I forget about my condition and about Mama being in the hospital. For those moments, I'm just me again—happy.

"David?" I say, still trying to catch my breath.

"Yeah?"

"Thank you."

"For what?"

I shrug my shoulders even though he's not looking at me. "For sharing this day with me."

"It wasn't a big deal, but you're welcome."

"I mean it." I roll on to my side and prop my head on my arm. "You have no idea what life has been like for me, how things have been so dark and hopeless. And yet when I'm with you, somehow I've got a reason to smile again. I don't know how you do it."

David rolls onto his side, too. We look into each other's eyes. I wonder what David sees when he looks at me.

"Mira, I knew there was something different about you the first moment I saw you. And then when I spotted you at your father's fundraiser hiding behind that horrible plant, I had to take a chance. I wanted to know you. I can't begin to put myself in your shoes, with your mother being sick and all, but I'd like to try to understand if only you'll trust me enough to let me in."

Trust him. How do I do that? I haven't trusted anyone in such a long time—except Mama.

"All right, you want to understand me?" I stand up, brushing the sand from my clothes. "Then come with me."

I start walking toward his car. David's up in a heartbeat, walking beside me.

"Okay," he says. "So… where are we going?"

# 18

THE HOSPITAL ROOM SMELLS faintly of roses thanks to the fresh bouquets I've kept beside Mama's bed, but it does little to mask the pervasive scent of ammonia and urine that follow us in from the hall.

Mama lies on her back, her arms resting on top of the blue blanket that covers her body. If someone didn't know any better, they would think she was taking a nap. Except for the gray circles that have formed around her eyes and the respirator attached to her mouth, she looks just the same as she did that morning I tried to wake her.

David stands beside me at the foot of Mama's bed. "She's beautiful," he says quietly.

Hearing him say those words makes me happy. She is beautiful. But then he adds, "Like mother, like daughter."

His comment takes me off guard. Fortunately, the nurse comes in before David can notice that I'm blushing.

"Hey, Mira," she says as she checks Mama's IV level. Jessie is one of several nurses assigned to Mama's care. She's young, in her early twenties, with bright-blue eyes and a comfortable smile. "You brought a friend?"

After I introduce her to David, Jessie removes the wilted purple roses from a glass vase on the nightstand. David drops in the fresh bouquet of yellow ones we picked up on the way, and Jessie gives me a wink and thumbs up behind his back. I feel my cheeks turning red all over again.

"All right then," says Jessie, "I'll leave the three of you alone. If you need anything, just buzz." She points to the button on the wall over Mama's bed, more for David's benefit, I guess, than mine.

After Jessie leaves, David pulls up a stool and sits down. "I've met the nurse," he says, making a show of smoothing down his hair and straightening an invisible tie, "now for the real test ... the parent."

I lean over the bed a little to make sure she can hear me. "Mama?" I say. "Mama, this is David, a friend of mine."

"Nice to meet you, Mrs. Ortiz." David gives a little wave, but there is nothing apprehensive or condescending in the gesture or his tone. "You know, Mira," he continues, "I think your Mama would like me."

"*Would* like you? I'm sure she likes you now."

"Is that so?"

"Yes, most definitely."

He lets out a soft laugh, like the news pleases him.

"You don't believe me?" I ask.

"Sure, I believe you, Mira." His tone is more serious now. His gaze fixes on mine. "I really am sorry about your mother. I shouldn't have made light of it."

He looks down at the floor. He's ashamed, though I'm not sure why. Does he think he's offended me? Does he believe I'm so sensitive that I can't enjoy a little humor?

"David, it's all right," I tell him. "I wasn't kidding when I said Mama likes you."

"But she never met me. Not officially anyway."

"She's meeting you now."

"Mira, she doesn't know I'm here."

He's starting to look concerned. I realize that now is the time. This is the moment I've been dreading, but it's all or nothing. I might as well get it over with.

"This is why I brought you here," I begin. "You said you wanted to understand me."

"I do."

"Okay then."

I hesitate. No matter how many times I do this, I can't get used to it, just like you never get used to getting burned. Finally I will myself to reach out my right hand and simply lay it on top of my mother's hand. The electric shock tears through me, but I ignore the pain.

"Mama does like you, immensely," I say to David. "She likes your voice. It is ... *amable*?"

"Kind? I thought you didn't speak Spanish?"

"I don't."

David looks at me intently. He glances to my mother and back to me. I can tell he doesn't know what to make of this.

I look at Mama, and I feel my face go warm with embarrassment. I have to remind myself that Mama is in a coma.

"Mama, no," I tell her.

"What?" asks David.

I'm sure my face is bright red now. "Mama wonders if you've been a gentleman with me. She wants to make sure we haven't…"

A look of comprehension crosses David's face, which quickly turns red as well.

"No!" he says, nearly laughing. "No…" But then his expression changes. He stands abruptly, pressing his fists into his hips, and his voice gets a little louder.

"Mira, what are you doing?"

"I'm trying to show you."

"Show me what? That you can make a joke out of this? Your mother is in a coma for crissake!"

"She's still here." I let go of Mama, and the pain subsides.

David sits down again. He's whispering now, not wanting others to overhear. "Of course she's still here. I'm sure you've been told to communicate with her, right? Let her hear your voice? I get it."

"No, you don't get it. This isn't about Mama. It's about me. I'm not like anyone else."

"That much we agree on."

"David," I begin, my voice quiet and slow. "When I touch people, skin to skin, I see everything inside them. Thoughts, feelings, memories … all of it. In a single instant, that person's psyche enters my own. See how I touched my mother's hand? She's in there, David. She's comatose, but she's still thinking! New things every day. The smell of ammonia when the janitor comes in to mop the floor, the sounds of the heart monitor and the murmured

123

conversations between the nurses, the feel of this blanket against her skin. She's taking it all in."

David doesn't respond, so I continue. "This is why I see Dr. Walsh. It's why I went to that clinic today. I don't understand it any more than you do, but that doesn't make it fake."

David nods his head and rises from his stool. "This is why you won't kiss me?"

"Yes."

His eyes betray how hurt he feels. This is not what I expected. But what did I expect? For him to shout hallelujah and take every word I say as gospel truth?

"Now I do understand," he says as he walks to the door. "But you didn't have to go to so much trouble to get rid of me. All you had to say was goodbye."

And with that, David walks out.

The truth hits me like an arrow that's been shot through my heart. He doesn't believe me.

# 19

I FOLLOW DAVID OUT INTO the hospital waiting room and find him sitting with his face cradled in his hands. I take the chair beside him. Then... I wait. It doesn't seem right for me to speak. I've already said enough. He needs time to process it.

After a while he straightens up and leans back in his chair. He doesn't look at me when he speaks. "I'm sorry," he says, the fingers of his right hand drumming against the chair arm. "I just needed a minute."

The drumming stops and he leans forward again, clasping his hands in front of him. "I like you, Mira. If you don't feel the same about me, I have to respect that."

"You've got it wrong, David. That's not it at all."

"What then?" He looks directly at me. His gaze is intense, as if his eyes alone could draw from me some hidden truth.

"I told you—in there. Something happens to me when I come in contact with other people. I know it's hard to believe," I continue. "I can't expect you to believe me, but whether you do or don't, it doesn't change the fact that it's true. And if it helps at all, you should know that I hate it. I hate it so much that I—"

For some reason, I can't say it. He already thinks I'm insane. If I tell him I'm suicidal, too, he'll probably run for the nearest exit. I can't say I'd blame him. I'd do the same thing if I was in his place. I cover my face with both hands. I want to scream. I want to cry. This is like Craig all over again. And Mama. No matter what I do, I always end up pushing people away. I always end up alone.

David remains silent for some time, staring at the floor. After a while, he finally talks. "So, if I touched you," he says in a quiet voice, "you'd know everything about me."

I nod slowly. He breathes out with some force, the way people do when they're thinking about something serious.

"I just—" He stops.

"Yes?"

"I don't know, Mira. It's a lot to take in."

"I know."

David looks at me again, but his expression—apologetic and resigned—cuts deep. Then, before either of us can say anything more, the ER doors open and in walks Papa with Jordan right behind. I can tell from the stern expression on his face that he's not pleased to see us here.

"Hi Papa," I say, jumping to my feet, but he ignores my greeting completely.

"What are you doing here?"

"What do you mean? You know I come here every day."

Papa glares angrily at David. "I meant *him*."

"Hello, Mr. Ortiz." David extends his hand, but Papa doesn't take it. He's fuming.

"Papa, you remember David from the fundraiser. He works at the convention center."

"I know who he is," Papa says. "I thought I told you not to bother us."

"You did, sir. Mira just brought me here to introduce me to your wife."

"Papa? You told him not to talk to me?" I ask, angry now. "When? Why?"

"Because you don't need anyone interfering right now."

"Interfering? What are you talking about? David isn't interfering with anything. He is my friend—and a perfect gentleman. You have nothing to worry about."

Papa doesn't say anything more to David. He turns to me instead. "Get in the car, Mira. Jordan will take you home."

"But David and I have plans."

David interrupts, "It's all right, Mira. I've gotta run anyway. I'll see you around."

Giving me a half-hearted smile, he strides purposefully out of the hospital without glancing back. Although I know it's best that I obey my father, whether I want to or not, I can't help but wonder if I'll ever see David again.

I spin toward Papa, anger roiling inside me, like a volcano about to erupt. "I can't believe you went behind my back! After everything I've been through—"

"Mira—"

"David's the only real friend I've got right now, the only person I can talk to, and you're trying to ruin it for me."

I turn for the doors intending to stomp out, but Papa grabs my shoulder to stop me. As I pull away, his fingers slide down my arm to my hand. He grips it reflexively for a moment, and then snatches it away, the emotion draining from his face.

"I'm sorry," he whispers. "I—"

I've never seen him look so shaken before. Though he claims he doesn't buy my condition, he does everything he can to avoid touching me. But he shouldn't bother. I've known it since the beginning when this all first began. I just haven't told him because I can't explain it, and he has a hard enough time dealing with me without my throwing in a curve ball like this. And the fact is, I'm still trying to figure out why, when I touch him, I see absolutely nothing.

# 20

WHEN I FOLLOW JORDAN OUT to the car, I don't bother looking back to see if Papa is watching. I know he's not. I slide into the passenger seat, slam the door shut, and shove my hands into my pockets. My fingers collide with something cold and hard—David's cell phone. I'd forgotten that he asked me to hold it for him at the park.

Jordan gets in and starts the engine. "You shouldn't take what your dad says too hard. He's got a lot on his mind. He's worried about you, about you're spending so much time at the hospital when you could be out doing other things."

"Like what? Hanging out with friends? He seemed pretty angry about my doing that just now."

"I know," Jordan sighs. "He saw your boyfriend and overreacted."

"David's not my boyfriend."

"I'm glad to hear it."

Jordan starts the engine and backs out of our parking space. A jagged shadow falls over me through the car window. I look up at the Rawley wing, the sun blazing through the windows on the lower floors and the mesh of girders above. I notice that some of the windows on the fourth level are dark, covered from the inside with a reflective lining.

"Why are those windows covered up?" I ask.

Jordan leans over me to peer up at the building. "We've been moving things over from the old lab. The light isn't good for the specimens."

The car eases out of the parking lot. We wait at the red light before merging into traffic, the reflection of the wing still visible in the car's side view mirror.

"What's in there?" I ask, half to myself.

"Just your typical lab stuff," Jordan answers with an indifferent shrug. "Bunsen burners, microscopes, jars of dead babies…"

"What? Ewww!"

Jordan's lips twist into a devious grin.

"That's just gross, Jordan!"

"Should've seen your face." He laughs. "Priceless."

The signal turns green, and the Benz jolts forward. We continue on for a while before stopping at another signal. Jordan's gloved fingers tap at the steering wheel.

"By the way, Mira, there's something your dad asked me to talk with you about. He got a call from your mother's attending physician, Dr. Zimmerman. He says you've been asking questions—about the blood test results."

"Papa suggested I should."

"He didn't mean for you to actually… Mira, you know you shouldn't question the doctors that way. It smacks of disrespect."

"But I think there was a mistake. The results were wrong."

"Wrong how?"

"I just think it's odd they found Trazodone in her sample, that's all."

Jordan glances at me for a second, and then turns his eyes back to the road. "What's so unusual about that? Lots of people take sleeping pills. The bottle was right there on her nightstand."

"But she hardly ever uses them."

"She used them that night."

"No, she didn't."

Jordan snorts, actually snorts. "How would you know?"

"I just know." My words come out more defensively than I intend. I take a second to calm myself. Jordan's watching the road, but he is listening.

"Jordan, I need to talk to someone. I can't talk to Papa. Every time I try—he won't take me seriously."

Jordan nods. "You can always talk to me, Sunshine. You know that." He rests his left elbow near the car window and leans his head against his fist. It's his thinking pose, what he does when he's considering something important. "Go on."

"Papa thinks my—condition—is a bunch of bull. Maybe you do, too, but it isn't. I've seen Mama's mind. The last time she took Trazodone was more than a month ago when she had a bad headache and needed to sleep it off. She hasn't had any since, and she didn't take any pills the night of Papa's fundraiser."

The light turns, but Jordan doesn't seem to see it.

"It's green," I tell him.

"Oh," he says. Easing off the brake, he starts across the intersection, returning both hands to the steering wheel.

"And there's something else," I continue. "The doctor said she took too much insulin and that's why her blood sugar dropped so low. But she didn't take any insulin that night either. Without the insulin, her blood sugar should have been too high, not too low. It doesn't make any sense."

While I've been talking, Jordan's jaw muscles have clenched. I can tell he doesn't like what he's hearing.

"Not to be disrespectful," he says as his voice tightens, "but your mother was stone-cold drunk that night. She may have taken the pills and the insulin and not remembered."

"She wasn't drunk, at least not as drunk as she appeared to be," I add. "She only had a couple glasses of champagne."

"Or maybe it was your father who gave her the insulin. Even you've done that for her in the past."

"But if he did, why hasn't he said so? Why would he keep insisting she did it herself? And that still wouldn't explain all the Trazodone."

"Stop it, Mira." Jordan's voice is loud. The sharp tone takes me by surprise.

As we approach the next signal, it turns yellow. Jordan presses on the accelerator and the car speeds toward the intersection. But before we reach it, the light turns red. Jordan slams on the brakes. My body jolts forward, my seatbelt snapping tight as the car screeches to a stop. The car behind us blares its horn.

Jordan takes a deep breath and lets it out through clenched teeth. When he speaks again, he's calmer, but there's still an edge in his voice. "What are you doing, Mira?" His hands grip the wheel. "Are you accusing your dad of—?"

He looks at me, his eyes searching mine.

"No!" I say, realizing what he's asking. "No, it's just that…"

What *am* I doing? Could someone really have hurt Mama on purpose? When I think about it, the idea does seem farfetched. We drive in silence for a few minutes before arriving at our gate. It swings slowly open, and the Benz makes its way up the gravel drive, finally coming to rest in front of the porch. We sit there with the engine idling.

"When I was a kid," says Jordan finally, "my mom had—problems. I don't think she was ever properly diagnosed or anything, but she would get mad sometimes. I mean, like, she'd go into a blind rage over the smallest things. Once, I came home from school with a note from my teacher. I'd left my spelling book at home. Mom freaked out, screamed right in my face. She didn't hit me that time, but I was scared half to death. When she finally burned herself out, she dropped to her knees and begged me to forgive her. She cried like a baby when I said I would.

"Other times Mom was excessively happy. She'd get these urges to go shopping and come home with all sorts of junk. She bought this parrot one time, a macaw, I think. That thing was huge. Its beak was as big as my fist, and it chewed through every piece of furniture in our apartment. When it chewed up the piano, Mom let it go."

"Let it go?" I ask, shocked.

"Yeah. Just opened the front door one day and let it fly off. Crazy, huh?"

133

Jordan smiles at the memory, but then gets really quiet. "Life with her was a complete rollercoaster—at least until the day she hung herself in her bedroom closet."

Outside the car, I notice the sky is growing darker. I watch as the colors of day pale to gray. Jordan leans his head against the back of his seat. His jacket falls open, and the metal of his pistol barrel glints in the fading sunlight.

"I know you miss your mom," he continues. "I miss her, too, and so does your dad. It's only natural you'd want to find some explanation for what happened, Mira. I wish there was an easy answer, but there just isn't."

Maybe he's right. Maybe I *have* been reading too much into Mama's thoughts. I silently chastise myself for letting my imagination run wild.

"Whatever you may think about your dad, don't forget about all the good he's done. If Gaudium had been around for my mom... No one should have to endure what she did ever again."

"But my dad didn't discover Gaudium," I remind him. "He's a businessman, not a scientist."

"He's the face of Rawley Pharmaceutical. I know he doesn't work with us now, but to the public he still *is* Rawley. And once he becomes governor, we're practically ensured funding for continued research. There's no telling how far Gaudium can go—the number of lives it can save."

I climb out of the Benz and shut the door.

Jordan rolls down the passenger side window. "I've got to get back to the hospital to pick up your dad," he says, his hands still gripping the steering wheel. He manages a half-hearted smile. "Tell Helen he may not make it back for dinner. And Mira, hang in there, okay? We're all in this together."

I watch Jordan drive away. As for me, I'm already regretting our conversation. It was thoughtless of me to say what I did. I hadn't meant to accuse Papa of anything. I wonder if Jordan will tell him what I said. But then I think, who cares? It would serve him right. But I feel a little guilty, too, because I also know how deeply Mama loves him. She would never do anything to hurt him, and yet that is exactly what I've done.

# 21

THE HOUSE SEEMS UNUSUALLY QUIET when I enter, but then I hear the telltale sounds of Helen in the kitchen, the clang of metal pots, running water, and a half-muttered *bugger*. I push through the swinging door and find her chopping vegetables with a rather intimidating chef's knife. The smells of onion and celery fill the air.

"There you are," she says, tossing a carrot top into the garbage. "I was wondering if I should bother with dinner tonight. Haven't seen hide nor hair of you or your father all day."

"Papa won't be here," I tell her dutifully. "But I'm famished."

"Very well, then. How does a nice steaming pot of Arroz con Pollo sound?"

Chicken and rice has always been a family favorite, and Helen relishes making it for us.

"Can I help?" I ask her.

"I've got it under control. It'll be ready within the hour. How about you find something to keep yourself busy until then? You know, I wouldn't mind listening to that French music you had on yesterday."

"You heard that?"

"Your father's office is right down the hall. Couldn't help but hear it. Hope you don't mind." She tears a stalk of celery from the bunch on the counter and rinses it in the sink. "Here," she says, handing it to me. "That should hold you over until dinner."

"Thanks." I take the celery and fetch a small tub of whipped cream cheese from the fridge before heading down the hall to Papa's office.

The record player still sits open on Papa's desk. I hadn't bothered putting it away, knowing I'd probably want to use it again soon. I slip the LP out of the *Les Mis* cover and turn on the music, loud enough so that Helen can hear it in the kitchen. I settle into Papa's overstuffed leather office chair and prop my feet up on his desk.

When I lean back, the chair bumps into the filing cabinet behind me. Too close. I sit back up in order to shift the chair away from the cabinet and notice that the bottom drawer has popped open. I thought Papa kept these drawers locked, but maybe the bump jostled the lock free. The music thumps along in a heavy, persistent rhythm. I should just shut the drawer. I could easily push it closed with the heel of my foot. That's what I should do. But instead I'm frozen there, staring at the one-inch opening.

Papa isn't here, I tell myself. He won't be home for hours. What would I find anyway? Tax records most likely, or nothing at all. But then I think of the Rawley scandal, all the things the media says about him. Papa, of course, claims none of it is true, and I believe him. But what if…?

I turn the chair so that I'm facing the cabinet and slide my fingers into the drawer, but I can't open it more than a few inches because the chair is in the way. I'd have to move it to be able to open the drawer completely. And for some reason, I'm afraid to do it. What if Papa comes home, walks in, and finds me on my knees searching through his private things? With the music blaring I wouldn't hear him coming, wouldn't have time to put the chair back in its place. No, it's better to leave things as they are. But curiosity finally gets the better of me.

Slipping off the chair and onto my knees, I peer into the drawer, but it's too dark to see much. The smells of old paper and stale air leak through the opening. I stick my hand in and feel around. My fingers touch paper and cardstock, file folders and loose documents. I remove a few, pulling them out through the narrow gap, and flip through them. Just as I suspected. Photocopies of old tax records from years ago, and a nest of sales receipts, mostly from office supply stores and gas stations. I set them on the floor beside me and go fishing again.

I pull out two more files just like the first and set those aside as well. On my third try, I find only the cold metal bottom of the cabinet. Empty. What was I expecting to find anyway? I'll just put the folders back and shut the drawer. I feel stupid now thinking there'd be anything interesting in there. But then again…

One last time, I plunge my hand into the dark recesses of the cabinet drawer. This time my arm sinks up past my elbow.

I feel around the bottom again. Nothing. Then I reach back further. My fingers trace the line where the bottom and cabinet back meet. As I near one corner, I stop. There's something there, something not quite as stiff as cardstock.

It's tucked securely into the metal corner. I tug it free, and bring it out into the light. I'm surprised to find a photograph in my hand. The image has a matte finish, and the edges are worn. One edge is ragged, like a piece was torn off. There are two people in the picture, a man and a woman. I recognize the man immediately as Papa, a younger version, but most definitely him. He's smiling and has his arm around a woman with long, blonde hair and bright, smiling eyes. She's resting her head against his shoulder. They wear bright pink leis, not the cheap plastic kind like you'd get at some silly office party, but real ones made of flowers. They are holding champagne glasses and, from the expressions on their faces, it looks like they are having a really good time.

There's something familiar about the woman's face. I'm certain I've never met her before. I don't know who she is. But Mama does. I'm sure of it.

I climb back into the office chair and examine the photo more closely. The woman is so familiar, but I have to dig deep into the part of her lodged in my mind to find the memory. And then I put a name to the face. The woman is Jackie Beitner, the temp secretary Papa told Mama he hardly remembered.

There's a date written on the back of the photograph in pencil, but it's hard to make out. Turning on the Tiffany desk lamp, I hold the photo beneath it. The picture was taken less than a year before I was born.

139

# 22

I SPEND THE ENTIRE WEEKEND obsessing over Jackie Beitner. What was she doing in that picture with my father? Why did he lie to Mama about her? The questions nag at me so much that I can hardly sleep at night.

At first I consider just putting the picture back where I found it. Maybe some things are better left unknown, but no matter what I do, my mind keeps going back to it. Finally, I decide I have to tell someone. I consider calling my friend Krista, but we haven't spoken since before school let out. After I ignored her texts and calls for so long, she finally stopped trying. It would be beyond awkward to contact her now. It's not like we were ever really close anyway. The only one I really want to talk to is David, but calling him is impossible since I've got his cell, which is dead, so he can't even call to track it down. I need to return it, but after seeing us together at the hospital, Papa and Jordan have been watching me like proverbial hawks.

Saturday Papa insists we take that drive up the coast. It's a beautiful day and the sky is blue and clear, but he and I hardly speak a word to each other the entire time. At one point, I actually pull out the photo of him and Jackie Beitner. I want to ask him about it, but I just can't bring myself to do it. He lied about Jackie, that much I know for certain. What else might he be lying about?

I slip the photo back into my pocket and leave it there. After stopping for some ice cream, we turn around and come home. I hope he'll go out somewhere, anywhere, but he stays home all weekend. But when Monday rolls around he tells me that he'll be in court most of the day, and then he's jetting up to Sacramento to deal with some campaign issues at the Capitol office. He won't be back until tomorrow morning.

Though he seems disappointed about this, I couldn't be happier. The moment Papa drives away I head for the garage. Mama's car keys still hang on their hook by the door. Technically, I'm not supposed to drive on my own since I've only got a permit, but David doesn't live far. Just a few minutes down the freeway. If I hurry, I can be there and back in half an hour, long before Helen comes in for the day.

I pull the cover off Mama's VW Bug. No one's driven it since she's been sick. It would make Mama cry to see it sitting here collecting dust like this. She would want someone to take it out, let it stretch its wheels.

I ease into the driver's seat, touching two fingers to the dashboard and then my lips, just the way Mama would if she were here. Before long I'm heading west on the freeway with the radio up full blast, singing along with the familiar putter of the engine.

I take the Lowell Drive exit and follow the road through the mountains into North Hollywood. David was right about not being able to miss his house. It's smaller than my garage, but the front of it is completely welcoming. Painted a warm shade of brown with red trim, it stands in stark contrast to the peeling exteriors of its neighbors. And just like David said, there are plants—lots of plants, covering nearly every spare inch of the front porch. I'm not exactly sure what kind they are, but they are all lush and green, obviously given meticulous care by someone who loves them.

I rap at the front door. I hear footsteps inside and the dull *clack* of a lock being unlatched. The door opens, and David is there, staring at me.

"Hi," I say with a nervous little wave. "I—um—you forgot your cell phone."

I hold the phone out, but David doesn't take it. Instead, he opens the door wider and leans out into the sunlight. To my relief, he's smiling.

"Hey, Mira," he says, his eyebrows raised curiously. He glances behind me at Mama's car. "Did you drive here yourself?"

"Yeah."

"I thought you couldn't drive."

"I can drive all right," I tell him. "I just don't have a license yet. But I won't tell if you don't."

Laughing, he opens the door all the way. "Come in," he says, stepping aside.

I'm still holding the phone out. He takes it as I pass by him into a room that resembles a tropical rainforest. Just like outside, there are plants all over—on the floor, on the window sills, hanging from the ceiling, sitting on the piano.

"My uncle," explains David as though he can read my thoughts. "He loves to garden. Back in Guatemala he owned a pineapple plantation. I think he still misses it."

Also on the piano is a glass terrarium complete with sand, heat lamps, and a lizard.

"Hey, Charlie," I say, tapping on the glass with my index finger. "I remember you."

Charlie blinks and waggles a little pink tongue at me.

"I was just getting ready to take my uncle to the grocery store," David says. "I need to check on him. I'll be back in a second, okay?"

He excuses himself and vanishes through a doorway. The plant on the piano is one I actually recognize. The deep, velvety-green leaves and rich-purple petals look just like the African violets Mama had in our home when I was small. I brush my fingertips across the soft leaves, and then let them skate down the glossy finish of the piano. I trace the curves of the wood and pull my thumb across a few of the keys. Four low notes release into the air.

"Do you play?" David's voice startles me.

I turn abruptly to face him. "Uh, no. Not really."

"Not really?"

"I took lessons for a few months when I was nine, but I never practiced and my parents didn't want to waste any more money on me, so…"

David laughs. "Ramón will be out in a minute. Needs to put himself together."

"I'm sorry for just dropping by. I should have called first, but that would have been kind of hard, under the circumstances."

143

He smiles. "I was wondering what I did with my phone. Thanks for bringing it back. Why don't you take a seat, and I'll get us something to drink."

I wander across the tiny living room to the worn corduroy loveseat while David heads for the kitchen. I hear him open the refrigerator door, shift things around, and pop open two soda cans. The clink of ice against glass and the fizz of the soda being poured makes my mouth water. When David returns he hands me a glass already coated in condensation.

"What about you?" I ask. "Do you play?"

David tips his head to one side and considers me for a second. There's a look on his face I haven't seen before, a little bit cocky, yet a little self-conscious. Setting his glass on the coffee table, he positions himself on the piano bench. He wriggles all his fingers in the air before letting each one alight, like a bird, on the keys. Then … he plays.

The notes are staccato, vibrant and cheerful. His fingers dance up and down the keys, the melody teasing and toying with the harmony line.

"I know this song!" I call out over the music. David glances at me over his shoulder, which moves with the rhythm his hands are making. "Why can't I remember what it's called?"

"*Maple Leaf Rag*," he replies. "Scott Joplin."

I tap my feet to the music for a few more measures before the song comes to a rousing end. But David doesn't stop. His hands slow, and the music transforms into something melancholy. It's beautiful, though, like someone's broken heart translated into a melody.

At the end of this piece, I clap my hands and call for an encore. "Where did you learn to play like that?"

"I taught him," says a deep voice to my right. I turn to see an older man, perhaps in his seventies, standing in the doorway. David's uncle Ramón is a small man, just a little over five feet tall, with skin that's brown and weathered. But his eyes sparkle, and the corners of his mouth are turned up into a perpetual smile.

"Tio!" David stands and embraces him, leading him over to me. "Tio, this is my friend Mira," he says, introducing us.

"Ah! The governor's daughter."

"He's not the governor yet." I chuckle.

So, David's mentioned me to his uncle?

Ramón holds out two thin, trembling hands. Mine are in my pockets, and I keep them there.

"I'm sorry," I say sheepishly, thinking of some plausible excuse not to touch him. "I've got a cold."

Ramón nods and pats me gently on the shoulder instead. "That is all right," he says. His English is very good, despite his heavy Spanish accent. "So, you got my David to play the piano for you, eh?"

"I didn't know he could play until just now."

"He never told you?" Ramón casts David a look that is both critical and playful at the same time. "Ah, well, he likes to keep things to himself. I can hardly coax him to play for me anymore." To David, he says, "I haven't heard you play Solace in so long. It is my favorite, you know."

"I know," replies David. His fondness for his uncle is evident in his voice. "When I was a kid," he continues, addressing me now, "I used to visit Tio Ramón every summer. He was a good teacher. All I had was a cheap keyboard back home, but I did the best I could. It was great moving here and being able to play on a real piano anytime I wanted."

"You should do it more often," says Ramón.

"I'll try to find more time, Tío. I promise."

"He's busy," Ramón tells me. "He goes to school all day. He works all night. Good things, but leaves little time for music."

David, clearly embarrassed, empties his glass and excuses himself for a refill.

"Don't you like to hear us talk about you?" Ramón calls out, laughing.

"No, I don't," says David from the kitchen.

"All right," Ramón gives me a playful wink. "Then perhaps I will play a little myself."

Ramón eases himself onto the piano bench and raises his hands. He holds them there for a long time, suspended just above the keys. I wait for the notes, but they don't come. Instead, Ramón's face tightens in frustrated confusion.

David returns carrying two glasses. He sets them down on the coffee table and comes to stand beside his uncle who looks up at him like a child, pleading and ashamed. But David only smiles and places his hands beneath Ramón's. Together, their fingers descend onto the keys and play a slow, simple melody.

When they're finished, Ramón lets out a delighted laugh. He pats his nephew's arms and then turns on the piano bench to face me.

146

"So, David, you don't like us to talk about you?" he says, grinning. "Let's talk about your *friend* then."

His emphasis on the word 'friend' is stronger than it should have been. I can't help but blush a little.

"Wish there was something interesting to tell," I begin, still in awe of the brief moment shared between them. "I like music, but just listening. I only speak a little Spanish, which drives my parents crazy, and I love all your plants."

"Ah, yes!" says Ramón. From beside the bench, he picks up a plastic watering canister, which he uses to refresh some of the plants closest to him. "Do you have a favorite?"

"Your violets are beautiful," I respond.

Nodding, he pours a little water beneath the leaves.

"Hey, I promised you could see Charlie," says David. He reaches into the terrarium and lifts out the lizard. "I guess you two already know each other."

Charlie is about a foot long from her nose to the tip of her tail. She's mostly dark gray, with vicious looking thorns and ridges all over her.

"Hi Charlie." I stroke the spot between her eyes. "I think she likes me."

"Why wouldn't she? I've told her all about you."

Ramón has taken a seat at the end of the sofa. "I believe Charlie knows more about David's life than anyone else. Perhaps because she is such a good listener."

David places Charlie back in her tank and finishes off his drink. There's a lull in the conversation which I take as my cue to leave.

"I'd better get going," I tell David. Turning to Ramón, I add. "It was a pleasure to meet you."

147

"I am very glad to have met you, too, Mira," Ramón says with a smile so warm and genuine I almost want to hug him. "You know, your father is good man," he continues, "A *héroe* to our people. I will vote for him come the election. It is one of the few things worth leaving this house for. Perhaps he could give me a bumper sticker?"

"Tio, you don't drive anymore," David reminds him.

For a moment, Ramón looks bewildered, but the smile soon reappears. "Well, I've always wanted one."

I can't help but laugh. "I'll see what I can do."

David walks me outside to the car. He doesn't say anything until we reach it.

"I hope you don't mind my Tio," he says, the corners of his mouth turned up ever so slightly. "He—uh—he's in the early stages of Alzheimer's. One of the reasons I live with him. It's not too bad yet, but I like to keep an eye on him, you know?"

"Sure," I reply. I can't help but think about Gaudium and how Papa keeps saying its next big advancement will be the cure for Alzheimer's. Maybe someday it will help Ramón.

We stand looking at each other for a few seconds. I decide to take a chance and tell him the real reason why I've come.

"David, I need to talk to you." I take a deep breath, pulling nervously at my sleeve. And the rest of the words just come tumbling out. "I'm sorry about the other day. I really am. But I found this picture in my father's desk, and something's just not right about it, and I don't have anyone else I can talk to, but then I realized I had your cell phone, and—"

"Whoa. Hold on a second," he says. "Slow down. You found a picture?"

"Yes, of my father and another woman, but…" I stop talking and squeeze my eyes shut. What am I doing? I take another deep, calming breath. I need to be rational about this or else I might scare David off again. "I just wondered if you could spare some time to talk with me about it. But I'd totally understand if you're busy—or you don't want to."

David opens my car door for me. I take his silence as a 'no'. Embarrassed, I quickly climb in behind the steering wheel. But then David is leaning over, smiling at me.

"Mira, I'm glad you came today."

"You are?"

"Yeah. I acted like a real jerk at the hospital. It was just, you know, kind of a shock." He squats down so his face is level with mine. "What I mean to say is that, I'm sorry. I like you, I really do, and I don't want whatever you're dealing with to come between us."

I stare at him, dumbfounded. "All right," I say numbly.

His smile grows wider. "Good. Now, I've got to run my uncle to the store, but I'll come by your house afterwards so we can talk, okay?"

I nod a little too enthusiastically. He closes my door, and I start the engine. When I catch a glimpse of my watch a jolt of panic shoots through me. I've got ten minutes to beat Helen home.

"Bye!" I shout through the window. "See you later!"

Releasing the parking brake I shift into gear, jerking Mama's VW forward. As I drive off, I look in my rearview.

# CONTACT

David's watching me, a perplexed but happy expression on his face.

# 23

DAVID ARRIVES AT THE MANSION about an hour later, and while Helen prepares breakfast for both of us, I tell him about how I came across the photo of Papa and Jackie Beitner.

"I'm not sure what I should do." I drag an absentminded finger down the side of my juice glass. A trickle of condensation forms a little pool on the table. "Maybe I should try to find her, talk to her. What do you think?"

"Would you mind passing the syrup?"

I unscrew the little red cap and hand David the bottle. Then I watch in awe as he smothers his pancakes with the viscous brown liquid.

"This stuff is really good," he says. "Better than any syrup I've ever had."

"At twenty bucks a bottle, it better be," I tell him. "It's real maple syrup, not that sugary junk they sell at the market. Papa orders it from Vermont. Now, would you mind turning a little attention away from your food and focusing it on me?"

He takes a rather large bite of dripping pancake, and chases it down with a few gulps of freshly squeezed orange juice.

"All right," David mumbles, setting down his glass and wiping his mouth with a napkin. "I'm all ears."

"Really? For the last few minutes I could swear you were all mouth," I say with a hint of playful sarcasm.

David grins before taking one last triumphant bite of his breakfast. "There. My plate is now clean. You have my undivided attention."

"Finally," I say, tossing my unused napkin at him. "I'm just wondering where to start? All I know about Jackie Beitner is that she worked for Papa while he was at Rawley, but she was a temp and didn't work there very long."

"Let me see that photo again." He pushes his plate out of the way. I pass the picture across the table and watch as he studies the image on the front for a minute before turning it over. "This definitely seems odd. Since when do temps get so buddy-buddy with their bosses?"

"That's what I think, too." I take the photo back. "He claims he hardly knew her."

"What does your mom think about her?"

"What?"

"When you see your mom's thoughts, I mean. Does she have any suspicions?"

His question startles me, and I'm not exactly sure how to respond. "Not about Jackie. She actually liked her, though she did wonder about her and Gregory Stark, that researcher who conducted those tests. But Mama never had any reason to think Papa and Jackie were—involved."

Just then the door to the kitchen opens and Helen comes in to clear the table. "How was it then?" she asks, collecting David's plate and the empty hotcake platter.

David proceeds to gush over the meal, telling her how much he enjoyed every bite. His compliments are sincere, and Helen blushes from them all. When she takes my plate, she gives me a chastising look.

"I'm sorry," I tell her. "I guess I wasn't that hungry."

"I'll let it slide this time." She offers me a slight look of disapproval before sending David an almost flirtatious smile. "You've got a nice beau here, Mira. Hope you'll bring him around more often."

I feel my face flush. "He's just a friend," I say quickly, but Helen doesn't buy it. She raises her eyebrows and hums a little on her way out.

"I'm sorry about that," I tell David once we're alone. Glancing at him, I realize that he's studying me. He doesn't say anything, and I wonder what he's thinking.

"David, I need to explain—about the other day." I recall how he walked out of Mama's room, how upset he was thinking that I had blown him off. But then I think of his hand on my knee and the tender way he looked at me just then. Maybe he could believe me if I give him a chance.

David sets both elbows on the table and folds his arms, listening intently.

"I told you the truth—about me," I continue. "And about Mama. There's something wrong with me."

"There's nothing *wrong* with you, Mira," he says quickly. "I'm sorry I reacted the way I did. I just didn't understand, that's all. But I want to."

153

He leans close to me until we are only inches apart. He's so near I can smell the musk and vanilla of his cologne. "How did this happen to you?"

"I'm not sure," I answer honestly. "I think I was born with it, but it didn't hit full force until recently—after I got immunized."

"You mean this is a reaction to Happy Juice?"

I grin at hearing Gaudium's nickname. "Maybe."

"But I thought it didn't have any side effects. The perfect cure, right?"

"So they say."

"Jeesh, I'm glad I didn't get it."

"You didn't?"

"Not yet. The regulations for immunizing at sixteen went into effect late last year. I'm eighteen. I have to wait for the new batches along with the rest of the *grown-ups*."

I hadn't considered the fact that David hasn't been given Gaudium, nor have any other adults. Just us teens. I wonder how the Rawley scandal will affect the drug's future? Until those deaths became public there was little, if any, opposition to it eventually going mainstream.

"You know," David continues, "I never understood how you can cure things like Bipolar Disorder and Autism, but we still can't cure the common cold."

"That's simple, actually," I explain. "The cold, the flu, things like that are caused by viruses. Viruses mutate, so every time we're exposed it's like getting a whole new illness. There are vaccines, of course, and some diseases have been completely eradicated, like small pox and polio. But for other things like the flu, you have to get immunized every year."

"And Gaudium is different how?"

"Mental illnesses and even some developmental disorders are caused by chemical deficiencies or imbalances in the brain. Gaudium repairs the damage that causes those deficiencies. Except it didn't quite work right with me for some reason."

David leans back in his chair, thinking out loud. "So, this thing about Jackie Beitner could be solved pretty easily. If you just touch your Dad once, you'd save yourself a lot of trouble."

"In theory, yes. But in actuality—no."

"But I thought you said when you touch someone—"

"Except my dad. For some reason it doesn't work with him. I have no idea why."

"He's the *only* exception?"

"The only one so far."

David nods, contemplating all this. "So, what's it like, this mind hacking thing?"

*Mind hacking?* I flinch at the distasteful term.

I take a deep breath and let it out in a measured stream. "Have you ever been burned?"

"Sure. The worst, I think, was when I burned my finger on my mom's iron." He sucks in some air through his teeth. "Man, it hurt for a week."

"Okay," I tell him. "Now imagine that burn all over your body, inside *and* out."

His eyes become more focused. He's concentrating on me, wondering.

"And the pain?" I continue, leaning in for emphasis. "Triple it."

David stares at me with such seriousness that I can't help but crack a smile. It seems to set him at ease a little.

"But that's not the worst part of it. Getting a life's worth of pain and sorrow, joy and fear, dreams, and nightmares dumped all at once into my brain, which has more than its own fair share of all that—it's horrible."

"So your mom, when you visit her, you touch her to—"

"To reassure myself that she's still in there somewhere." I realize that David looks sad, almost depressed. What I've told him is more than he expected to hear. He needs time to—as he says—process.

"So, back to Jackie Beitner," I say, hoping to get his mind back on track.

"Right. Right." David sighs, his trance broken. "Let's see. If Jackie was a temp, then she probably was a local, but in L.A. local could mean one of dozens of towns within an hour radius."

"Actually, she was from Bakersfield, a couple hours north of here. Mama remembers Jackie mentioning that she planned to go back there when she stopped working for Rawley."

"It wouldn't hurt to look for her there. Why don't we start by checking the internet for listings?"

He pulls his phone from his pocket.

"Why don't we use my computer?" I suggest. "The screen's bigger."

David follows me up to my room. I feel incredibly grateful for Helen who has picked up after me. There's no trace of my pajamas or the wet bath towel I left on the floor this morning.

156

I sit down at my desk, a relic from my childhood that's. Painted bright green to match my lime and Pepto-Bismol walls, it's an eyesore as well as an embarrassment.

"I just have to turn the computer on." I see David in the oval mirror above my desk. He stands so close behind me I feel his chest lightly brush up against the back of my head. "It takes a sec to warm up."

He doesn't say anything, but he's looking at me again. I can't help but look at him, too. It seems safer to look at each other in the mirror, as if it were a magic barrier shielding me from getting too close. I let my eyes study his face, something I haven't allowed myself to spend much time doing before. Right now his expression is conflicted. I watch as he slowly raises his hand behind me. He hesitates before resting it on my right shoulder. I feel his warmth through my hoodie.

"This is all right, isn't it?" he asks. "No skin."

"Sure. I'm good." Though my heart's thumping so fast I can hardly bear it. Then his hand shifts, and his fingers stroke my hair. It's just the lightest of touches but sends pleasant shivers down my neck.

"And this?" His voice is as gentle as his touch. His fingers burrow deeper into my hair, careful to avoid contact with my scalp. I close my eyes, leaning my head back a little. My mother used to run her fingers through my hair but hadn't done it since my problem got too strong for me to handle. David's hand leaves my hair and slides down my shoulder to my back, massaging in small circles just below my shoulder blade. It feels so nice. I open my eyes to look at him again, and I'm startled by the desire that stares back at me. He wants to touch me as much as I don't want him to.

157

The computer emits a loud beep.

"It's ready." I try to keep my voice from trembling. David's hand drops to his side. The magic between us evaporates. "There's a chair in the corner," I tell him.

I mean for him to bring the chair close so we can both look at the computer screen. Instead, he walks over and drops down on it. He looks dejected.

Trying to ignore the empty feeling sprouting in my stomach, I Google Jackie Beitner— Bakersfield, California.

"Nothing."

David stretches out his legs and arms in front of him. "Is she on Facebook?"

I log onto my Facebook account and type in her name and several variations of it. "I don't see a single one."

"That doesn't necessarily mean anything. Lots of people don't have Facebook accounts. Let's look up the Yellow Pages."

"David, there's no guarantee she still lives there after sixteen years. She could be anywhere by now."

I stare at the computer screen, tempted to just shut it off. So I found a picture of my father and some woman. So maybe he cheated on my mom. Aren't all politicians the same? Should I have expected better of him? What am I trying to prove by digging in his dirt? Mama accepted Papa for who he is. Why can't I?

"What are we doing?" I glance at David sitting by the window. He looks amazing with those eyes and strong shoulders. And when he smiles, those dimples of his send little zings through me. Refocusing on the computer, I silently hope he didn't notice me staring at him.

"I don't know, Mira," he replies. "What *are* we doing?"

"So Papa keeps an old photo of her hidden away," I say out loud, as if giving voice to my concerns will make them vanish. "It might not mean anything." I realize my tone is defensive, a little angry even. But I'm not angry at David. I'm angry at myself for letting my imagination get the better of me, and for butting into my father's business.

"What are you going to do?" David asks.

"I'm going to put this picture back where I found it and forget I ever saw it."

"If that's what you want, Mira, then do it. But maybe you should reconsider."

"Why?"

"Because of *that*."

David stands and walks up beside me. Reaching around me, he clicks my mouse, minimizing the Facebook page. In its place is a listing of current news stories. David drags the cursor toward the bottom left hand corner and points to a headline in bold letters: *Evidence Links Rawley Scandal to Political Candidate.*

"Think about it, Mira. What if he's not the man you always thought he was? The picture proves he lied about Jackie Beitner. What if he lied about this, too?"

"You mean what if he sanctioned those Gaudium trials after all?"

"That's exactly what I mean. People died, Mira." David's voice is full of concern.

"Papa had nothing to do with that. He couldn't have."

David walks back across my room to the window. Outside, the promised storm is finally making its appearance.

159

"Maybe that's true," he says. "But what if he is guilty? What if he did what they claim he did? Either way, maybe this Jackie Beitner knows something."

I look at the photo again and consider what he's saying. What if Papa is found guilty? Would he go to prison? What would happen to me? To Mama? If this woman had a relationship with my father, she might have information that could hurt him, but it's just as possible she could help clear his name.

"So where do we go from here?" I ask out loud, not really expecting an answer.

David turns from the window, his hands in his jeans pockets. Shrugging his shoulders, he says matter-of-factly, "We go to Bakersfield."

# 24

DAVID NEEDS TO RUN HIS UNCLE to a dentist appointment, but he promises to come back later once he's finished. We're going to drive the two hours to Bakersfield and see if we can track down Jackie Beitner. I search for addresses in Bakersfield and find one for a Robert and Marie Beitner—the only Beitners listed in that town, so they might very well be related. The phone number is unlisted, so we'll just drop by and take our chances.

After printing out the address and directions from Google Maps, I power down my computer. I still have a little time to spare, so I take a shower and put on a clean tank and jeans. I reach for my hoodie and my backpack, then head downstairs.

On reaching the entryway, I notice movement in the dining room. I swing in to tell Helen goodbye but find the room empty. Except for the lingering aroma of maple syrup, all traces of breakfast have been cleared from the table. A gray suit coat is draped over the back of a chair, a pair of black leather driving gloves peeking out from a pocket. Have

Papa's plans changed? If he's home early, how will I leave with David without him knowing?

I pick up the jacket and walk through the kitchen toward Papa's office, but instead of Papa I find Jordan standing at the desk, rifling through an open manila file full of papers. He jumps when he sees me, startled.

"Mira," he says, laughing uneasily, "I didn't know you were here."

"I've been here all morning," I tell him, "but I am going out later."

"I see," he says with a hint of disappointment. "Helen saw your friend's car drive away. I just assumed you'd gone with him."

He knows David's been here? If he knows, then it's a good bet Papa knows, too.

"I thought you both went to Sacramento. Did the flight get cancelled? Is Papa here?" I ask, peering back down the hall.

"No," Jordan replies. "I had some business at the lab to take care of so I stayed behind."

He spots his jacket in my hand and reaches for it. I give it to him, and he thanks me as he slips it on before turning his attention back to the papers. "Listen, Mira, would you mind getting me a glass of water from the kitchen?" he asks. "I'm parched, but I'm in a bit of a hurry."

I'm relieved to know Papa isn't here, and that he doesn't know about David after all. At least not yet.

I set my backpack down on the desk. "What are you looking for? Anything important?"

162

"I'm afraid not." Jordan smirks and rolls his eyes, his usual expression when Papa asks him to do something trivial. But Jordan never says 'no' to Papa. No matter what.

I enter the kitchen and find a six pack of cold water bottles in the fridge. I take one out for Jordan and a couple more for the trip to Bakersfield. When I get back to Papa's office Jordan slips a folded piece of paper into his jacket breast pocket and takes a bottle.

"Thanks," he says. "I'm off then." He starts for the door, but something inside me doesn't want him to go. Not yet. There's something I need to know first.

"Did Papa cheat on my mother?" I blurt out the words before I can change my mind.

Jordan freezes, a look of amused shock on his face. "What—?"

"I need to know," I continue. "You and Papa have been friends forever. If he ever did anything like that he would have told you—wouldn't he?"

Jordan stares at me for a few moments, as if debating with himself whether or not to answer me.

"Did your mom tell you that?" he asks, finally. I don't answer. I simply wait. "He never meant for her to find out," Jordan says after a while. "He thought he was being discreet."

"So you knew all along?"

"I've known your dad a long time, Mira. We were in the 2$^{nd}$ Battalion together."

"I know," I reply. He and Papa have told me dozens of stories about their experiences over the years.

"After the war I wasn't doing so well," Jordan continues. "Your dad got me a job at Rawley Pharmaceutical as a lab tech. Obviously, I've done pretty well there, thanks to him. What I'm trying to say is he's a decent guy, Mira."

"Then why did he have an affair?"

Jordan sighs and pinches his lips together. He doesn't want to go into this, I can tell, but he will.

"Early on," he begins, "your parents were mad about each other. But they had problems. They couldn't get pregnant. It caused a real strain in their marriage. Your dad … Let's just say he made some mistakes. But then things turned around. You came along. He's been devoted to you and your mom ever since."

Hearing Jordan confirm what I'd already guessed only hurts more. Between the endless hours away from home as Rawley's CEO, his campaign, and now the inquiry, the one thing Papa hasn't been is a devoted husband and father.

"Give your dad a little credit," Jordan adds. "He's a good man at heart. Your mom knew—knows that."

There is a long stretch of silence between us. Behind him, the metal filing cabinet where I found that photo stands as the only witness to Jordan's revelation. I wonder what other secrets it might still hold. I notice that Jordan's eyes are on me, narrowed and probing.

"Mira, there's something else, isn't there?" he asks. "What else did she tell you? Did she know who?"

The question is vague, but I understand what he wants to know. The photo of Jackie Beitner and my father is stiff in my back pocket. I could pull it out right now and show him. Jordan steps closer and peers down at me, his expression suddenly hard and menacing, as if a demon was waiting just under the surface. I leave the photo where it is.

"Mama only suspected he'd been unfaithful," I lie. "She doesn't know the woman's name."

Jordan relaxes a bit, and his lips pull up at the corners, relieved. Turning to the desk, he straightens the file he'd been searching, and then slides it into a desk drawer.

"So, you've got plans this afternoon?" he asks, abruptly changing the topic.

"Yeah, sort of."

"With that boy?"

"His name's David. And I'd really appreciate it if you didn't mention him to my father?" I frame the request like an appeal. "He thinks I'm better off quarantined than spending time with people my age."

Jordan tugs on his driving gloves while giving me the reproachful look I know all too well. So I amend my comment, "All right—*boys* my age. But David's really nice. Papa would like him if he'd give him a chance, but all he cares about is his campaign."

"The campaign isn't all he cares about, Mira," says Jordan. "But it is very important right now. The future of Rawley Pharmaceutical—of Gaudium—hinges on his success. With your father as the governor, he will have a great deal of influence in getting state and possibly federal funding for Rawley's research."

Hearing Jordan explain it, I almost feel guilty for doubting Papa at all. "But the investigations, those deaths," I say. "What if they hold Papa liable? What if he's arrested?"

"Your father won't be arrested," answers Jordan, his voice firm.

"But even so, he could still lose the election after all this."

# CONTACT

Jordan steps up to me and places a gloved hand against my cheek. I smell the leather and something else I can't quite place as he traces the side of my face with his thumb. The gesture takes me by surprise and sets me on edge.

"He won't lose," he says, his pupils contracting to small black points which seem to pierce right through me. "I'll make sure of it."

# 25

AFTER JORDAN LEAVES, I WAIT impatiently for David. My conversation with Jordan left me feeling unsettled.

I'm relieved when I climb into the car beside David. I consider telling him about my conversation with Jordan, but I just don't feel much like talking. It was one thing just suspecting Papa of being unfaithful to Mama, but hearing Jordan confirm it has left a solid void in the pit of my stomach.

The drive up to Bakersfield is a quiet one. We don't say much, but the radio's volume is turned up high, filling the space between us. Halfway to our destination, a light sprinkle of rain begins to fall. David turns the wipers on, but the weather doesn't dampen our spirits.

When we get closer to Bakersfield, I reach into my backpack for the map I printed. "Crud," I say with a frustrated huff. "I must have left it at home."

"Do you have your phone?"

I dig in my purse some more. "Of course I don't have it. I never have it."

"No problem. We'll use mine."

After looking up the Beitners' address again, the GPS on David's phone leads us to a quiet, middle-class, suburban neighborhood with nicely kept lawns and homes painted all the same drab shades of beige and brown.

"That's it," I tell David, pointing at a house with a bay window and an apple tree in the yard.

Pulling a u-turn, David parks in front. "So what's the plan?"

"I don't have a plan," I tell him. "I thought you'd have a plan."

"Me? Why would I have a plan?"

This is going nowhere. Stepping out of the car into the drizzling rain, I jog up to the front door. David's beside me a few seconds later, shaking the water from his hair. I ring the doorbell. From behind the door there's a light scuffling sound, then the click of the lock being unlatched. Finally, the door opens a few inches, and the face of an elderly man peers at us through a pair of thick, rectangular shaped lenses.

"Yeah?" asks the man in a scruffy voice. "If you're trying to sell me another vacuum cleaner, I don't want it. The last one ate up my carpet and scared my cat away."

"We're not here about vacuums," says David. I can tell he's trying to stifle a chuckle. He clears his throat and quickly regains his composure.

"We're looking for Robert Beitner," I cut in.

The old man squints at us both. "I'm Robert Beitner."

"And Marie Beitner?" adds David.

"That's my wife. You want my wife? Mar!" The man turns and shouts into the house. "Mar, there's a couple a kids here to see you!"

"Actually, we just had a question—" but the man's moved aside and his wife, a frail-looking woman wearing a yellow apron and fuzzy, pink slippers, appears at the door.

"Yes?" she says cheerfully.

I look at David. He shrugs. So I guess I'm in the spotlight.

"Mrs. Beitner, my name is Miranda—" I'm about to tell her my last name, but then decide against it. "Miranda Johnson. And this is my friend, David."

Marie Beitner looks at me a little funny, but waits patiently for me to continue.

"We're looking for someone who may have lived in this neighborhood a long time ago. Did you know a Jackie Beitner by any chance?"

At the sound of Jackie's name, Marie's face goes white. She raises a trembling hand to her lips and closes her eyes for a moment. When she opens them again, a tear escapes and gets lost in her wrinkled cheek.

"I'm sorry," she says. "It's been so long, but I still miss my Jackie as much as ever. Why don't the two of you come in and set a while. I just baked a loaf of lemon berry bread. I'll slice you up some, hmm?"

How can we turn down such a kind invitation?

The Beitner home smells of spiced apple and old newsprint. I spot some potpourri in an electric warmer near the front door, not far from several waist-high stacks of newspaper. Mrs. Beitner leads us along the pathway between the stacks into a small yet comfortable living room dominated

169

by a baby grand piano at the window. The piano and fireplace mantle are draped with white crocheted coverlets, the perfect backdrop for the dozens of framed photos arranged on them both.

"You can imagine how hard it's been for us without her," Mrs. Beitner says, lowering herself into a wooden rocker beside the piano. David and I sit on a yellow, flowered loveseat while Mr. Beitner heads toward the kitchen in the back. "Jackie was our only child."

David and I exchange astonished glances.

"*Was* your only child?" I ask, trying to be as tactful as possible.

"Yes," replies Mrs. Beitner. "She passed away sixteen years ago."

My heart drops. "I'm so sorry. We didn't know."

I notice the display of framed photos on the mantle. They are all the same girl at different ages, most likely Jackie. There's one when she's a teen holding a violin under her chin, another as a girl riding a bicycle, and still another in a black graduation cap and gown.

"How did she die?" I ask cautiously.

Mrs. Beitner goes silent. She remains polite, but I can tell she's a bit wary of us.

"I'm sorry," I tell her. "I guess I should explain why we're here." I cast a quick *help me* glance at David. "Uh, well, we're from the local high school, you know. And we're..."

"We're on the committee for the school paper," interjects David.

"Reporters?" asks Mrs. Beitner.

"That's right," I say. "We're doing a piece on—the upcoming election. We understand that your daughter used to work for one of the candidates."

"Oh? I don't recall—"

Mr. Beitner comes in carrying a plastic silver-colored tray. "Just a minute, Mar," he says with a pleasant smile, "let our guests sample some of your cooking."

He first offers the tray to me. I help myself to a thick, golden slice of warm lemon bread dotted with large, purple blueberries, and a Styrofoam cup of apple juice.

"Thank you," I say. "This looks delicious."

David takes his share too. Mr. and Mrs. Beitner take the remaining slices of bread and cups of juice, before abandoning the tray on the piano. The bread is as tasty as it looks. I should ask for the recipe before I go.

"Did I hear you say you write for your school newspaper?" asks Mr. Beitner.

"That's right," I say.

"They want to know how Jackie passed away," explains his wife. Then she turns to us. "She died of a brain hemorrhage—caused by a tumor."

"Again, we're so sorry to hear that." I'm sure the disappointment must show on my face. Jackie Beitner is dead, and any information she might have had about my father is dead, too. I want to leave, but the Beitners seem to be enjoying our visit. I need to find some polite way of ending this.

Rising slowly from the couch, I try to think of something to say, when David speaks up. "Do you know if Jackie was

171

seeing anyone before she died?" he asks while finishing off his lemon bread. "Did she have a boyfriend?"

Mrs. Beitner pauses, her forehead creasing in thought. "I didn't know much about her private life," she says. "Jackie didn't tell us much. She lived on her own, had a job with a temp agency doing secretarial work."

"She worked for Rawley Pharmaceutical, didn't she? I mean the candidate, Mr. Ortiz, mentioned her in an old interview once." This is a complete lie, but I'm hoping the Beitners won't notice.

Mrs. Beitner looks to her husband, who nods. "Yes," he says. "For a short time. Don't you remember, Mar?"

"That's right. She did mention it once or twice. Rawley... I think I remember hearing something about it on the news. Didn't we, dear?"

Mr. Beitner nods again.

"But you asked about a boyfriend," continues Mrs. Beitner. "She must have had, though we never met him. She did introduce us to one of her co-workers once. A nice young fellow. We met them for lunch when we were in the Valley one day. We were shopping for a new car, weren't we, Bob?"

I look at David. He raises his eyebrows and gives a slight nod of his head, encouraging me to go on. "Could you tell us what the man looked like?" I ask.

"Young," says Mrs. Beitner, "and very tall. He had red hair, I remember that distinctly about him, and a birthmark under one of his eyes. He was very nice."

I look back at David, conveying my disappointment. Red hair. Tall. Definitely not Papa.

Stepping over to the mantel, I take a closer look at the photos. There's one I hadn't noticed before. It's not framed, just a snapshot leaning against the wall.

"Who is this?" I ask, picking up the photo. In it, a young girl about two years old sits on Santa's lap smiling directly into the camera. She has dark curls and wide dark eyes. I know this girl—this picture. And she is definitely not Jackie Beitner.

At first it seems as though the Beitners are going to ignore my question. But then Mr. Beitner glances at his wife with a resigned expression on his face. Marie lowers her eyes, but not before I see more tears in them.

"That's our granddaughter," says Mr. Beitner, "the baby Jackie gave up before she died."

# 26

MY HANDS TREMBLE AS I SET the photo back into place. I suddenly feel weak and even a little lightheaded. I should sit back down, but I'm too numb to move.

"Jackie didn't tell us about the baby until she was too far along to hide it anymore," continues Mr. Beitner, sharing a tender look with his wife. "By then she'd been having headaches for several weeks. She was naturally worried and came to us for help. She said she'd been seeing a doctor—for the headaches—but whatever he was doing for her wasn't helping. Not long before the baby came, she was diagnosed with the tumor. We told her we'd raise the baby if anything happened to her, but she refused. She'd already signed the adoption papers. We tried to convince her to change her mind, but she was adamant."

Mr. Beitner reaches for his wife's hand. "We were there when the baby was born. But on Jackie's insistence, the baby was taken away. We never met her adoptive parents."

His voice cracks, and he stifles a quiet sob. Tears roll down his cheeks, and I worry that some might start rolling down mine, too. Mr. Beitner pinches his eyes and pulls himself together before continuing.

"Jackie passed away a few weeks later. After that we got pictures of the baby in the mail from time to time, but eventually they stopped coming."

There is a moment of silence that seems expected for the Beitners, as if it is customary for them to pause in remembrance when discussing their daughter. For me, it feels like a massive void just opened up and swallowed me whole. My reaction to their story is as physical as it is emotional. It takes all my effort to keep myself together.

David must sense the sudden change in me. He looks at his wristwatch. "It's late," he tells me, his voice tender. "We've got to head back."

The Beitners walk us to the door. I find myself wanting to embrace them, to tell them not to be sad anymore. But the distance between us remains rigid. I cannot close the gap— not now—not yet. But suddenly Marie slips her aging arms around me and pulls me close, pressing her cheek against mine. I'm too startled to resist her.

"You're a sweet girl," she says before releasing me.

David and I thank the Beitners for everything. David shakes their hands and walks with me to the car. It's dark now, the sun having set not long ago, and it's raining—hard. I slide into the passenger seat and shut the door as David gets into the driver's seat. We sit for a few moments in silence before he starts the engine. Then, he eases away from the curb onto the dark, rainy street.

"So, what do you think?" he asks.

175

Already I feel the tears burning behind my eyes. I have to say something, and I have to say it out loud. "I can't..." I stammer. I clear my throat and try again. "This can't be happening."

"What do you mean?"

My throat constricts like a fist, but I force the words out. "That photo of the little girl, the Beitners' granddaughter—it's me."

David does a double take. "What? How do you know?"

"Because that same picture is hanging on my bedroom wall, that's how. Mama took it on Christmas when I was two years old."

"Are you kidding? Are you sure? Wait. She touched you, didn't she—when Mrs. Beitner hugged you goodbye. What did you see?"

I shake my head furiously and swipe away a tear. "Nothing. I saw nothing."

"Nothing at all? You mean like with your dad?"

"I think—" My voice catches in my throat. "I think that's why I couldn't see him before, why I can't see Marie. They're related to me. They're my family—my *real* family."

We reach a stop sign, and the wipers bat futilely at the torrent of rain pelting the windshield.

"We should go back and tell them," David says as he begins to turn the steering wheel.

Quickly, I grab hold of it. We go straight through the intersection.

"I can't just announce who I am to these people. I'm a complete stranger to them. For all they know, I might be some lunatic escaped from the mental hospital. And I still have no evidence that Jackie and Papa…"

Jackie Beitner is—was—my mother. And the two wonderful elderly people I just met are my grandparents. But *is* Papa my real father? Did he and Jackie Beitner have an affair that resulted in me? It would make sense that he would take me in if he knew she was dying, and even more why he'd keep the truth from Mama. And yet something doesn't quite fit, or more like a piece of the puzzle is still missing—a big piece. I just can't put my finger on what it could possibly be.

David keeps glancing in his rearview mirror. He looks concerned.

"What's wrong?" I ask him.

"Nothing, I think. It's just that those same headlights have been behind us ever since we left the Beitners' house."

I look over my shoulder at the car trailing behind. Through the fogged-up back window all I can see are the lights and a vague outline of the vehicle. It's too dark to tell what color or make it is. But what I can tell is that it's way too close. Right on our tail.

"What the heck?" David presses his foot down on the accelerator. Our car picks up speed, but the car behind us keeps pace.

I realize that after leaving the Beitners I forgot to buckle my seatbelt. I grab for it now, my fingers fumbling with the buckle. I hear the sharp click as it locks into place, then I grab hold of the dashboard with my right hand and David's shoulder with my left.

We near another intersection. The road is nearly deserted, just a few cars parked alongside the road. The signal turns red, but David doesn't stop. He hits the accelerator and speeds through the light. I turn to see if the car behind us stops. To my relief, it does. We drive a few more blocks before turning onto a side street.

"It's gone." I lean back against my headrest and let the anxiety seep out of my body.

David pulls the car into a gas station and turns off the engine. The lights above the gas pumps are bright, a beacon in this dark, wet night.

I'm still holding onto David's shoulder, so I let go. "I'm sorry," I tell him. "I didn't mean to grab you so hard."

Leaning forward, he rests his head on the steering wheel. "It's gonna leave a bruise," he says, laughing nervously. He sits up and takes a couple of deep breaths. We look at each other and giggle like little kids.

"For a second I thought…"

"Me, too."

David smiles, relief in his eyes. We're both feeling a little silly. Why would anyone want to follow us? Who knew we were even here in Bakersfield anyway?

"I need a soda," I tell David. "Do you want anything?"

"No, but I might as well fill my tank while I'm here. It's a long drive back."

While David pumps the gas, I go into the mini-mart. I've got a ten dollar bill burning a hole in my pocket. I wander down the aisle of junk food while an acne-faced attendant eyes me warily. Glancing up at him, I smile, which seems to set him at ease a little. I grab a couple of candy bars and head for the refrigerated section. Opening the frosted glass door, I reach for a Coke.

I don't know what makes me look up just then, but I do. David's right outside the window leaning against the trunk of the car, his hands buried in his pants pockets. And ... is he whistling?

The refrigerator door swings shut. I haven't taken anything. I'm not thinking about Coke right now. I'm thinking about the pair of headlights that just turned onto this street a block down, two small orbs of light floating in the darkness. David's facing the other way. He doesn't see them.

I take a step toward the window. The rain comes down like a hurricane, blurring the headlights. Suddenly, the lights jolt forward. In a spasm of speed they race toward the gas station—straight at David!

I drop everything and run, shouting out the mini-mart door.

"David!" I scream. "Get out of the way!"

David jumps when he sees me, but he doesn't move. He's staring at me, confusion in his face. The headlights—the phantom car—is close now. Its tires skid as it turns into the gas station parking lot with an ear-splitting squeal.

The car, now fully illuminated by the station lights, is an older black sedan. David turns and sees it just as I reach him. We grab each other and run back toward the safety of the mini-mart, but the car swerves directly into our path as if it means to hit us. Shifting our course, we bolt out of the beacon of light into the rain. We run down the deserted road, our feet slamming against the pavement in unison, icy water splashing against our legs. The headlights are on us like spotlights. We're fleeing prisoners without a chance in the world of escape.

179

# CONTACT

The street we're on is narrow, lined with brick storefronts all closed and dark for the night. Only the pale, yellow glow of intermittent street lamps and the harsh glare of the lights behind us cut through the night. There's nowhere to go. No alley to duck into. No bridge or magic porthole in which to hide. The car is going to mow us down like road kill, and all I can think of is, *why?*

Suddenly I feel a sharp jerk on my right arm as David grabs me, yanking me right off my feet. There's a loud crash, the sound of shattering glass. I hit the ground so hard it knocks the breath out of me. The air splits wide open as a piercing alarm sounds. Tires squeal once again, peeling out against the wet black top of the road. Then the sound of the car engine fades as it speeds away.

I blink open my eyes. The alarm is so loud my eardrums are pulsing. I try to sit up, but something crunches beneath me. Glass. I'm lying on a bed of glass shards, and I'm no longer outside. I'm inside—inside a shop staring at the wide jagged opening where a window used to be. All around us I see the dim outlines of sofas, dining tables, and rocking chairs. We're in a furniture store. I lift my hands, not wanting to get cut, but in the dim light leaking in from the street lamp outside I can see crimson spider webs on my palms and fingers. Then, suddenly, there's a third hand grabbing my sleeve and pulling me to my feet.

"Are you all right?" David asks, his voice filled with fear.

"Yeah," I reply shakily. "I think so."

"Did you get a good look at the car?"

"Sort of," I tell him, wishing now that I'd had the sense to look at the license plate.

"Did you recognize it? Or see who was driving?"

"No."

David hisses through his teeth, and I can't tell if it's because of pain or frustration.

"We've gotta get out of here," he says, "before the police arrive—or that guy, whoever he is, comes back."

# 27

RUNNING AGAIN. HUGGING THE shadows. Back to David's car at the gas station. My hands throb from the dozen or so shallow cuts on them. I think I may have one or two on my face as well, since my right cheek hurts, too. But that seems to be the extent of my damage. David, on the other hand, is limping—badly.

We reach the gas station but hesitate before leaving the safety of darkness to step into the umbrella of light. Our eyes dart about in every direction looking for those hellish headlights, or worse, no headlights. In this ink-black night, a car is all but invisible until it's right on you. Not entirely satisfied, but desperate to get out of the rain, we make one last mad dash to the car. Sirens blare in the distance.

"Give me your cell," I say. "I'll call 9-1-1."

"What for?"

"What for? Someone just tried to kill us!"

David shakes his head. "We just busted into a store, Mira. We'll be arrested."

"Who cares about the store? We'll explain about the car. I'm the future governor's daughter. They'll believe me."

"Please. Don't call the police."

"Why the heck not?"

David doesn't respond. He just opens his door and slides in behind the steering wheel. Only when we're both inside with the doors closed do I notice his face. It's contorted in pain. David retrieves his key from his front pocket and tries to stick it in the ignition, but his hands are shaking too much.

"You're hurt." My words seem so obvious, so stupid. I should have noticed before, should have said something, but I was so scared. All I wanted was to get away. I turn on the overhead light so I can see better. The leg of David's jeans is sliced open from the knee to the hem. And there's blood. A lot of it. I carefully grasp the edge of the wet fabric and pull it aside. I gasp when I see the gash in his calf—at least five inches long, and pretty deep.

He looks at me and musters a half-hearted smile. "I cut it going through the window," he says apologetically.

"You need stitches. I should call an ambulance."

"No."

I had no idea David could be so stubborn. I huff impatiently. "We at least need to stop the bleeding. Just hold on."

I'm out of the car in a second and run into the store.

"First aid kits!" I shout. The kid behind the counter just glares at me. I ignore him and head up the toiletries aisle. Nothing but bandages barely big enough to wrap around a toe can be found. In frustration, I throw all the boxes to the floor. I do find one self-adhesive Ace bandage, the kind for wrapping a sprained ankle or knee. I go a little farther and snatch a bag of Kotex off the shelf. On my way out the door, I toss my ten dollar bill at the jerk.

Back in the car, I tear open the plastic Kotex package and pull out three pads.

"What are you doing?" David asks, his teeth clattering. It could be because he's wet, though the air is warm, or maybe it's shock. I'm not going to take a chance that it's the latter. After tearing open his pant leg the rest of the way, I place the three pads across his wound and wrap them tightly in place with the ace bandage.

"So, are you going to tell me why you won't let me call the police?"

David winces as I tuck the end of the bandage into place. "I'm, uh, not supposed to be here."

"What are you talking about? You mean here in Bakersfield?"

"No. I mean in this country."

I sit up and stare at him. "You're illegal?" I half laugh, half snort. "Oh, this just gets better and better."

"My uncle needs me." David's voice is pleading. "I'm all he has. I'm trying to get the correct legal documents, but the waiting period is so long."

If he had told me at any other time, I might have been angry, or at least irritated. But David just risked his life to protect me. And after what we've just been through, I don't have the heart or the time to hold it against him.

Instead, I hop out of the car and hurry around to the driver's side. "Move over," I order, opening the door. David manages to climb over the emergency brake and settle into the passenger seat. I turn on the ignition and crank up the heat.

"If you won't let me call for help then I'll have to take you to the hospital myself. We can look for one here or, if I step on it, we can get back to the Valley in a couple of hours."

"Let's get home," David says.

"Okay," I agree. "But I swear, if you pass out or something, I'm pulling over and dialing 9-1-1."

During the trip back to the city, I spend as much time looking in the rearview mirror as I do at the road ahead. I can't go any faster than I am for fear of hydroplaning. But my nerves are on edge waiting for that car to appear out of nowhere and run me off the road. Luckily, we make it all the way back without incident. At least the rain has stopped. It's after ten by the time we finally reach the ER.

The waiting room is full of people in varying stages of pain and illness, but when I tell the receptionist who I am, we're immediately escorted to a closet-sized exam room.

"We're kind of busy tonight," says the nurse, an Asian woman expressing a little too much enthusiasm for this late hour. "At least you'll be comfortable in here while you wait, away from all those people out there with the flu. These crazy summer storms always bring on the worst of it." She hands David a paper gown and instructs him to remove his pants. Her eyes roam across my face and down to my hands. "Better have the doctor examine both of you. Those cuts don't look so good."

There's a small TV mounted in the upper corner of the room. The nurse reaches up and turns it on. She flips through a couple of channels. For a split second I see Papa's face flash

185

on the screen, before the shopping channel appears with some woman demonstrating an onion chopper.

"This all right?" asks the nurse.

"Would you mind going back one?"

It's a recap of the nightly news. Papa's face is gone, but Rawley Pharmaceutical's logo is on the screen behind the reporter's head.

The nurse clucks her tongue. "You'd think since they cured so many other things, they could find a cure for the flu. Then I could go home early tonight." She laughs at her own joke, and then leaves the room, shutting the door behind her.

Whatever the news was saying about Papa and Rawley is over now. The news moves on to a story about a break-in at a furniture warehouse in Bakersfield. Officers arrived at the scene of the crime to find the front window shattered, but nothing was missing from the store.

I turn to David and find him fumbling with his belt buckle. His hands are still shaking.

"Here, let me do that." I release his buckle and deftly undo the button and zipper of his jeans.

"I feel so helpless," he says.

I turn back to the TV to give him some privacy. "Don't be such a baby," I say to him, but not in a critical way at all. I mean, he's probably still in shock. I hear him wrestle out of his clothes and slip into the gown. Next, I hear the crinkle of paper as he sits down on the exam table.

"All right," he tells me. "I guess I'm as decent as I'll ever be."

I grin when I see him sitting there wrapped in baby blue paper that barely reaches halfway down his thighs. One hand is behind him, holding the back of his gown closed.

"You do look helpless," I say, laughing a little.

David rolls his eyes. "Shut up."

I snatch a pair of surgical gloves from the counter and pull them on. I inspect the Ace bandage on David's leg and the lumps of Kotex underneath.

"That's going to be embarrassing." David cringes at the sight. "After the doctor sees that, what little is left of my masculine dignity will be utterly destroyed."

"Well, you can't beat them for absorbency," I say, stifling another laugh. I stand and look into David's face. He looks forlorn, like a sad, little puppy. Something about his expression tugs at me. I step closer, my stomach touching his knees.

"I don't think you have anything to worry about." I try and comfort him. "That maniac wanted to kill us—he would have killed us—but you saved us."

"I threw us both through a plate glass window. We could have died anyway."

"But we didn't. David, you saved my life tonight."

David's head remains bowed, studying the floor. What is he thinking? For the first time since I've met him, I really want to know what's going on inside his head. He blinks a couple of times and then slowly lifts his face until his eyes meet mine. Only inches apart, I can feel his breath against my skin. A prickly sensation races down my spine, and I shiver. From the corner of my eye I see his free hand rising, ever so slowly coming near. Inside of me, my heart pumps faster, every instinct telling me to back away. But I remain still, my eyes locked on David's. His eyes locked on mine.

His hand brushes against my hair. I feel the minute ripples of movement in my scalp. His hand is at my cheek, his palm a millimeter away from my skin—so close I can feel the warmth of him. His fingers trace the outline of my brow, the bridge of my nose, the curve of my lips—but not once does he make contact. It would be so easy. All I have to do is tip my face forward just the slightest bit. I could reach up and take his hand, press my lips to his palm... But I can't. I won't. My heart is wildly out of control, but the rest of me remains horribly, excruciatingly still.

He leans toward me, just a little, his face coming to rest so close to mine that I can smell peppermint on his breath as his lips graze the molecules of air between us. God, I can't stand it. To feel him so close, to want him so much—and yet we might as well be miles apart. It would be the same. No. Distance would be easier.

There's a light rap on the exam room door, and the gap between us instantly widens. I back away, pressing myself against the wall. The door opens, and a female doctor in her early thirties struts in. Her short, blonde hair is tucked casually behind her ears, and she's all smiles.

"Mr. Valdez? I understand you're in the market for some stitches. Is that right?"

She asks him a few standard questions, such as his address and date of birth. Then she begins to un-wrap the Ace bandage.

"Um... I'm going to step out, okay?" I say. In truth, I don't want to see the wound again. Normally, I've got a weak stomach for those sorts of things. I'd be better off in the lobby.

"That's fine," the doctor replies. She takes a quick glance at my hands and face. "My nurse told me about you. Those cuts don't look too bad, but I would like to put some antiseptic on them and maybe a Band-Aid or two. Why don't you check in at the nurses' station while I take care of your boyfriend?"

My boyfriend? I start to correct her, but then I shut my mouth. I actually like the sound of it. I smile at David before leaving. He smiles back, but his expression is a little fearful. If I could, I'd stay and hold his hand, but then I guess he'd really have no dignity left.

I close the door behind me and lean back against it. My heart is finally slowing down. I need a moment to get my bearings, to think straight. I feel like I've just stepped off the craziest roller coaster ride of my life. I look at the clock down the hall near the nurses' station. It's nearly eleven p.m.

I step away from the door through which I hear David asking something about a needle and how much it will hurt. This is probably going to take a while, so instead of going to the nurses' station, I head for the nearest elevator.

I want ... I need to see my mother.

# 28

IN THE ELEVATOR, TODAY'S EVENTS run through my brain: our visit with the Beitners, finding out that their daughter is my real mom, and nearly getting killed by some wacko. But as crazy as all that is, what my mind keeps coming back to is David. He wanted to touch me, kiss me. I saw it in his eyes, but he didn't do it. He could have, and he could have apologized later for touching me, for connecting with me even though I'd asked him not to. But he kept his distance. And for some reason that makes me want him in a way that is almost unbearable. I had to get away to think about all this.

The elevator doors slide open, and I head for Mama's room. From where I am I can see that the door is ajar and the lights are off. Strange. There's always a light on in there, even if it's just the one above her bed offering a soft glow for the nurses to see by. I remind myself how late it is and chastise myself for being stupid.

When I reach the nurses' station a tall, male nurse I've never met before glances up from a medical chart. He's on his feet in a second. "Can I help you?" he asks, planting himself directly in my path. The badge pinned to his blue scrubs reads *Colin*.

"I'm here to see my mom."

"Do you know what time it is, honey?" he says. "Visiting hours ended at nine."

I don't have time for this. I pull my hoodie up around my head and the sleeves down to my fingertips. Then I push past Colin.

"Hey! Hold on!" he calls out behind me. "You want me to call security on you?"

I stop, my feet suddenly cemented to the white tile floor. Every little sound is amplified—the elevator doors closing behind me, the voice on the intercom calling 'code blue', the nurse threatening me. I don't know how long I stand there. It can't be more than a few seconds, though somehow it feels longer—time stretches out in front of me, minutes and seconds strung along on an endless invisible thread.

My feet move again, slowly at first, then faster. I reach Mama's room and push the door open. The room is dark, but the unnatural brightness of the light from the hall slips past me in a sharp rectangle on the floor. My eyes adjust quickly, and I see at once that something is wrong.

Am I in the right room? I look at the number on the door. I back out of the room and turn toward the nurses' station where Colin waits with his hands on his hips.

"Has Ana Ortiz been moved?" I ask him. "To another room, I mean?"

Colin's face goes noticeably pale. "You're her daughter?" he asks.

I nod.

"Wait here a sec, okay, hon?"

His manner shifts from critical to almost motherly, exaggerated as though he were talking to a five-year-old. He walks to another room and sticks his head in. A moment later, a second nurse comes out of the room. It's Jessie.

"Mira?" Jessie asks. "What are you doing here?"

"My mom," I say. "Has she been moved? She's not in her room."

Colin turns away, busying himself with a stack of papers on the desk. I get the feeling that he doesn't want any part of this conversation. Jessie's eyebrows crease together. And there's something else—something in her eyes.

"Mira, are you all right? Maybe you should go home, talk with your dad."

"I don't want to go home, Jessie. I want to see my mom. Could you just tell me where they've moved her?"

She hesitates and glances at Colin, but he avoids her gaze.

"Listen, Mira," Jessie says to me, "I don't really have any authority to—"

"To do what?"

"Why don't I call Dr. Zimmerman? Or your father? He could come down and explain."

I'm not getting anywhere. Either she doesn't want to tell me, or she really can't. I make it easy for her. In half a second, my hand locks around Jessie's wrist.

The deluge of memories, thoughts and feelings burst inside me like shrapnel from a bomb, more than I can stand. More than I need. I quickly sift through chaos. I find all her early memories, everything before today, and shove them aside. And there it is—only a tiny fraction of Jessie's psyche,

192

just a splinter of her existence—but enough to destroy all of mine.

I let Jessie go and stumble back. My chest clutches, and I snatch breaths through the sudden onslaught of tears.

"You took her off—" The words are hot stones searing my tongue. "You took my mom off life support?"

My mind burns with the images—powering down the respirator, detaching the IV, watching the heart monitor flat line. It's not like watching Jessie do it. Jessie's thoughts are my thoughts now—it's like it was me—like I killed Mama.

Jessie stares at me, her eyes wide and wet with tears. "My God," she says, "you didn't know. I assumed—I thought you knew."

I'm shaking. Every cell in my body is on fire—rage, shock, and despair all bore a hole through my soul. My stomach wrenches. I'd vomit, but I haven't eaten anything since that piece of bread at the Beitners. There's nothing to throw up. I bend over anyway, my hands braced against my knees, and dry heave.

I hear Jessie's voice talking. "Colin, page Dr. Zimmerman."

But I'm seeing it all in my mind. The orders. The orders signed by Zimmerman—and another signature at the bottom of the page.

*Alberto Ortiz.*

I see the doctor standing by with a clipboard in his hand as a legal witness. I see Jessie flip the switch on the respirator, the cessation of air pushing in and out of Mama's lungs. I watch the peaks on the heart monitor grow farther and farther apart until finally there are none at all. And through all this, *where is Papa*? And I remember he's in Sacramento tonight. But how could they end her life without her husband present? The answer hits me like a cannonball. He's Rawley's former CEO, the hospital's primary source of funding. They do whatever he tells them to. All he had to do was sign a form. So he was conveniently absent when Mama died, as her soul slipped from her body. Coward! But where was I? I was in Bakersfield with David trying to find out why the bastard had cheated on her.

I straighten up, tears raining down my cheeks. He promised me he would wait. He promised!

Jessie's still beside me. Colin's on the phone. They both look very worried. I don't care what they think. I don't care about anything.

"I want to see her," I tell Jessie.

"Mira, I don't think that's such a good idea."

"I want to see her now!" I shout so loud that my vocal chords nearly burst.

Jessie turns to Colin. "Tell the doctor that I'm taking her down to see her mother." Then she leads me to the staff elevator at the far end of the hall. She inserts a key and turns it to call it to our floor. We go down, farther down than I thought we could go. The basement level lacks the bright blue walls and the new carpet smell of the upper floors. It's all concrete—the walls, the floors, the ceilings. Stark, mesh-covered lights hang from bare metal fixtures overhead. While the hospital above resounds with a variety of noises, down here it is oddly silent.

"We don't usually bring people down here," says Jessie, as if reading my mind. Her voice has a hollow sound to it.

The empty space here seems to swallow it up. "But it wasn't right, you know? I assumed he would have told you. You didn't get a chance to say goodbye."

I don't say anything, but I stay close. We follow one corridor to where it turns into another. Finally we reach a set of double doors. Jessie presses a round metal plate on the wall, and one side swings open. Just inside, a guard sits behind a plain steel desk. As we walk in, he glances up from the little TV screen perched on his desk. I can hear the thump of a bat hitting a baseball and the cheers of the crowd. The guard turns the volume down. "Replay. Sorry," he says.

Jessie shows him her badge. "Has Dr. Zimmerman called down the authorization yet?"

"This the Ortiz girl?" the guard asks. "All right." He hefts himself out of his chair, and walks as if he's got all the time in the world. "Wait here a minute." Then he disappears behind another set of doors.

We wait.

About ten minutes pass and the guard returns, dropping lazily back into his seat. He turns the volume on his TV back up before telling us to go right on in.

The room we enter now is a stark contrast to the bland, barren terrain we left behind. This is a softer room, with pale yellow and green wallpaper and dark wood trim. And there are chairs with green cushions in each corner. In the center of the room is Mama.

The gurney's metal wheels show beneath the white sheet draped over her body. That's what my eyes lock on. I can't seem to raise them any higher.

I feel Jessie's hand on my shoulder. "I'm so sorry," she says. I step away from her touch.

I hear the door open again. "Take as much time as you want," Jessie adds. "I'll be waiting just outside if you need me." The door closes shut.

For a long while I just stand there staring at the wheels. Then I force myself to look higher, to the hem of the sheet, and then to where the sheet bulges, covering Mama. My eyes are so blurred with tears I can hardly see. I wipe them dry with my sleeve, but more tears come. Finally I allow my gaze to wander to her face. From Jessie's thoughts, I know that it hasn't been long, just a few hours. Her color is just starting to fade. There are dark circles under her eyes, and a blue tint around her lips. But the shape of her face is the same, the same high cheekbones and straight Romanesque nose. I can't help but watch her chest to see if it will rise and fall.

It doesn't.

"Mama?" My voice is nothing but an empty whisper. "Mama, are you here?"

I blink, and more tears spill out of my eyes. It doesn't matter that I should have known this day would come. Papa tried to prepare me when he showed me that form, but I refused to accept it. But this day came anyway—nothing I did could have stopped it.

Still...

Could there be something left, even just a trace? *Please, God*, I whisper, *please*.

I raise my hand, holding it just above her cheek. She used to stroke my cheek when I was young to comfort me when I cried. How I long to feel her touch now, to have her wipe my tears away. What I wouldn't give to share one more memory with her, just one. Any memory would do. Please. Please, God. Don't let this be the end.

I lower my hand until my fingertips alight on her skin. The cold takes me by surprise, frozen and firm—not at all like Mama. I spread my fingers apart allowing my palm to caress Mama's cheek. I wait for the burst, the sudden shock of lightening. I wait for the impact of memories, of emotion.

I wait.

But nothing comes.

# 29

DAVID WAITS IN THE ER lobby with his bandaged leg resting on an adjacent chair, a copy of *Car & Driver* in his hands. He doesn't see me until I'm standing in front of him. He looks at me over the top of the magazine and smiles.

"Hey, I was wondering when you'd come back for me— *if* you'd come back for me. I was beginning to think you'd found some other dashingly handsome invalid to dote on." He pauses, his smile vanishing. "Mira? What's wrong?"

Swiping at my tears with the heel of my hand, I shake my head. I don't want to talk about it. Not here surrounded by a bunch of people I don't know, but who probably know more about me and my family than they should. "Let's go," I mumble, and head out the door.

Outside, I wait for David to catch up. He's hobbling along on a pair of crutches and looks like he could topple over at any second. "Wait here," I tell him. "I'll get the car."

"Aren't you going to tell me—?"

"Just wait here!" I don't mean to raise my voice at him, but at this point I'm not interested in restraining my emotions. I jog over to the parking structure and let myself into David's car. Alone, I grip the steering wheel in both hands and scream—a guttural, feral scream from the deepest part of me. I pound the wheel with my palms, let my tears splatter onto my lap leaving little dark stars on my jeans. Only when I manage to gain some self-control do I start the ignition and go meet David.

He's standing on the curb when I pull up. Luckily, the rain has stopped. I wait, staring forward into the darkness as David shoves his crutches into the backseat and gets in. He looks at me, but says nothing. He knows I don't want to talk, can't talk. He lets the silence between us alone.

I feel like a bomb ready to go off at the slightest touch. Fury brews inside of me, a raging storm churning in a sea of loss and agony. I've never felt this way before. My arms are stiff as they make the turns at the intersections. I have to force them to respond. David sees all this, but he remains quiet.

We pass the park—our park—which means we're nearly to my house. But I don't want to go home. Not where I have to walk by Mama's room. Not where Mama's things are still scattered everywhere, remnants of my shattered family. I pull to the curb and turn off the engine. Then I open the car door and start walking, my arms wound around myself as if they could somehow deflect the pain.

When I reach the play gym, I stop. I just stand there staring out into the void of night. Then suddenly my whole body ruptures into gut wrenching sobs. I collapse to my knees in the sand and batter the earth with my fists. I don't know how long I'm there, wailing like that, but eventually I

199

simply wear myself out. The sobs turn to weeping, which turn to desperate gasps. Drained of energy, I let my body crumple against the damp ground. Once I'm lying on my back looking up, I see David sitting beside me. He's been there all along, so close I can hear him breathe—watching, waiting, knowing I had to suffer alone, but refusing to let me be alone. He doesn't say a word. He doesn't have to. I see the pain in his face, the comprehension of what has happened. He knows.

David lies down beside me, and we both look up at the stars, faint because of the city lights, but still present. The moon peeks out from behind the clouds, casting a pale, silvery glow on everything around us. After a while, I start to feel a little normal again. At least I'm not crying anymore.

"David?" My voice almost feels like an intruder in the silence.

"Hmm?"

"Thank you."

He turns his head to look at me. "For what?"

"For just being here."

I look at him, and he smiles at me. I try to smile back, but it's hard.

"I didn't have much choice, did I?" he says, shrugging against the sand. "I mean I'm not in any condition to drive."

I crack a little smile at that and land a playful punch on his arm. I let a few more moments of silence pass, but the void left behind from my emotional breakdown is suddenly filled with a million words clawing to get out.

"Why did this happen?"

"What do you mean?"

"I mean me, David. *Me*. Why am I like this? Why am I so … different?"

"You're not so different, Mira."

"Yes, I am!" I roll to my side and get up. I can't lie still any longer. I need to move, to let the agitation I feel out somehow. I walk over to the tall slide, the one that curls around a center pole. I climb up and sit at the top of it.

"When I was a little girl, there was a slide just like this one at our neighborhood park. I was terrified of it," I call down to David. He's gotten up, too, and is trying to maneuver his way across the sand, but his crutches keep sinking, making the trek more arduous than it needs to be. I keep talking. "Mama used to stand at the bottom, trying to talk me into sliding down, but I wouldn't budge. Then one day she climbed up with me. Holding me around my waist, she pushed off and we both went down together. It was the most thrilling moment of my life up to that point. The rush of air against my face, hearing my mom's laughter, feeling so safe in her arms. After that I was never afraid again."

By now David has reached the slide. I push off, and my body careens around the curves and comes to a gentle rest at the bottom where he's waiting for me. I stand up in front of him, peering into his chocolate brown eyes.

"You *are* different, Mira Ortiz," he says. "You're different in all the right ways."

"I'm a freak."

"Not a freak. No, you're—you're amazing."

For some reason what he says sets me off. "Stop trying to make me feel better, okay? I don't want to feel better. I don't want to feel anything ever again! I should be dead, not her!"

"Don't say that."

Tears threaten to start up again. I swipe at my eyes, trying to hold them at bay. "Sorry." I try to smile. "You're right. I'm good. It's all good."

"No, it's not, Mira." David steps closer. "You're not *good* right now. You're hurting, but I'm here. Okay? You're not alone in this."

"Yes, I am!"

The earlier rainstorm has cooled the air. A little breeze carries the scent of damp grass and pine trees through the night.

"Don't you get it?" I continue. "God spared me and took my mother instead."

"What are you talking about, Mira?"

"It was too much. It was all too much, so I tried—" My voice catches in my throat, but I force the words out, "I tried to kill myself."

The expression on David's face is one of disbelief, shock. I grab the hem of my hoodie with both hands and jerk it up over my head. I throw it to the sand and thrust out my arm. The wound is healed now, but the deep red scar is still fresh and ugly.

"I was supposed to die! Not her!"

I don't know what I expect from David. Revulsion? Pity? But I see nothing like that in his eyes.

He lets go of one of his crutches, still holding it beneath his arm, and reaches for me. But then he stops—hesitating. He won't touch me. But I want him to. When he reaches out again I remain purposely still. The tiny hairs on my arm tingle as his fingers trace the air just above my scar. My skin aches for his touch.

It's too much—this ever present barrier between us—the barricade I've erected between me and everyone else. I'm tired of the isolation. I want—*need* to feel again—to know in some way that someone understands me, cares about me.

Slowly I raise my arms and slide my hands over David's shoulders. Lacing my fingers across the back of his shirt collar, I pull him toward me. He resists at first, a questioning look in his eyes. So I step closer, erasing the gap between us. Fighting my instinctive urge to turn and run, to protect myself from the pain and chaos, I press my body against his. I can feel his heart steadily beating in his chest, his lungs expanding and retracting with every breath. I close my eyes and lean into him.

The moment our lips connect my mind ignites with electric bursts. The burning is so intense I nearly pull away, but instead I kiss him harder. I see everything he is, everything he's experienced and felt and learned in a lifetime. A little boy running barefoot down a cobbled street in a small Guatemalan town, savoring the sweet tastes of mango and coconut, standing in the warm torrential rains, arms outstretched, head tipped back, mouth wide open.

But there are bad memories, too, ones he's buried deep. A father struggling to make ends meet, taking out his frustrations on his boy: a calloused hand, a leather belt, a wooden dowel, whatever was convenient and within reach. I feel the fear, the betrayal—too painful even for me. I move through them quickly only to discover an even darker void—

203

the trauma of leaving his home and family behind, of entering a new country, a new world, and trying to find his place in it.

His more recent memories slip around each other like ice cubes melting on fevered skin. I see him at school watching someone from a distance, a girl—*me*. He liked me then? The realization startles me. And I see Craig, my boyfriend, and David's intense loathing of him. Then there are his memories of seeing me at Dr. Walsh's office, the fundraiser, everything over the past few days. I feel the depth of compassion he felt watching me fall apart tonight, wanting so much to comfort me, knowing he couldn't.

And the longing—his agonizing longing—for me.

Our kiss ends, and I look up at him. I want to ask him, is this for real? But I know it is. I know everything about him. I know that his every thought is for me, that he wants so desperately for me to understand how he feels, but that he would never compromise my trust in him. Never.

I kiss David again, and this time he kisses me back—hard and passionate. My fingers brush up the back of his neck into his hair. I'm so consumed with him I don't even feel the pain anymore. His lips skim along my chin and throat, the tops of my shoulders. His hands caress my back—delicate, like a whisper. He smells so good—vanilla and spice. I breathe deeply, letting him fill my senses.

I hear the crutches hit the sand as David's arms slip around my body, holding me even closer. But I want more. Feeling a desperate hunger for contact, I grasp the hem of David's shirt and lift it, dragging it up his arms until it comes free. Warmth radiates from his russet skin, smooth and curved over joints and muscles. Wearing just my thin cotton tank top, I feel horribly exposed. Fighting the impulse to wrap my arms defensively around myself, I wrap my arms around David instead.

Touching him again, all I see is him. His passion envelopes me completely, like the shield of warm night air that surrounds us. My hands sweep over the contours of his shoulder blades and spine down to the small of his back. Gliding up again along his sides, my fingers graze a patch of raised, irregular skin—a scar.

At that moment something inside of David shifts—a change so subtle I might not have noticed if I weren't so connected to him. He stiffens ever so slightly in my arms, and a thought—no, not even that—an *impression* leaches from his psyche into mine:

Regret.

# 30

I HAVE JUST WITNESSED THINGS David has kept hidden for years, things too painful to exhume, let alone share—especially with someone he hardly knows. All this time I've been so worried about myself I never considered what it might be like for David—for anyone—to be so exposed.

I peel myself away from David. Stepping back, I put a distance of two or three feet between us.

"Mira?" His expression is one of surprise, confusion. "Is something wrong?"

Heat radiates into my cheeks. My throat constricts. "I'm sorry, David," I say, wrapping my arms defensively around my overly bare body. "I'm so sorry."

Part of me hopes I'm wrong, that I misunderstood what I felt—what *he* felt. But when his eyes briefly flit away, ashamed, I feel a sharp stab in my heart. I quickly lean over, scooping my hoodie off the ground, and shake the sand out of it.

"You're leaving?" he asks, half-smiling like he thinks I'm just playing a joke on him.

"Yeah, I'm leaving."

"But why?"

I take a moment to look at him, at his eyes full of stunned hurt and questions. For a second I almost want to stay, to ignore the fact that I've trespassed where I wasn't invited. But then I remind myself that everyone has secrets, and some of those secrets are best left buried.

"Have I offended you in some way?" David asks.

"No, of course not," I lie, knowing how hard he tried not to offend me. It wasn't him who broke off the kiss—it was me. "It's been a rough night, you know? I'm tired, and I just want to go home."

He probes me with his eyes, searching for evidence of my lie, but the anguish in my face, in my heart, is as real as anything. First losing my mother, and now losing him. It has been a rough night—a horrible night.

"Let me drive you." David snatches his shirt from the ground and slips it on over his head all in one smooth motion. Then he reaches for his crutches.

"No, you said yourself you can't drive," I remind him, my eyes aching with the threat of tears.

"I was teasing. I think I can handle it."

"I really would prefer to walk. All right?"

David drags his fingers through his hair, frustrated. "Whatever I did, whatever I said—"

"I'm good," I say, crafting a smile. "It's all good."

I pull my sleeves to my fingertips and head down Foothill Boulevard, walking briskly toward home. I don't look back.

The mansion is dark and still when I arrive. I let myself in through the back door via the key Helen keeps hidden beneath one of those fake plastic rocks in the garden. I don't bother turning on any lights as I wander through the kitchen and dining room. Slants of pale blue moonlight drift through the windows, casting an almost iridescent glow on everything. The face of the grandfather clock at the foot of the stairs glares accusingly at me, its hands nearing three a.m. Despite the late hour, I'm not tired. Emotionally spent, yes. Physically exhausted, yes. But having only just gotten news of Mama's death less than two hours ago, sleep seems a self-indulgent luxury.

The sick roiling in my stomach returns with a vengeance. I compel my legs, heavy with fatigue, to climb the stairs and carry me to my bedroom. Down the hall the door to my parents' room stands open. I recall again that Papa is not home. He's four hundred miles away in Sacramento. For once I wish he were home just so I wouldn't be alone tonight.

My room is dark except for the red numbers on the face of my iPod dock, which bathes the room in crimson shadows. Discarding my hoodie on the corner of my bed, I glance down at my naked arms, tinged the color of blood. Lifting my left hand, I slowly rotate my wrist until the narrow ropes of scar tissue gawk at me like lifeless worms affixed forever to my skin.

*I should have died. Not her.*

A cry catches in my throat when I think of Mama lying on that gurney, the white sheet draped so gracefully over her body. I think of Papa, fleeing to the Capitol to escape the burden of watching her die. I squeeze my eyes shut, hastening tears.

If I had died maybe Mama would still be alive. That stupid fundraiser would have been cancelled. Papa would have been home comforting her. She wouldn't have been alone. And David ... I would never have met David.

I cross the floor to my bathroom and switch on the light. The sudden brightness burns my eyes. I close them for a moment then slowly reopen them, letting them adjust. I stand at the sink, the oval mirror framed in carved oak beckoning to me like the magic mirror in the story of 'Snow White', but I can't bring myself to make eye contact. Avoiding my gaze, I jerk open drawer after drawer in the cabinet below. I find what I expect to find: toothpaste, toothbrush, hair-bands, make up. In one drawer is a three-week-old electric razor that my parents bought to replace the disposable ones I used to use. Papa and Mama both got one, too. There hasn't been a razor in the house since I was in the hospital. Mama's needles and lancets are gone. And Helen keeps the kitchen knives under lock and key—obeying Dr. Walsh's strict instructions. For the past three weeks everything sharp or even remotely toxic has been kept out of my reach. Until now I haven't cared. I don't even know where Papa keeps everything let alone how I'd get into it if I did.

Slamming the last drawer shut, I hunch forward, pressing the heels of my hands against the marble sink. I let out a frustrated, feral growl as I strike one hand against the counter hard enough to hurt. The collision sends a burning tremor up my arm. Finally I raise my eyes to the mirror.

What I see before me is unrecognizable. The face I know, but the person in front of me looks as hollow as a dry well. Eyes ringed red from crying, the souls of all those she has touched have driven her own soul away. Where is the girl I used to be, I wonder—before Mama, before Gaudium?

Balling the fingers of my right hand into a fist, I smash it into the strange girl's face. The glass splintering reminds me of a frozen pond cracking. When I lower my hand I see the fragmented face in the spider-web of minute fissures. I punch my fist against it once more. This time the shattered shards of mirror slough off the wall, landing on the counter and in the sink with delicate tinkles. I stare at the void left by the broken mirror, a desolate irregular circle of wall. But I'm not interested in walls. Walls, like secrets, should be left alone.

Instead I fix my gaze on a long, jagged triangle of glass resting against the faucet. I carefully wrap my trembling hand around it, feeling the sharp edges bite into my skin. How ironic, I think, that just hours ago these very hands were unwillingly damaged by shards like this. I lift the glass and bring its glistening silver tip to my wrist. I press down until the skin bows, creating a tiny bowl, and I recall how it was before, the blood droplets bubbling, swelling, merging into a single crimson line. Strangely I'd felt no pain. In fact, when I cut into myself I could almost feel the pain inside me being released.

But of course, it didn't release anything, didn't change anything, except how Mama and Papa treated me. I remember Mama coming into my room, me with the razor blade still pinched between my thumb and forefinger, my blood dripping onto the carpet. Her eyes had darted from my wrist to my face, comprehending in that single glance all the agony and desperation I couldn't express to her in words. I hadn't touched her in weeks, and yet I knew from that glance that she wouldn't judge me, wouldn't scold or condemn me.

I dropped the blade and reached for her. "Mama?" I cried, and she came to me, snatching the sheet off my bed, winding it tightly around my wrist, dialing 9-1-1 on her cell, and somehow embracing me all at once.

"You're all right," she repeated over and over. "You'll be all right, Mira. I swear on my own life."

I think of her now, the point of the mirror shard yearning to bite into my arm. And I know—I can't do this to her again. Not again. It would break her, losing me, like losing her has broken me. But she wouldn't want that—not for me.

"You're strong, Mira. You'll be all right."

I drop the shard into the sink and take a deep gasping breath as if I've just come up for air after being submerged in icy water. The smell of copper pricks my nostrils, blood filling the creases on my palm. I haven't cut myself, only reopened an earlier wound. I grab the towel hanging behind the bathroom door and wrap my hand in it. Then I turn off the light.

I lie down on my bed without bothering to fold back the covers or kick off my shoes. My head finds comfort in my pillow's caress. That's when I notice the swath of moonlight on the wall just across Mama's photo collage of me when I was young. I look at the faces and am reassured. I know that girl, the one my mother saw through the camera lens. If I can't connect with the girl in the mirror, at least I can connect with this one. I can see myself the way Mama saw me.

211

CONTACT

Finally fatigue claims me. I pull my knees up to my chest, close my eyes, and fall asleep dreaming of Mama and David—and of snow angels.

# 31

I WAKE TO A LOUD THUMPING sound. I hear a shrill bell, more thumping. The numbers on my iDock read 7:22 am. Four hours! I've been asleep four hours! Who the heck would be pounding on my door so early in the morning?

Rolling off the bed with a groan, I reluctantly make my way downstairs to the entry and open the front door. I'm greeted by the smell of sunrise and juniper, and to my utter astonishment, David is there leaning on his crutches, his fist poised for another round of thumping.

"Oh, hey," he says, lowering his hand. "You up?"

"I am now."

"You *saw* me, didn't you?" he asks without hesitation. "That's why you left last night. I didn't know what to do at first, couldn't figure it out, but I walked—hobbled around town all night—"

"What? Hobbled?" Still in a daze from the abrupt end to my sleep, I can't wrap my head around what he's saying. "You've been up all night?"

213

"Yeah. But then I realized what—*why* you—Mira, you didn't have to leave."

I don't know why, maybe because of surprise, maybe relief, but I want to touch him again. I move toward him, but he steps back, more an instinctive response than a conscious one. He looks down, embarrassed.

"Sorry," he says, tightening the grip on his crutches. The space between us feels awkward. I don't like it. I try to brush it off.

"Are you okay?" I finally ask.

"Yeah, I'm fine," he says uncertainly. "I liked it, you know—kissing you. I've wanted to kiss you for a long time. But I'm just not sure how I feel about—*that*, you know?"

"All right." I say it like it's no big deal, even though it hurts. "Then we won't do *that* again, okay?"

David looks up at me, suddenly concerned. "I've hurt your feelings, haven't I?"

Squashed my heart underfoot like a cigarette is more accurate.

His gaze drops again. He stares at the space between his feet. "I never wanted to hurt you, Mira." His voice is barely a whisper. "But until last night no one knew. Not even my mom. At least I never told her, though now that I'm older I can't imagine any mother not knowing something like that."

His eyes flicker to mine, and then back down again. "If she did know, she never did anything to stop him."

I respond cautiously, not sure how much he trusts me, if at all. "Your scar—"

He shrugs. "My dad came home drunk one night, grabbed a burning stick from the fireplace and hit me with it.

214

My shirt caught fire. Burned me before he put it out. I was ten."

The emotions I felt when I touched that scar come back to me, the shame and fear of a young boy, the resolute determination of the man to keep his weakness hidden.

"When Tío Ramón suggested I come live with him in California," David continues, "I jumped at the chance. I didn't care about getting a visa or any of that. I just wanted to get out as soon as I could. Ramón arranged it. I suspect maybe he felt the same urgency as I did."

He releases a slow, strained breath, and his eyes connect with mine.

"Mira, I care about you. I want to be with you. I just— I'm just not ready to—"

His eyes fill with need—a need for me to understand, a need for time, for forgiveness.

"It's good," I tell him. "It's all good."

And it is.

David relaxes, the rigid tension in his body melting away. "Okay," he says, smiling. He takes a deep, cleansing breath and laughs a little.

"So," I begin, stepping away from the door to invite him in. "Are you hungry?"

# 32

IT'S HELEN'S DAY OFF and one of those rare opportunities to take control of the kitchen. I remove a carton of eggs from the fridge along with some cream, butter, and grated cheddar cheese. David searches for a whisk.

"You know, we could go grab a couple of breakfast burritos from Bergie's," I suggest, though the thought of warmed-over powdered eggs and stale tortillas makes me cringe.

"Nope. I'm making you breakfast here." One corner of David's mouth creeps up a little. "And don't say 'no', or you'll hurt *my* feelings."

I can't resist his crooked smile, so I reluctantly agree.

"Ta da!" he says, brandishing a metal whisk in the air. "Perfect. Do you have any onions, tomatoes, mushrooms?"

"Onions in the pantry," I tell him. "Tomatoes there on the counter. You might find some mushrooms in the fridge."

"Great. Let me handle this then."

"What about your leg?"

"I'm fine, Mira. I'm not crippled. I can handle breakfast."

"But then what'll I do?"

"Shower." David makes a funny face at me, pretending to pinch his nose.

"All right. I do have sand in my hair. But when I'm done, there had better be a feast ready."

"I solemnly swear." He holds up three fingers, the Boy Scout sign.

I reach into the bag of cheese and withdraw a pinch of orange strands, tossing them at him, and then head to my room. After gathering some clean clothes, I lock myself in my bathroom. The mirror fragments still lay in the sink. I make a mental note to clean it up later. As I start to undress, my cell phone vibrates in my pocket. It's a text from Frank Felton, the doctor from the Cayce Institute:

I HAVE SOME MORE INFO. CALL ME. PLEASE.

Snapping the phone shut, I toss it onto the vanity. After I undress, I step into the shower and let the hot water cascade down my skin as my thoughts turn to last night with David. The physical sensations were the same as all the other times, the electrical surge, the explosion of images and feelings. But even though he made it clear how he feels about being seen that way, for the first time in a long time I didn't hate being touched. To be wanted, to be loved that much—and to know it with absolute certainty—was the most wonderful experience I have ever known. The only touch that ever came close was Mama's.

I lean my face into the spray of water and pull the steam into my lungs. I will miss Mama's touch. I will miss the intensity of her love for me. Her memories begin to surface, mingling with my own. An overwhelming emptiness swells inside me. Standing here, alone, I allow myself to cry again.

If only Papa loved me like she did.

After a while, I dry off and change into a clean pair of jeans and a t-shirt. The shallow cuts on my hands have already begun to heal, but I dab some ointment on them just to be safe.

When I come out of the bathroom, I can smell the sautéed onions and eggs coming from the kitchen. My stomach aching from hunger, I hurry back to the dining room and take a seat. David comes in carrying identical plates.

"Here you go," he says, setting them on the table. I sit down in front of the biggest omelet I've ever seen with a dollop of sour cream on top. He spears a clump of egg and tomato with his fork and holds it out to me. "Try it."

I take a bite. The blend of onions and mushrooms is unbelievable. "It's got a bit of a zing to it."

"Do you like it?"

"I do," I answer, helping myself to more—with my own fork this time. "What is it?"

"Pepper sauce. Just a little, though. Bet you didn't know I could cook?"

Actually, after last night, I did.

"It's delicious," I tell him.

"Good." He pulls out a chair and sits down beside me, resting his arms on the table. "So," he says, his voice taking on a more serious tone, "how are you feeling?"

I swallow before answering. I'm not sure if he's asking because of my mother or because of what happened between us at the park. I don't really feel like talking about either one. "Good, but I am starting to get a headache. Too much stress and not enough sleep, I guess."

Before I can say anything more, David hobbles out of the dining room back into the kitchen. He returns with a glass of pineapple juice and two little white tablets.

"There's a first aid kit in there," he informs me, dropping the pills into my palm. "They're just aspirin. Wish they were something stronger."

I cradle the pills in my hand and think about how a few months back I tried to kill myself with pills like these. I failed miserably, of course. I should have snuck a handful of Mama's sleeping pills instead. Now I'm glad I didn't. The second time I tried, I thought for sure I'd succeed. I was so determined to die. But after last night I feel differently.

I down the aspirin with the juice and dig into my omelet. I start chewing, but then something hits me—a thought, an image, I don't really know what—but it's like a light bulb has turned on. It must show on my face because David shoots me a puzzled look.

"What is it, Mira?"

"Pills!"

The words start spilling out of me faster than I can string them together in my head. "I don't know why I couldn't see it before. I guess there were just so many pieces floating around in my head I couldn't put them all together, but it makes sense. It's horrible, but it makes sense."

"Whoa, whoa!" David holds his hands out in front of him. "Slow down. You're *not* making any sense. And maybe you should put down your trident before you stab someone."

219

I hadn't realized I was waving my fork around. I set it down and try again.

"The night of the fundraiser, you remember?"

"Yeah?"

"Mama was drunk when we left for home. I'd never seen her drunk before in my life. I mean, I know she was drinking, but she's never had so much that she lost control. And she didn't have any more to drink that night than usual, but she was totally out of it. Then she went into the coma. Dr. Zimmerman said he found traces of Trazodone in her bloodstream, her sleeping medication—which she rarely used anyway. And she had taken extra insulin to cover the alcohol, but she was so deeply asleep she couldn't wake up when her blood sugar dropped."

David stops chewing. "Where are you going with all this?"

"Mama was practically unconscious by the time we got her home. She wouldn't have taken any sleeping pills—couldn't have."

"You think someone else gave her the pills?"

"I think someone slipped them to her during the fundraiser. Maybe in her drink."

"And the insulin?"

"Papa could have given Mama the injection. He's done it lots of times. So have I."

David and I stare across the table at each other. My appetite's gone, and from the fact that David's put down his fork, I think his has, too.

"But there's more."

I tell David about the Authorization to Terminate Life Support, how Papa had brought it home and wanted to talk about *options*.

"He promised me he wouldn't do it," I add. "Not until I agreed to it. But last night…"

Until now, telling David all this had seemed easy. But when it comes to describing how I found out about Mama, how she'd been taken off life support, I can hardly get the words out. By the time I'm finished, I'm crying.

David hands me a napkin. I wipe my nose and crumple it into a tight ball. I wait until I'm more composed before I continue.

"He wasn't there, David," I tell him finally. "I saw it, Mama's last moments, through Jessie. Papa just signed her life away. He didn't even have the decency to watch her die."

I pick up the photo of Papa and Jackie Beitner, which I'd set on the table last night when I got home. It's creased in several places now.

"Mira," says David, his voice a little shaky and quiet. "Are you saying what I think you're saying?"

Am I? Do I dare put into words what all the evidence so blatantly suggests? This man, my father, a revered member of the medical community, public leader—is it possible? Could this all be real?

I pick up the picture and look into my Papa's eyes.

"Yes," I pronounce "I think Alberto Ortiz murdered my mother."

# 33

"THAT'S CRAZY!" DAVID PUSHES away from the dining table and stands up. He starts collecting our plates even though we've hardly touched the food on them. I don't think either of us feels much like eating now.

"What about Bakersfield?" I ask. "Whoever was driving that car wanted us dead."

"But you said no one knew we were there."

"My dad has a GPS locator on my phone. He keeps tabs on me."

"You didn't have your phone that night, remember?"

"True," I reply. "But someone did try to kill us that night. He said he went to Sacramento, but what if that was a lie?"

"Your dad's not a murderer, Mira," David says, swiping some stray eggs from the table to his plate. "He couldn't be."

I lean back in my chair, my shoulders slumping.

"I mean, think about it," he continues, "you're talking about your *father*."

"But you're the one who suggested I consider the possibility."

"Yeah, the possibility that he was involved in the Rawley scandal, the medical trials. You're talking about killing people—on purpose."

With his hands full of dirty plates, David pushes through the kitchen door. While he's gone I'm left alone with my thoughts. He's right of course. So Papa had an affair—so my parents didn't have a perfect marriage. Papa wouldn't *kill* Mama. And he wouldn't try to kill me.

Would he?

David returns, drying his hands on a dish towel. He cringes a little as he walks. His leg is hurting, and I realize I should have been the one to clear the table, though I doubt he would have let me.

"I admit it does sound kind of crazy," I tell him, "but that doesn't change the fact that he terminated Mama's life support when he promised me he'd wait."

David flips the towel over his shoulder. "You have every right to be pissed at him for that."

"I'm more than pissed, David."

"All right," he replies. "Why not tell him so?"

"Because if I do I'll probably say some things I'll regret."

"Like what? What would you say to him if you had the chance?"

David's question catches me off guard. What would I say to Papa? "I don't know," I answer, burying my face in my hands. "I don't *want* to talk to him. I don't ever want to see him again."

"That's impractical," says David. "You happen to live in the same house. Eventually you'll bump into each other."

Right again. I was beginning to get irritated. I let out a defeated sigh as I run my thumb over the photo's one torn edge, stiff and irregular.

"I can't confront him," I tell David. "Not now."

"So what are you going to do?"

I get up from the table and walk toward the kitchen. I pause at the door a second, glancing back. "I'm going to put this picture back where I found it and forget the whole thing. I'm sure Papa had his reasons for letting Mama go. Maybe it's time I do the same."

I leave David in the dining room and head for Papa's office. It's just as I left it, the record player sitting open on his desk, *Les Misérables* on the turntable, Papa's leather chair still beside the file cabinet. I push the chair out of the way and kneel down in front of the drawer. Then I pull it open as far as it will go. The photo was stuck into the metal seam at the back. I'll have to tuck it back in. I remove the stack of file folders, setting them on the floor beside me, and then reach my hand in to feel for the seam.

As I run my fingers along the shallow depression, they stop at the touch of something I didn't expect to find there, something not metal. Paper. The uneven torn edge of stiff paper. In my other hand I hold up the photo. When I'd removed it, I hadn't thought much about the torn edge, nor had it occurred to me that the missing piece might still be stuck in the drawer. But that is exactly what this must be.

The scrap of photo is wedged in tight. Careful not to tear it further, I gingerly work it loose a little at a time. It takes several minutes, but finally it slips free from the metal, and I pull it out of the drawer.

It's not much, maybe an inch wide. Holding it beside the photo of Papa, it's a perfect fit. I can see now that whoever snapped the photo had centered it on Papa and Jackie Beitner, but there's a third face to their left, the grinning face of a red-haired man in a yellow polo shirt. It looks like he leaned into the shot at the last second, just as it was snapped.

I close the cabinet drawer and pull the chair back to the desk. Opening the top drawer, I retrieve a roll of scotch tape and carefully secure the two pieces of the photo together.

David's not in the dining room anymore. He's sitting in the living room watching a commercial for laundry detergent on Papa's 56-inch flat screen. I sit beside him, and he glances down at the photo in my hand.

"Changed your mind?" he asks.

I hand him the photo. He flips it over, studies it for a moment, and hands it back to me. "Who's the other guy?"

The commercial's over, and a female anchor appears in a newsroom. On the corner of the screen is the Rawley Pharmaceutical logo. David and I both take notice.

"Turn up the volume, please?" I lean forward, intent on the screen. David wraps his arm around me, careful not to touch my skin. On the TV the Rawley logo is replaced with footage of Papa coming out of the courthouse. Jordan's beside him, fending off a horde of reporters.

The news anchor delivers her spiel with a statuesque pose.

"The inquiry regarding Alberto Ortiz's alleged sanctioning of illegal medical testing finally came to an end yesterday. The District Attorney's office announced that all charges against Rawley Pharmaceutical's former CEO have been dropped. The man deemed responsible for the testing that led to several deaths has himself been dead for sixteen years. In response to the announcement, Ortiz will address the public this morning in a location befitting the event, the new Rawley Wing of the Memorial Hospital. The speech is scheduled to begin at 9:00 a.m. Pacific Standard time, and we'll be broadcasting it live right here."

"I guess it's over then," David says, settling back into the sofa. "That must mean he had nothing to do with those experiments after all."

I send him a glare. "You say that as if it's a bad thing."

David shrugs. "Not for your father, obviously. I just feel bad for the other people who were involved. You heard what the news said before, some of those people died as a result. It was all swept under the carpet for a lot of years. I feel sorry for them—for their families. That's all."

On the TV screen a full size image of my mother suddenly appears. She's dressed in blue, and she's smiling. It's a photo from one of Papa's political rallies. Seeing her stops me short. I stare at her, and my guts clench up like they're being squeezed in a vise. I miss her so much it feels like dying. I stare at her, recalling every horrible detail of last night. Am I really so vulnerable? Could it really have been so easy for Papa to let go?

All the emotion, the heartache from before threatens to overwhelm me again. I struggle against it, but I already know it's a struggle I will lose. I can't let go. I just can't. Not yet.

The newscaster is talking about how Mama took ill after a fundraiser a few weeks ago and remains in a stable, yet comatose, condition.

David casts me a bewildered look. "That's odd, don't you think?"

I have to agree with him. Though I'm relieved at not having to hear a public announcement about her death, it is strange that the media wouldn't at least mention it.

"Maybe your dad is keeping quiet about it until after the press conference," David suggests, "or he'll make a statement there."

The photo of Mama fades and another image takes her place, the image of a young man with unruly red hair and a birthmark under his eye.

"Hey, that's the guy in the photo with your dad," David announces. And he's right. The man in the photo is Gregory Stark, the researcher responsible for Rawley's illegal experiments. Below the TV image is a set of dates, the first is his date of birth and the second his date of death. The image is only on for a couple of seconds, and then it's gone.

I've seen the guy a dozen times before on the news, but I purposely didn't pay attention. Mama didn't like hearing all the things the media said about Papa, so when the reports came on, we usually turned them off.

"Did you see that?" I ask. "Red hair. Birthmark. The Beitners said Jackie introduced him to them a while back. Papa said he never met Stark, but he's in this picture with Jackie and Papa. And did you see those dates?"

"No, I didn't catch them."

"Do you have your phone?"

"Yeah. Of course."

"Would you mind Googling Gregory Stark?"

"Sure."

# CONTACT

David types Stark's name into his phone's search engine. "Okay," he says, "what do you want to know about him?"

"Those dates. Or, more specifically, when he died. I have to make sure."

He scrolls down a little then turns the screen so I can see it. When I do, I feel both triumphant and sick at the same time. Gregory Stark died sixteen years ago, two days after Jackie Beitner's death—and just a week after I was born.

# 34

THE DRIVE BACK TO THE HOSPITAL is the longest ever. I can't seem to stay away from that place. It's like a gigantic magnet, and I'm nothing but a paperclip.

"Mira, are you sure you want to confront your father like this?" David asks for the third time. He gives me an odd look, one that suggests he just might think I'm crazy. But I'm way past crazy.

"Yes, I'm sure, damn it!" But then I bite my lip. My anxiety level has been building since we left the mansion. "I'm sorry," I immediately apologize, and I mean it. "It's just that the pieces are all falling into place. The fact that Gregory Stark and Jackie Beitner died so close together *could* be a tragic coincidence, but I doubt it. Wikipedia said Stark died in a car accident. The autopsy found high levels of alcohol and a sedative in his bloodstream, just like what they found in Mama. There wasn't anything about Jackie Beitner online, but I just know they're connected."

"And you're convinced your dad's responsible?"

"Yes."

"But why?"

"The affair for one thing."

There's a twinge of doubt in David's voice. "He'd risk prison, risk his entire career to cover up a love affair?"

"It's not just the affair. It's the Gaudium trials, too. It's all linked somehow."

"What about you? Why would he spend the past sixteen years raising you only to try to run you over? It wasn't even his car."

"But it was too dark to tell for sure. Besides, he could have used a rental."

"In that case, it could have been anyone. Even just some crazy person who mistook us for someone else. But, your dad? It doesn't make sense, Mira."

He has a point, but there are just too many coincidences to ignore. "Whatever the truth is, the only way to find out is to talk to him—face to face."

After hitting every red light in the city, we finally reach the hospital. My father's presence here is confirmed by the hordes of news vans and protestors gathered at the entrance. Several police officers hold them at bay, but the crowd seethes like a kettle left on the burner far too long. Some are here to show support for my father while others are enraged. Either way, getting through them and past the police will be impossible.

"We need another way in," David says.

"Let's go around the back." I point to a side street that leads away from the hospital, but I know that it doubles back to the south side of the building. "We'll use the ambulance entrance."

David parks the car on the nearly vacant street. We get out, and David pulls his crutches from the backseat. I nod toward the skeletal remains of the Rawley wing.

"The news said the press conference would be held in the new wing," I remind him as we slip through the doors. "I'm assuming they meant the lobby, since the upper floors are still off limits. It's not far from here."

I lead us both down a deserted hall. We make the first right turn and run nearly headlong into the biggest, hairiest nurse I've ever seen. Built like a linebacker, this guy towers above me. And with his thick, smoke-colored beard, he looks like he should be wearing deerskins instead of scrubs.

"Excuse me," I say, trying to sound as nonchalant as possible. If we look too nervous we'll attract undue attention, but it's too late. Nurse Mountain Man takes a stance directly in front of us, effectively blocking the entire hallway.

"Where are you two heading?" His eyes narrow suspiciously.

I glance at his name badge and blurt out a greeting. "Hi Carrey." *Carrey?* "Actually, I'm a little turned around. We're supposed to meet our dad in the ER. Our brother's there with a broken arm."

David interrupts, "Fell out of a tree, poor little guy."

"But we didn't get any breakfast, so I thought we'd, you know, get something from the cafeteria. I could have sworn it was this way."

"I told you we should have turned left," says David, rolling his eyes. I play it up, too, letting out an exasperated sigh.

Carrey glares at us, and then raises his meaty arm, pointing back the way we came. "Cafeteria's near the front entrance. Take this hall all the way to the end and hang a right."

"I knew it," says David, slapping my shoulder.

I slap him back. "Knock it off."

We continue our feigned sibling bickering all the way back down the hall. Twice I look over my shoulder, but Nurse Mountain Man is not far behind. Finally he disappears down another corridor. We wait a minute before turning back, peering around the corner just in time to see Carrey slip into the men's room.

"Come on!" I grab David's shirt front, urging him to move faster. With his injured leg and crutches, he's walking at a snail's pace. "At this rate the press conference will be over before we get there."

Luckily it hasn't even started yet when we arrive. The vast room in which it's being held is crammed with reporters and cameramen jostling to get closer to Papa who sits behind a narrow table at the front of the room. His clasped hands rest on the royal blue tablecloth. The stress he must be feeling shows on his face. Standing behind him, off to one side, is Jordan, and on the other is a security guard. From the looks of it, it's going to be a few more minutes before things get rolling. But that still doesn't leave me much time.

I feel a gentle push from behind, David urging me forward. Maneuvering my way through the crowd isn't easy, but finally I reach the table.

"Papa." The din in the room is so loud that even though I'm right in front of him, he doesn't hear me. I shout louder.

"Papa!" Finally his eyes connect with mine. He sees me, but he's not smiling.

"Mira, what are you doing here?"

"Papa, I need to talk to you."

"This isn't the time or place, Mira. It will have to wait until later."

"No, not later," I tell him. "Now."

I hold up the photograph. The moment he sees it, all the color drains from his face. I can tell he wants to ask where I found it, but he already knows the answer.

"I can explain," he says.

A technician steps up beside him and clips a mic to his lapel, telling him that it will be switched on once the press conference has begun. I wait until he leaves to fiddle with the podium mic before speaking to my father again.

"I want to know why," I say, lowering my voice to make sure no one else will overhear. "I need to know why you killed Mama."

# 35

PAPA'S EYES WIDEN, AND A THIN sheen of perspiration forms on his brow. "What are you talking about, Mira?"

"You promised me you'd wait. You promised."

He stares at me, speechless. The expression in his eyes is not what I expected. I thought he'd be angry or defensive. Instead he seems bewildered—as if he doesn't know what I'm talking about. But how could he not know?

A man in a gray business suit steps up to the microphone and announces that the conference will begin shortly. I'm still holding up the picture, and Papa is still staring into the faces of Stark and Jackie Beitner.

"You knew them both," I tell him. "You lied."

Papa looks away from the photo and out over the crowd before turning back to me. "I can explain—" he tries again.

"I want to know about my mother—my *real* mother. I want to know how she died."

For a moment, I think Papa is going to answer me. But then someone's got me by the elbow, a grip so strong I'm sure it will leave a bruise. I'm being pulled away from the table, away from Papa. I look up and see Jordan dragging me through the crowd, his leather-gloved hands digging painfully into my arm through the fabric of my hoodie.

"Papa!" I call out. "Papa!" But the hum of voices and cameras drowns me out. I try to wrench free from Jordan's grasp. He takes both my arms in his fists.

"Stop it, Mira!" he demands, his face right in mine. "Let your father do his job."

"I have to talk to him, Jordan!"

"Not now, Mira." Jordan pulls me through the crowd toward the door. "We'll go somewhere quiet and wait until this is over. All right?"

I don't respond. I'm straining against his grip, wanting to go back to Papa, but Jordan grabs me tighter and gives me a firm shake. "All right?" he says again. I stop resisting and nod my head.

We snake our way through the swarm of reporters toward the doors. I spot David through the sea of bodies. He gives me a questioning look, wondering if he should follow us, but I shake my head.

Jordan and I exit the room, and the doors slam shut behind us. The hall outside is deserted and eerily silent. We walk a few yards to a little alcove near a window. The space is complete with blue upholstered chairs and several potted plants.

Jordan turns to face me. "Now, tell me what's going on."

The anger I felt just moments ago melts into grief. "It's Mama," I tell him. "She's gone."

"I know," he says. "I'm so sorry, Mira."

I'm about to fall apart. I've got to hold myself together. There's too much at stake. I swallow back the emotion and remind myself why I came here in the first place.

"Papa isn't who you think he is, Jordan. All those people in there who believe he's innocent." I nod toward the conference room doors. "They're all wrong. Papa is guilty."

Jordan's grip on me tightens, but I keep talking.

"He killed my mother, Jordan, and I'm pretty sure he's responsible for at least two other deaths."

The muscles in Jordan's jaw tense up. "What other deaths?" he asks. "You mean the Rawley trials? Gregory Stark was responsible for that. They found no evidence linking your father to him."

"They didn't," I say, gathering my courage, "but I did."

I slip the photo of Papa, Jackie and Stark out from my pocket. Jordan takes one glimpse of it, and his whole demeanor changes. He's suddenly furious.

"Put that away!" he orders He glances nervously up and down the empty hallway. I do as he says and shove the photo back in my pocket. "What the hell are you doing with that?"

"It's Jackie Beitner and Gregory Stark."

"I know who they are."

"Jordan, Papa drugged my mother and then authorized to have her life support terminated. Papa is linked to Stark's death and Jackie Beitner's, too. What is going on? I need to face my father and demand he tell me the truth."

I try to pull away, but Jordan jerks me back hard. "You're not going back in there."

"Yes, I am. Now let me go."

"Think about what you're doing, Mira! Your father is the face of Rawley Pharmaceutical—of Gaudium. It has already restored thousands of autistic kids to normal function. Teen suicide rates have bottomed out. And there's the very real possibility of curing Alzheimer's! Mira, don't you see? We are on the verge of changing the world!"

"But at what cost?" I ask, peering directly into Jordan's eyes. "Mama, Stark, Jackie Beitner, those women who died—how many lives lost are *too* many? I have to talk to Papa, Jordan. This has to end."

Jordan suddenly squeezes my arms so hard I can feel his fingers against my bone. Seeing him this angry frightens me. "Stop," I gasp. "You're hurting me!"

"Knock it off, Mira!" he shouts, shaking me again. His voice has turned into a cruel hiss. "Nothing is going to stand in our way. Not you, and sure as hell not your dead mother!"

My dead mother…

When I accused Papa of killing Mama he looked honestly surprised. But when I told Jordan, he said he knew. How could he know and not Papa? Yesterday Jordan was looking through Papa's papers for something. What if that something was Mama's Termination of Life Support form?

"You?" Rage flares up inside me. "You filed the authorization without Papa's knowledge? You killed her!"

In a burst of strength, I wrench my right arm free from Jordan's grasp. Before I even realize what I'm doing my hand strikes his cheek with all the force and bite of a rattlesnake. The power of the impact causes Jordan to stumble back a step. He releases my other arm, but already it's too late for me. In less time than it takes for the burn of the slap to radiate across my palm—I know.

I see...

Everything.

# 36

JORDAN'S PSYCHE IS MANGLED and distorted, like a thousand threads all knotted together. My brain struggles to sort out his thoughts and memories, picking through the most lucid of them. My mind lines most of them up into a somewhat comprehensible pattern.

From the time Jordan Cummings was six-years-old, he knew he was special. He had a knack for science and chemistry. His father pushed him to go to medical school, but after two years Jordan dropped out to join the Marines. America was embroiled in another war in the Middle East, and he felt obligated to do his part. His father said he was wasting his talent, so after the war Jordan returned to school and barely managed to get a degree. After a failed marriage and a series of dead-end jobs, he asked his old war buddy, Beto Ortiz, for help and was hired on at Rawley Pharmaceutical when it was nothing more than a sprouting drug manufacturer. He was assigned to work in one of the development labs as an assistant to Gregory Stark.

CONTACT

Meanwhile, Alberto Ortiz quickly rose through the management ranks of the company, but he maintained his friendship with his fellow Marine. They'd make a point to go out for drinks on occasion, and sometimes Stark would even tag along.

It was on one of these occasions that Stark flapped his tongue a bit more than he should have. In his research, he had isolated a variable that affected the production of dopamine and serotonin in the brain. Those who presented this variable inevitably developed mental illness in one form or another. All of the illnesses, he proposed, were on the same linear path. In other words, depression, schizophrenia, Alzheimer's were all symptoms of the same basic problem, just differing degrees of it. The cure, he insisted, was to be found not in treating the symptoms, but in repairing the neural damage. And that could be achieved through injections of a new isotope he'd engineered in the lab.

It all sounded fantastic, and the three men congratulated each other and downed their beers. In a few years, a decade at most, Stark's discovery would make Rawley the world's leading medical research company and would make all of them very, very rich.

But then something happened that sent their world into a tail spin. Alberto had an affair with a member of the secretarial staff, which was not unusual for him. Only this time, he claimed to love the girl. There was only one problem. Jackie Beitner suffered from Bipolar disorder. One day she'd be pleasant, fun, and affectionate, the next she'd explode like an atomic bomb, cursing and breaking things. Then she'd apologize in tears. Life was an emotional roller coaster, but

Alberto loved her just the same. He convinced Stark to try out his new therapy on her. Stark hadn't even reported his findings to the company yet, but after a great deal of coaxing on Alberto's part, Stark agreed. After only a couple of weeks, Jackie showed marked improvement in her condition. Jordan and Stark decided to try it out on a few more test subjects without Alberto's or the corporation's knowledge. Unapproved trials were unconventional, but once they had collected proof of the isotope's success, they would be hailed as geniuses.

The first few months went well, but then, one by one, the test subjects developed complications: seizures, memory loss, and headaches. They were all diagnosed with grade four Glioblastoma. The tumors were embedded so deep inside the brain tissue they were deemed inoperable. Jackie Beitner was no exception.

To make matters worse, Jackie announced to Alberto that she was pregnant.

During that last month of the pregnancy, Stark and Jordan watched helplessly as each test subject died. When Jackie finally gave birth, the child was adopted by Alberto and his wife, who had no idea of the child's true identity. Jackie died shortly after.

Two days after Jackie's death, Gregory Stark broke. He had agreed to help her, thought he could make a difference, but now he found himself responsible for at least a half-dozen deaths. They'd all signed affidavits swearing them to secrecy. The treatments were administered under the table at no cost to them. None were ever aware of the others, or of the connection between their illness and the treatments, and

241

none ever broke their silence. But it was too much for Stark. He would go to the authorities and turn himself in. He would do the right thing.

Jordan argued with Stark. If word of this got out it would mean tens of millions of dollars in lawsuits against Rawley Pharmaceutical. Not only would they lose their jobs, they would go to prison. Stark didn't care. The guilt clawed at him from the inside out. Frantic, Jordan's mind raced with all the possible outcomes his confession could have—none were good.

It was easy slipping the pills into Stark's drink, and later that night his car rolled eight times before coming to rest at the bottom of a steep embankment, crushed like a soda can. In the morning, Jordan got a call from Alberto telling him the news of Stark's tragic death. Alberto believed it was a suicide—couldn't blame him, after all. Losing both Stark and Jackie so close together, Alberto considered doing the same. But now he had Jackie's little girl to watch over. She gave him a reason to live.

After Stark's death, Jordan was promoted to his position. Eventually, Stark's original formula was granted approval. In time, Rawley perfected the therapy and christened it Gaudium. The company went on to international fame and fortune with their cures. Alberto decided to go into politics, asking Jordan to help him. Jordan proved to be instrumental in navigating the political arena. Everything was going well until the investigation went public. Now Alberto and Jordan's futures were both at stake.

When Mama started talking about Jackie the night of the fundraiser, Jordan feared she had put two and two together.

With Papa's gubernatorial race in full swing, a divorce would prove fatal. On the other hand, public sympathy for a devoted husband and father might sway public opinion in his favor.

That night, in my parents' room, Jordan slipped some of Mama's Trazodone and insulin into his pocket. He put a few pills into Mama's drink and injected her with insulin, the combination that resulted in her coma. But a new complication arose when I became suspicious.

When I tracked down the Beitners, Jordan knew things were about to go terribly wrong. I claimed that when I touched people, I could read their minds. He'd never bought into it before. He thought I must have mental issues, like my birth mother. But now Jordan wasn't so sure. What if it *was* true? If I could read Mama's mind, and if Mama had any knowledge of Papa's affair with Jackie Beitner, then it would only be a matter of time before I connected Jackie to Jordan as well.

The answer was to get rid of Mama—and me.

Here, Jordan's mind again becomes distorted and twisted, like someone has taken a roll of movie film and scrunched it up into a giant knot of images. It's as if he isn't exactly sure what he's thinking and feeling. I see nothing but rage and a tenacious appetite for control. Is this what being crazy—truly crazy—looks like from the inside out?

My eyes lock on Jordan's, dark and menacing. The images and emotions are turbulent, difficult to decipher, but in that fraction of an instant I know one thing for certain.

I have to run.

# 37

I SPIN AWAY FROM JORDAN and take off running down the hall.

"Mira!" Jordan shouts, his rapid footsteps echoing behind me on the tile floor. "Mira, come back here!"

I have to find someone, anyone, and tell them—what? That the future governor's best friend is some sort of mad scientist hell bent on doing everything he can to get what he wants—even if it means killing innocent people? Who would believe it? I can hardly believe it myself.

The most obvious place for me to go is back into the conference room, but Jordan's right behind me. If I stop now he'll reach me before I can get my hand around the doorknob. I'll call David's cell—Crap! My pockets are empty. I've left my stupid cell at home as usual.

I run down the corridor toward the main section of the hospital. When I turn a corner at full speed, I suddenly collide with a woman coming from the opposite direction. In a pale green pantsuit and heels, she looks as surprised to see me as I am to see her.

"Dr. Walsh?"

"Mira!"

"What are you doing here, Dr. Walsh?"

She hesitates. "I'm meeting a friend for breakfast at the cafeteria." The smile she offers is pleasant, but she averts her gaze. "I heard on the news that your father's holding a press conference. Has it started yet?"

"No. I mean, yes, but I need to get help—"

"Help? Why?"

"There's a man chasing me—I need to call security!"

Dr. Walsh takes me by the shoulders and looks at me with patronizing concern. "You know, Mira, I'm glad I bumped into you. I was planning to call you later, you know, to make sure you're all right. When I heard about your mother, I was naturally worried—"

A cold finger of fear stabs my chest. "Who told you about my mother?"

"I did." Jordan steps up behind me. "Hello, Emma."

Leaning past me, he kisses Dr. Walsh's cheek. I recoil at seeing them together—an image somehow not unfamiliar to me. My brain ransacks Jordan's jumbled memories and finds what I failed to notice before: a business card, phone calls, and discussions about me. I see other things, too, impressions too strange to be real. Dreams maybe—or nightmares?

"Mira—" Dr. Walsh's voice slices through Jordan's psyche, bringing me back to the present. "Mira, are you okay? I know losing your mother is a horrible tragedy, but it isn't your fault," she says. "Mr. Cummings called me because he's worried about you. He's afraid you might be having another breakdown."

"I'm not having a breakdown! Dr. Walsh, please listen to me. Jordan is not who you think he is."

"Why don't you just calm down, Mira." Jordan's voice is now calm, filled with fake concern. "Do you see what I mean, Emma?"

"He's a murderer!" I shout. "People have died!"

Dr. Walsh's eyes narrow, studying mine. She believed me once. Would she believe me now?

Jordan snatches my arm in a vise-like grip. "I think you need to sit down, Mira. We can talk about this in private, all right?"

"Let me go!"

He turns me back toward the conference room and practically drags me down the corridor. His hold on me is so tight that my fingers throb from the constriction of blood flow.

"Please, Dr. Walsh!" I try to jerk myself free to no avail.

"Stop wriggling!" Jordan snaps.

Through the closed conference room doors I hear a man's voice over the PA system declaring what everyone has already heard: Alberto Ortiz has been cleared of all charges.

When we reach the elevator, Jordan presses the recall button. A bell sounds as the elevator doors slide open, and he shoves me inside.

"Wait!" Dr. Walsh slips into the elevator after us. She gives Jordan a cautious, chastising glance. "I'll go with you, if you don't mind," she says.

When the doors close, Jordan lets go of me. I rub my arm to get the circulation flowing again.

"Where are you taking me?"

His glare is cold. "Up," he says.

# 38

I'M PRETTY SURE THIS ELEVATOR is the one I've seen leading to the upper levels of the Rawley wing of the hospital. The numbers near the elevator ceiling light up one at a time. We reach the fifth floor, one of the partially completed levels of the building. The moment the doors open, Jordan shoves me out onto the bare concrete floor. I land on my hands and knees, reopening several of the cuts on both palms.

"Jordan, please!" says Dr. Walsh. "There's no need to treat her this way." She kneels beside me to inspect my hands, but despite her kindness, fear bubbles up inside me.

We're surrounded by stacks of drywall and rolls of insulation that look like cotton candy wrapped in silver paper. Wooden wall-frames have been erected, making the area look like a three dimensional labyrinth. PVC and copper piping are visible in some of the framework, plumbing for future installations of bathrooms and drinking fountains. Bouquets of colored electrical wires sprout from the ceiling and walls.

Dr. Walsh forages in her purse and pulls out a clean white tissue, dabbing at my cuts. "Jordan, you asked me to come here to help you with Mira. We're all here now, so we might as well get this settled."

Over Dr. Walsh's shoulder I watch as Jordan looks around, paying no heed to her words. His gaze stops on a coil of electrical wire tossed haphazardly nearby. He picks it up and unwinds about a yard of it, then turns toward us with a jerk.

"Dr. Walsh, look out!"

But it's too late. Before either of us can do anything to stop him, Jordan slips the wire over Dr. Walsh's head, tightening it around her neck. She doesn't even have time to scream. She struggles futilely for breath as the wire cuts into her skin.

"What are you doing?" I scream. "Stop!"

I lunge at him. My nails dig into the flesh of his hands as I try to pry open his fingers. He lets go only long enough to push me off. My back hits the floor, sending a shudder of pain down my spine. I roll to my side, ready to pounce on him again, but Dr. Walsh's body convulses and goes limp. Collapsing to the floor, her face lobs to the side, eyes open wide and unfocused. A thin, crimson line encircles her throat like a discolored necklace.

Panic claws inside me and escapes in a blood curdling scream. "You killed her! My God! Somebody help us! Please help—"

My pleas come to an abrupt end as Jordan's shoe hammers into my gut.

"Shut up!" he shouts. "No one can hear you!"

I curl my knees into my chest, trying to shield myself from any more kicks that might come my way. I'm not screaming now, but a few silent tears slide down my cheeks—not for me, for Dr. Walsh. I understood her better than anyone ever did. From the moment she touched me in the ER, I knew her deepest regrets and pain, and I knew how much she wanted to help me.

Jordan glares at me, wrapping the ends of the wires around his hands. He takes a step toward me. I sit up, holding my stomach, and scoot backward until a wooden wall frame and some plumbing block my retreat. I feel behind me and find a thick pipe with a valve on it. Wrapping my fingers around it I try to twist, but it's on too tight.

"Don't do this," I say, attempting to stall Jordan long enough to figure out what to do next. "Everyone in that room saw us leave together. If I turn up missing they'll know you're responsible."

Jordan takes another step towards me. "Those reporters were focused on one thing and one thing only—your father." He pulls the wire taut between his hands. "And *he's* too busy saving his own skin to worry about you right now."

"But I thought the charges against him were dropped."

"They were, but these sorts of scandals have residual effects. He may have convinced the D.A. that he's innocent, but now he's got an entire state full of voters to convince. Though I'm thinking news of his wife's death will prompt a wave of support. Everyone loves an underdog."

I struggle to loosen the valve, but I just can't get enough torque with my hand behind my back.

"What about me?" I continue talking, wondering if there's any chance I can reason with him. "I want Papa to win the election as much as you do, Jordan. Let me go, and I won't tell him what you've done. I swear it."

"What about you? You're my secret weapon, Sunshine. You are the proof that Gaudium can be administered in the fetal stages of development."

To my surprise, the valve gives a little in my hand. "I don't understand. What do you mean?"

"We gave your mother, your *real* mother, Gaudium during her first trimester," he explains. "I didn't think much of it at first—until you started in with that no contact thing. Beto thought you were nuts, just like Jackie. But I knew better. I knew Guadium had changed you, made you special. Imagine what we could accomplish if we gave it to every pregnant woman. Guadium may actually alter the genetic codes linked to all those illnesses we're trying to eradicate. That is the ultimate cure, isn't it? The genes for Autism, Alzheimer's, or Bipolar would simply cease to exist. They would be completely wiped out in a single generation."

"But Gaudium didn't work that way with me," I tell him. "It screwed up my brain."

"That's why we call them early testing *trials*. Sometimes they succeed, and sometimes they fail. But research will go forward, new vaccinations will be perfected. Of course, it will all take a great deal of money, which is precisely why your father needs to win this election. With him as Governor, continued funding for Guadium research is all but guaranteed."

"If I'm your secret weapon, why did you follow me to Bakersfield to try and run me down?"

Jordan squats in front of me and runs a glove-clad finger along my jaw. The wire in his hands brushes my skin, leaving behind a smear of Dr. Walsh's blood. I draw back in disgust, but he just smirks at me.

"I wasn't sure how much your mother really knew," he tells me. "I couldn't take the risk of you reading her mind and discovering that I was the one responsible for killing Jackie and Gregory Stark."

"If you want me dead, why don't you just shoot me?"

Jordan's eyebrows arch as if considering the suggestion, but then he shakes his head. "Too messy. How would I hide all the blood?"

Before I can react, Jordan drives the wire against my throat, strangling me. The wire presses into my esophagus, slicing into my skin. My lungs burn from lack of air. Blackness swirls around me.

They say at that moment just before death your whole life passes before your eyes. I see my life and many others—Craig, Dr. Walsh, Mama, Jordan, David. Countless random memories zip through my brain, some popping up and bursting like bubbles, other fading in and out so fast I can hardly keep up. The images are distorted, the emotions and recollections all jumbled together in a tangled mess. The pressure builds as if heading toward an inevitable climax.

And then…

*Whack!*

I smash the heavy copper valve against the side of Jordan's skull. The skin instantly splits, creating a deep red canyon. A thick river of blood gushes down his face, and he reels backward, crashing through a sheet of drywall. My body reacts on instinct, gulping for air, but I don't wait for Jordan to regain his footing. I sprint for the elevator and pound my fist against the button, recalling it to this floor. I don't have the seconds it will take for it to arrive. Standing here waiting for it, I'm like a deer in a meadow on the first day of hunting season.

I listen for the bell, signaling the elevator's arrival. I steal a glance behind me to look for Jordan, but I don't see him. Maybe I hit him harder than I thought. Maybe I knocked him out.

Then I hear it. The bell—followed by the slow swoosh of the elevator doors sliding open. I jump inside and turn to push the button—any button that will take me down. I look for Jordan again, but still nothing. As the doors start to close, I allow myself to feel a moment of relief. But then, just as the doors are about to seal shut, a hand slips in between them. The doors make contact with it and retreat again. Jordan steps inside, a depraved grin on his face. He reaches into his suit jacket and pulls out his Colt pistol.

As he takes aim, his words are clear, "Damn the blood."

# 39

WITHOUT THINKING, I THROW my full weight against Jordan. My assault surprises him and he teeters off balance just long enough for me to push past him out of the elevator. I run at full speed, darting back and forth between two-by-fours and pipes. Two shots ring out, but I don't stop until I've buried myself deep in the maze of half-built walls and unfinished plumbing. Reaching the far wall of the vast space, I slide down to the floor, gasping for air. I need a moment to breathe, to think, to get my bearings.

What have I gotten myself into? How could I have been so wrong about Jordan? I berate myself for being so naïve and for thinking all along that Papa was to blame. If I get out of this, I tell myself, I swear I'll make it up to him—somehow.

I try to slow my breathing a little, forcing my desperation and panic to subside. I need to think clearly. All I have to do is find some other way down. The stairwell must be around here somewhere.

Behind me, from the direction of the elevator, Jordan's voice taunts me. "Mira! Come out, come out wherever you are!"

I squat on the concrete floor with my back braced against a two-by-four, hoping I've put enough space, enough wall frames behind me to block Jordan's view. I just need some time to figure this out, but time is the one thing I don't have.

I listen for his approach but hear nothing. Where the hell is he?

Scattered all around me is an array of small discarded objects: bent nails, stripped screws, fragments of wire and metal tape. I gingerly pick up a handful of the ones I can reach and weigh them in my palm. I glance to my right, to the vast vertical forest of lumber growing in this cavernous fifth floor. Maybe I'll take another shot at the elevator. No, I'll never have enough time to get in before he reaches it. It's the stairwell or nothing. I peer through the wooden maze and spot a door in the far left corner about twenty yards away. That's got to be it.

The absence of sound is maddening. For all I know he might be standing right behind me. He's near. I can feel it. Any second he'll see me, if he hasn't already. I chuck the scrap metal toward the far right wall. The items land with a light clatter. Then there's the faint scraping sound of footsteps abruptly changing directions, rubbing against the grit on the floor, heading to the right.

Scrambling on all fours and staying low to the ground, I scurry through the skeletal walls toward the door. Behind me, I hear an angry grunt and a loud clang. He's thrown something to the floor, a box of tools maybe.

255

"I've had enough of your games, Mira!" Jordan's voice is taut with frustration. A moment later, the air all around me comes alive with the music of hundreds of nails colliding with the concrete, the wood, and the pipes. Several land on me before dropping to the floor. Next, a white plastic bucket flies past me and hits the wall. It drops with a loud thud and rolls to a stop at my feet.

"Where are you, Mira?"

His voice is closer now. I'm on my knees, crawling through the mess of nails around me, not caring how they cut into my hands. Ten yards away, the door beckons to me.

And then, close enough to hear his breath, I hear—

"Peek-a-boo! I see you!"

I spring for the door like a sprinter at the start of a race, but then suddenly, I hit the floor. The impact knocks the wind right out of me. Jordan's got me by the ankle.

I look down and see his black-gloved hand wrapped around my leg. His expression is rabid.

"Where do you think you're going, Sunshine?" he says, leering at me.

I don't think. I just kick as hard as I can with my free foot and hit him square in the nose. He grunts in pain, and his grip on me loosens. Lurching forward, I slam my body against the door's metal bar and throw myself into the stairwell. Getting to my feet, I leap over the first few steps. Then I stumble, half-tripping, half-sliding down the rest.

On the very last step I feel a sharp stabbing pain as my left ankle twists beneath me. I scream out, but I remain standing. Getting down the next four flights of stairs like this will be impossible. So instead, I pull open the door on this landing, the fourth floor of the Rawley Wing, and slip inside.

# 40

As I step through the door, lights flicker on in succession overhead, illuminating a massive warehouse-sized laboratory. Stacks of crates and wooden pallets occupy the wall beside the door. Also nearby are several large cardboard boxes marked with colored labels and words that are foreign to me. Certain that Jordan will come looking for me, I push my weight against the pallets and slowly slide them in front of the door, effectively blocking the entrance. Jordan will have to either move them out of the way one at a time, or climb over them to get in. If I'm lucky, he'll assume I continued down to the first floor and skip the lab altogether. Either way, I've bought myself a few extra seconds.

Turning, I quickly take in the room. In the center are a dozen wide, flat tables decorated with microscopes, computers, and other complicated looking apparatus. The lab's walls are smooth and white with dark gray tiles on the floor and ceiling. At the far end of the room, near the elevator, are eight or nine blue cylinders reaching from floor to ceiling, each about a foot in diameter. Metal pipes run from each cylinder across the ceiling to the workstations. More pipes extend from the bottoms of the cylinders through the wall behind them. I wonder if these are gas tanks of some kind.

This is the floor I noticed that day with Jordan, the one with covered windows. From in here I can see that all the windows have been blocked with dark plates to prevent sunlight from entering.

*The light isn't good for the specimens.*

The one thing I don't see in here, however, is specimens, but I don't really care about that. The only thing that concerns me now is whether or not I can reach the elevator. I lift up my pant leg to inspect my ankle, which is already starting to swell. Suddenly the distance between me and the elevator seems as wide as the Grand Canyon. I could try to hide or look for some way to call for help. Once again I berate myself for leaving my phone at home.

I decide to search for somewhere to hide, though I know it's futile. If Jordan does get into the lab he's sure to find me, unless—

Maybe I could fool him into thinking I've taken the elevator.

I tear open one of the cardboard boxes. Inside are dozens of smaller white ones. I don't care what's inside. I remove two of the boxes, open them, and fling their contents in the direction of the elevator. Dozens of Petri dishes smash against the floor, glass shards scattering everywhere. At the very least, Jordan will have to go to that end of the room to inspect the mess.

Next, a place to hide.

CONTACT

There's a narrow closet door at the back of the lab. I try
to open it, but it's secured by a coded key pad. Time is short,
I know, but I punch in something anyway—*Rawley*. Nothing.
I try *Gaudium* next, and *Jordan*...

Jordan.

A thought surfaces from the mess of Jordan's memories
swirling in my brain. My muscles tighten and my jaw
clenches. I punch in *Sunshine*.

The lock clicks open.

When I slip inside, a fluorescent light automatically
switches on overhead. Surprised, I spin around, searching for
a button to turn off the damn light—but then I freeze.

I'm not in a closet but another room, much smaller than
the lab, maybe twenty-feet square. I realize I've seen it before
in Jordan's psyche. Glass cabinet fronts line the three walls
opposite the door. Above each cabinet is a computer screen
with a black background, numbers, and green peaked lines
racing across them. And there are sounds—faint beeping
sounds coming from the screens.

I've seen computers like these before in the hospital. I
think they're heart rate monitors. But if so, what or who are
they monitoring?

Curious, I step up to the first cabinet. Its interior is dark
behind the glass. I narrow my eyes, just making out the
silhouettes of something on the shelves inside, cylinders the
size of mayonnaise jars. There is something familiar about
them—something not right. It comes to me just as I reach
for the metal cabinet handle. The moment my hand comes in
contact, a deep red light begins to glow, illuminating the
inside of the cabinet. I step back, horrified.

Each of several dozen clear glass cylinders contains a fetus only four or five inches long. Tiny legs are folded up to their chests, little arms and hands held near their over-sized faces. A bundle of wires protrude out of each cylinder with one wire inside it attached to the back of the fetus's head.

Jars of dead babies.

Jordan's comment made in jest comes back to me with a wave of nausea. I spot a printed label on the upper corner of the cabinet door: *20 weeks*. Each cabinet has a similar label: *10 weeks, 30, 38*. I touch each handle and the lights come on. I am surrounded by a room full of human babies at differing stages of development. So this is what Jordan meant about eradicating mental illness once and for all. But where did they all come from? Are they post-abortive babies? Were they conceived in the lab for research?

I approach the cabinet with the *38 weeks* fetuses. These are the largest specimens, fully grown babies in larger jars. If they weren't on display suspended in fluid they would look like any other babies. I peer closely at one, its little cheeks plump and pink. Suddenly its leg twitches. And then its tiny fist unfurls to reveal five perfectly formed fingers.

"My God." I gasp. "They're alive!"

# 41

BILE RISES IN MY THROAT, and my stomach churns. I have to get out of here. I have to tell someone. I will have to take my chances with the elevator. I stumble backward out of the storage room, my eyes locked on the horrendous collection of human lives. Stepping through the doorway, I collide with something behind me. I start to scream, but a hand clamps over my mouth. Instinctively I bite down on a finger. My captor shouts, releasing me. Despite my injured ankle, I make a break for the elevator not daring to look back.

"Mira, wait! It's me!"

I skid to a stop and spin around. "David!"

Holding his injured hand to his chest, he hobbles toward me on his crutches. I'm so astonished and happy to see him that I throw my arms around him.

"Thank God I found you," he says, clutching me to his body.

I'm nearly giddy with relief. "How did you get here?"

"When you didn't come back to the conference room I came looking for you. I saw Jordan and some woman force you into the elevator."

"But how did you know I was here on the fourth floor?"

"I didn't, actually. I watched the numbers light up above the elevator and they stopped at the fifth floor. I found a security guard and we went up together."

David's gaze drops and his voice gets quiet. "We found the woman."

"Jordan killed her," I explain.

"The guard went back for help. You can imagine what went through my head when I saw her. I'd have searched every floor until I found you. Where's Jordan now?"

"I'm not sure—"

*Crash! Crunch!* The sounds of snapping and splintering wood resound through the lab. "I know you're in there, Mira!" Jordan shouts, kicking and pushing at the pallets blocking the stairwell door.

I grab David and shove him back in the direction of the elevator. He doesn't even bother with his crutches, limping as fast as he can beside me, but neither of us are fast enough. I glance back to see Jordan squeeze through a narrow opening in the door and climb over the stack of broken pallets. He takes aim with his pistol.

"Get down!" I pull David to the floor as a shot rings out. The bullet pierces one of the tanks near the elevator. A stream of high pressure gas hisses out of it, the white haze obscuring the path in front of us.

Another shot ricochets off the tile floor just inches from where David and I lay. We're not far from the elevator, just a few yards, but if we try to make it now the chances of getting shot are all but certain. Instead we dive for cover behind the nearest work station.

I hear the sound of Jordan's slow, methodical steps approaching. My heart palpitates wildly as I listen to him come closer and closer. The hiss of the gas and the sound of my own rapid breathing only heighten my fear. I wait until his steps are right beside us, then I motion to David to slide around to the side of the workstation.

"There's no use hiding, Sunshine," Jordan's foul voice makes the air toxic. "Why don't you come out and—*play!*"

Jordan leaps forward, expecting to catch us by surprise, only we're not there anymore. We've already crawled past several workstations and left him behind. All that's left is a quick dash across empty space to the stairwell door.

I look at David, his crutches lying beside him on the floor. How will he make it, I wonder? How will I make it? There is no way for David to get on his feet, make it to the door and down the stairwell fast enough to outrun Jordan and his gun. But if I can draw Jordan away from him, get him to chase after me, maybe David could make it to the elevator and get help.

I dare a peek around the corner of the workstation and see Jordan peering through the haze of gas, searching for us. I use the moment of distraction and sprint for the door.

"Mira!" David whispers after me, but there isn't time to explain. I just have to hope he figures out what I'm up to.

Pain stabs at my ankle, but I reach the door and heave several pieces of the broken crates out of the way. Hearing the commotion, Jordan turns and fires. I feel it the same moment I hear it. A scream claws its way out of my throat as a searing pain tears into in my right thigh. And then, I hear David.

264

"Mira!"

Jordan spins and fires again, this time at the far corner of the room. The bullet strikes a light bulb, sending a shower of sparks into the air. In that single sliver of a second, Jordan realizes what he's done and lunges head-first behind a workstation. The sparks ignite the gas that's been filling the room. A red hot streak of flame zips through the air toward the white cloud hovering near the elevator. With a tremendous *boom*, the gas, tank, and pipes explode. A massive ball of fire inflates like a balloon, briefly engulfing everything in the lab.

I jump through the stairwell door just in time to avoid the deadly assault. Seconds later I dare a glimpse into the lab. The fiery sphere has already retreated, though the ceiling of the lab is blackened, and much of the apparatus and computers are melted or otherwise destroyed. The wall near the elevator is engulfed in flame, and where the lower pipes once were is now nothing but a gaping, jagged hole of fire.

# 42

THE PAIN IN MY LEG SENDS my head spinning, but I fear the worse for David. Fortunately my fears are quickly alleviated when I see him crouching behind the workstation, which acted as a protective barrier from the explosion. He gives me a shaky thumbs-up, and I feel a wave of relief wash over me. I'm about to come back in, to go to him, when I see a dark silhouette rise in front of the flames.

"You're not leaving already, are you, Mira? Why, the party has only just begun!"

Jordan, his face scorched and smeared with blood, tears after me with the speed of a jaguar. Ignoring my pain, I retreat to the stairwell.

The smoke hits me as hard as a solid wall. I glance over the railing and see orange flames undulate like reveling demons below. The explosion must have traveled through the pipes, spreading fire to the floor beneath us. I can't get down that way, and I can't face Jordan. I'd never survive.

Behind me, the door starts to open. I throw myself against it, trying to force it closed, but Jordan is much stronger than I am. Grunting with the effort, I brace my feet against a railing and use my full weight. Jordan pushes harder. There's no way I can win this.

I jump away from the door and head up the stairs. Maybe if I make it to the next floor I can get to the elevator, if it's still functioning. I keep climbing, the pain in my leg pulsing with every heartbeat. The smoky haze is getting thicker, too. I can hardly see anymore, but I know Jordan isn't far behind.

"I'm right behind you, Sunshine!" Jordan turns my fear into reality.

Instinct and self-preservation propel me on. Jordan starts to cough. The smoke is getting to him. It's getting to me, too, but I fight against my lungs' natural urge to expel it. If I stay quiet, maybe he won't be able to locate me. It's far from silent, though. The roar of the fire below is deafening.

A shot rings out. I know I need to keep moving, but terror paralyzes me. My body shakes with silent sobs, and I cling to the stairs with a death grip.

Not far below, someone calls out my name.

"Mira? Mira, are you in here?"

"David!" I shout. The deep breath I take makes me cough. "David, go back! Don't follow me—"

Jordan fires again.

"David? David!"

No response.

My God, did Jordan shoot him? The thought makes me sick. I manage to move up a few more steps to the next floor landing. My leg hurts so much I'm afraid I'm going to black out. I feel weak and lightheaded, not just from bullet wound. The smoke is so thick I can scarcely breathe.

Suddenly, my body is crushed against the stairs, solid right angles digging into my throat, my chest, my stomach. Something hard presses into my temple. Jordan's pistol.

"C'mon, Mira," he says between coughing spasms. "Be a martyr—for the greater good."

Jordan's full weight pushes down on me, but my hands are free. In a blind surge of desperation I reach back and grab Jordan's wrist, twisting it away from my head. All of sudden, I feel the vibration of something striking Jordan's body. A cry of pain erupts from his throat. I rotate just enough to see David land a blow directly on Jordan's face. I try to wrench the gun from Jordan's hand, but his grip tightens. I don't know which direction it's pointing when it goes off. I can hardly see more than a few inches in front of my face, and the terrible percussion of sound sends stabbing pains into my ears.

For a second I think it's me that's been hit, but then Jordan collapses on top of me, the skin of his face brushing against mine. I see a moment's realization of pain and a flicker of memory as Jordan's life ebbs away. I feel his body roll off me, and I turn in time to see his dark silhouette fall into the flames below.

# 43

I LAY MY FACE AGAINST THE WARM concrete step and close my eyes. Conflicting emotions churn inside me. I'm relieved that Jordan's gone, that I'm safe from him now, but I also feel sick knowing what he's done—and sad that the man I once trusted and cared about never really existed at all. I think of Mama, Dr. Walsh, Jackie Beitner, and David.

David.

Someone grabs me by the shoulders. In a sudden panic, I try to squirm away, but the pain in my leg makes me cry out instead.

"Mira, it's just me. We've got to get out of here."

David wraps my arm around his neck and helps me to my feet. I lean on him as we make our way up the next few steps. The going is awkward, both of us limping, grunting in pain. But eventually we burst through the door on the sixth floor landing. My chest burns, and I cough uncontrollably as we both hobble our way to the elevator. I press the DOWN button. Waiting has never been so hard.

My thigh throbs painfully. I look down and see that my pant leg is completely soaked with blood. David sticks his fingers into the small tear in my jeans and rips open the wet denim to inspect the wound. Blood oozes from the raw, tattered flesh on the outside of my thigh.

"It's not too bad," he says. "The bullet just grazed you."

I hadn't noticed before, but David's face and arms are splotched red with minor burns. I can tell from the strained expression on his face that he is hurting.

"What happened to your crutches?" I ask him.

He shrugs. "Lost them somewhere between the fourth and fifth floor landings. It's kind of hard to climb stairs with them anyway."

The realization of what could have happened, what I thought had happened, rolls through me like tidal wave. I grab his shirt sleeves in my fists, desperate to hold on.

"I thought he shot you."

David takes hold of my arms with that same gentle way he had with Ramón. His touch, even through my hoodie, instantly calms me.

"Yeah, well, he didn't," he says, smiling at me. "And I wasn't going to let him shoot you again either. I was reaching for the gun when it went off."

I will a smile to match his. "I'm glad you're all right."

He squeezes my hand. "Me, too."

The bell rings and the doors slide open. To our horror, however, the car is filled with smoke. If we take it down, we could descend into an inferno.

We let the elevator doors shut, and I collapse against a stack of concrete bags, mentally and physically drained. We're surrounded by steel girders. No walls yet, or glass in the windows, just a concrete floor and ceiling with the same copper plumbing as the floor below. From up here, through the building framework, we can see the entire city.

"I'll try 9-1-1." David pulls out his cell phone and enters the number, then he holds it up to his ear. "Damn it!" he says a moment later. "It worked earlier. But that was before the explosion, or something's messing with the signal up here."

He looks around, sizing up our situation. "The staircase and elevator are both useless. We have to find some other way down."

I look around me but all I see is a stack of lumber, boxes of nails, and an assortment of pipes. Why couldn't there be some rope in here? Or a ladder.

The ringing in my ears had subsided a bit, but now it starts up again.

"Do you hear that?" asks David, his voice turning hopeful. "It's a siren. Fire engines!"

David does his best to help me to my feet again. We move to edge of the floor and spot the crowd of onlookers below. Two fire trucks and an ambulance are down there. I wave my arms frantically.

"Hey, we're up here! Up here, guys!"

But everyone's rushing back and forth, hosing down the flames, evacuating the lower levels. No one suspects anyone is on the upper floors. Why would they? This part of the building has been neglected for months now. But then I remember what David told me earlier about the security guard going for help. Maybe he's told them about us. Maybe...

Behind us, smoke pours out from around the elevator and collects against the ceiling. With no outer walls to trap it in, the smoke curls up and around the steel girders, rolling out across the ceiling like an upside down river. David squats and places his palms against the floor.

"It's hot enough to burn," he says. "Won't be long before the fire finds its way through, and there's plenty of lumber in here to feed it."

Heat radiates off all the metal—the girders, the pipes, the elevator doors. I swear I'm baking in an oven. Pulling my hoodie sleeves down around my hands, I grab hold of the steel building frame and lean outside a little. On the exterior of the building a loose sheet of plastic flaps against the waves of hot air pushing past me.

"Hey!" I shout at the crowd below. I'm starting to shake, whether from fear or desperation or both, I don't know. "Please! Somebody look up here!"

And someone does.

People far below gather around, shouting and pointing up to where David and I are waving frantically. It seems like forever for the rescue worker to make his way up to us on a ladder rig. He wears a heavy yellow firefighter jacket and thick, soot-smudged gloves. I step into his arms and let him hold me close. I bury my face against his chest and smell the fire and ash on him. David climbs on beside us.

"Please," I beg the rescuer, "there are more people on the fourth floor—babies!"

"Babies?"

"Yes! You've got to send someone to save them!"

272

I quickly explain where the room with the fetuses is located and give him the access code. The firefighter relays the information to someone below as we slowly descend to the ground.

Once we arrive, David and I are immediately wrapped in warm blankets. The air explodes with sound: the clamor of sirens, shouts of emergency crews, reporters and onlookers talking over the din. I feel lost amid the chaos, like a toy boat battered by stormy ocean waves. Through the blanket, my rescuer has me firmly by the arm, leading me toward the safety of a waiting ambulance. The pain in my leg reminds me that's where I need to go, but then I realize David's gone. We've been separated.

"Wait," I say, hoping I'm loud enough to be heard. "Wait, please. My boyfriend was with me. Where is he?"

The stranger doesn't answer, but keeps pulling me through the bustling crowd. A suit-clad reporter followed by a cameraman backs into us, nearly knocking me over.

"Excuse me," he says, moving off in another direction.

I scan the crowd for familiar faces, but the throng of people is too dense to penetrate, and the frenzied activity all around me is far too overwhelming.

"David!" I shout. "David Valdez!" I call his name over and over, shouting until my throat is raw from the smoke and the strain.

A fireman in full gear hurries past, bumping hard against me. The force of the impact breaks the rescuer's hold on my arm. I quickly dart away. I keep shouting David's name, but no one answers or even notices me. And then, I see his face in the crowd.

"David!" I call again, pushing my way to him. He sees me, and soon I'm crying in his arms.

After a few moments, he pulls away and looks into my face. "Mira, you're going to be okay. You need medical attention."

"But what about you?"

"I'm fine," he says. "But your leg—let them help you."

I do feel a little woozy. Suddenly, my knees buckle beneath me. David catches me and lifts me into his arms. He carries me toward the ambulance where gentle hands lay me on a gurney. An EMT snaps an oxygen mask across my face. I hear people talking about the evacuation of patients to two other hospitals in different parts of the city. The EMT informs me I'll be going to one of them.

I peer through the open ambulance doors to look at David. He smiles at me before stepping away. For a moment, I panic. I can't lose him again. But then another face pops into view.

Papa.

He climbs into the ambulance. "Hey, Pumpkin," Papa says in a shaky voice. He looks pale and worried. "Thank God you're safe. You're going to be okay, I promise."

"David—" I try to talk, but it's difficult with the oxygen mask and the pain in my lungs.

"What is it, Mira?" Papa asks, leaning close.

"David saved me. If it wasn't for him, I wouldn't have made it."

Nodding, Papa turns to a security guard standing nearby. "Bill, see that boy right there? His name is David. He's a hero, and he's to be given the best care possible. Is that clear?"

A moment later, the guard is gone, and I know everything's going to be okay.

Papa turns back to me. He manages a weak smile.

"When that explosion happened, I thought—" His voice breaks, but he struggles on. "I thought I'd lost you." He clasps his hands together and presses his forehead against them. I can't see his face, but I could swear he's fighting back tears. Clearing his throat, he continues, "Jordan took you out of the conference room. Is he—alive?"

I slowly move my head from side to side. Papa's eyes glisten. I should tell him the truth about Jordan, but now is not the time. He's lost so much—a friend, his wife. He deserves a chance to mourn. I'll tell him soon, when the time is right.

A tear trails down his cheek. "It's all right," he says, brushing it away. "I'm just so relieved you're okay."

Papa holds out his hand to me—his bare hand. I hesitate, but I lay my hand in his. The ride to the hospital seems to take forever, but I don't mind. Papa's got his hand tight around mine. And I know—no doubts and no regrets—that he loves me.

# 44

AFTER SPENDING THE NIGHT in the ER where I got eight stitches in my leg and a breathing treatment, Papa and I head for home. It is early morning when we arrive. The sun hasn't even come up yet. I'm exhausted, so I make a beeline to my room and crawl into bed. I don't even bother taking off my clothes. I'm asleep before my head hits the pillow.

My dreams are jagged slices of memory, flames and explosions peppered with disjointed images from Jordan and Papa's lives. At times, I see myself falling from that stairwell platform instead of Jordan. I hear screams and gunshots. And then there's Dr. Walsh's lifeless body lying on the floor in front of me. I reach out with my hand to roll her over, but it's my face I see instead of hers—my lifeless eyes staring back at me.

Then I wake up.

I gasp and blink against the sliver of sunlight escaping from between the curtains.

I'm alive. Thank God I'm alive.

Getting up, I stumble into my bathroom. I discover my cell phone on the vanity, right where I left it. The power's about gone, but I check my messages and find a text from David. He sent it just after midnight:

R U OK?

I text him back:

IM FINE. U?

I don't know how long it will be before he gets it. He might still be asleep. There's so much I want to tell him, but I want to say it person. I send one more text before plugging my phone into the charger:

HEADING 2 THE PARK

The delicious fragrance of maple hotlinks and poached eggs wafts into my room. I am fully awake now and starving. The pain in my thigh throbs something awful. It's wrapped in a swath of white gauze, and I'm extra careful as I change into a pair of sweats and a t-shirt. I reach for my hoodie, but instead of wearing it, I drape it over the back of my desk chair.

After putting on my sneakers, I make my way downstairs to the dining room. The table is set for a feast. Papa rises from the table when he sees me. He wraps his arms around me and kisses me lightly on the top of my head, his lips just brushing my hair.

"How did you sleep?" he asks, pulling out a chair for me.

The TV's on in the other room and the sound of a reporter's voice draws me in. Papa follows me to the living room and we both watch as images from yesterday's near disaster are replayed.

"An explosion rocked the Memorial Hospital yesterday, igniting a fire on the ground floor of the new Rawley Wing, still under construction. Alberto Ortiz, candidate for governor, was giving a press conference at the time. Some believe the blast may have been a failed assassination attempt. Our field reporter caught footage of a dramatic rescue from an upper floor. Speculation has it that one of the rescued may have been the Ortiz's daughter. More than two dozen people were taken to other local hospitals with minor to moderate burns, and two bodies were recovered from the wreckage. One was identified as thirty-two-year-old Emma Walsh, a local psychologist. The other is Gerald Haight, a reporter from local radio station K-JKR."

"What?" I pick up the remote and turn up the volume, but the news anchor has already moved on to another story. "They didn't find Jordan's body?"

Papa turns off the TV. "No, not yet."

"You did tell the authorities about him falling down the stairwell."

Last night in the ER, I told Papa where and how Jordan had died, but I didn't tell him everything. I tried, but I just couldn't bring myself to say it.

"Yes, Mira, they searched the stairwell, just like you said." He looks at me hesitantly, but then resigns himself to continue. "There was nothing there."

278

I want to say that's impossible. Jordan was shot. He was dying. I saw him fall… didn't I?

"Don't worry. They'll find him," Papa assures me.

"What about the babies?"

A deep crease appears between his eyebrows. "Yes, the babies. I've been up all night dealing with that. Rescuers managed to get the fire under control and called in a science team from Rawley headquarters. They determined that it was safer to keep the younger fetuses where they are to allow them the best chance at reaching viability. Those already viable were transported to the ICU at Children's Hospital."

"What will happen to them?"

"I was told that suitable adoptive parents will be located. And since I know you're concerned about this, you should know that none of them had been given Gaudium. We accessed their records and learned the trials weren't set to begin until everything had been moved into the new lab. In other words, they're normal."

Normal.

The word makes me cringe, but thankfully Papa isn't looking at me just now. He runs his fingers through his hair, shaking his head. "I just can't believe this sort of thing could ever be approved at all. You have to believe me, Mira, I knew nothing about this. Nothing."

"I know, Papa."

"And I swear that the first thing I'll do when I'm elected is to push for legislation to prevent this from ever happening again. In the meantime," he adds with a tremor in his voice, "there are other things I do want to discuss with you—things I never told you that you deserve to know."

He glances down for a second. "Your mother—" The words catch in his throat and his eyes well up. "I miss her."

I'm not sure if he's referring to Jackie Beitner or Mama, but it doesn't matter. I feel myself getting choked up, but I don't want to cry. Not here. Not now. The next few days will be filled with making arrangements for Mama's funeral. It could be a huge media event, but Papa wants something more private. I'm sure we'll work it out after we've had a little time to recover from the blow of losing her.

But right now, I want—I need—something else.

"Papa, would you mind if I went out for a while? Just for a walk. Then we'll talk over breakfast. Okay?"

He nods and smiles weakly. "Okay," he says. "But are you sure you can walk? Your leg, I mean."

"I'll take a painkiller first, and I'll go slow."

"All right," he agrees. "But please take your cell phone with you in case you need me to come pick you up."

"I've got it," I tell him, holding it up as proof.

I turn to go, but then Papa says, "Maybe later we could go out for ice cream or something."

He gazes at me in a way he never has before, as though he wants to say something so important it just can't be put into words. He starts to reach for me, but hesitates. Instead, he cautiously touches a strand of hair near my face, his fingers gently sliding down the length of it. I close my eyes for just a moment, remembering how Mama would touch me that way.

"Ice cream," I repeat softly. "Yeah, I'd like that."

# 45

THE WALK TO THE PARK takes longer than I expected, but I use the time to enjoy the fresh air and the beautiful weather.

When I arrive, I see two little girls chase each other down the slide. Their giggles fill the park. Their mother sits on a nearby bench engrossed in a paperback novel. I keep my distance, leaning against the trunk of a tree. A warm breeze brushes against my skin. I close my eyes and savor the feeling. Leaning my head back, I breathe in the smell of fresh cut grass and pine. I sense a change in the air around me, a slight shift in space, and I know I'm not alone.

I open my eyes. David stands in front of me, his face relaxed and smiling, his dark eyes gazing into mine.

"I got your message," he says. "I've been worried about you."

"I'm fine," I tell him, pointing at my leg. "Nothing too serious."

He points at the new bandage on his own leg. "We match."

The red splotches have already faded a bit, but there is a square of gauze taped to the side of his jaw. I gently touch it, but he flinches.

"I'm sorry," I say, withdrawing my hand.

He looks suddenly concerned and apologetic. "No, it wasn't you—your touch. It just hurts a little."

"Oh. Of course."

He continues gazing at me in a curious way that draws me to him so that I can't look away.

"I wanted to thank you for coming for me," I begin, gazing right back into his warm, brown eyes. "I don't know what would have happened if—" I can't bring myself to finish the thought. The tears I fought to keep at bay earlier now spill down my cheeks. It hits me all at once, losing Mama and Dr. Walsh, discovering the truth about Jordan.

"Hey, it's all right," he says, gathering me in his arms. "You're safe now."

I lay my face against his chest. Feeling him so close somehow calms me. When I've stopped crying, he pulls back a little to look at me. David's eyes are soft and sensitive. We're so close that I can see the specks of gold and brown dancing in them. One corner of his mouth lifts slightly in an enticing grin, and my heart beats madly in response.

The attraction between us grows stronger. The spicy smell of his cologne tugs at my senses. He leans toward me, hesitant, waiting for me to meet him halfway. I want to kiss him—badly, but I take a step back instead.

"David, I can't—" I tell him. "My condition, reading your mind—whatever the heck you want to call it—I won't do *that* to you again."

He doesn't move, and his smile widens. "I know you won't," he says. "But I've actually been doing some thinking about *that*."

He leans in closer.

"And?"

And closer still.

"And," he repeats. "I've got nothing to hide from you, Mira Ortiz."

His kiss is long and gentle. His fingers slide around the back of my neck up into my hair, and his other hand reaches around my waist and presses me against him. To my surprise, our connection causes less discomfort than the first time. He just feels too good. Time seems to stop altogether while the whole world melts away. I don't want it to end, but it does all too soon.

From across the park, I hear loud giggling. The two little girls watch us from behind the slide. They point and then run to hide.

"We have an audience," David says, laughing.

I slip my chin onto David's shoulder and wrap my arms around him. I want to tell him that I know him, I know everything about him. I've seen it all, felt it all. I want to tell him that I understand him, that he can trust me with his secrets and his hurts. I want to tell him most of all that I believe in him.

Instead, I brush my lips against his ear. "I love you, too."

MAMA'S FUNERAL IS HELD on a bright, sunny Tuesday. The clouds from the previous week skitter away like frightened cats, and in my mind I curse them for their cowardice. It should have rained today. The sky should have opened up like they did for Noah and drowned the whole world. That might have made me feel a little better. Instead, I stand between my father and a white-haired priest, baking in a black crepe dress and high heels that keep punching holes in the grass.

Mama's high heels. And they're still too big.

Papa managed to keep the service private, which means that the crowds and the cameras are outside the locked mammoth gate gawking at our small, solemn gathering of close friends and family. I don't really care anymore. When you have a condition like mine, privacy is irrelevant.

The priest ends the service by reading a passage from the Bible: "'The Lord is my light and my salvation; whom shall I fear? The Lord is the strength of my life; of whom shall I be afraid?'"

I remember all the moments Mama and I had together, some of which she captured on film, and others I captured on contact. I am deeply grateful to have those memories now, to feel what she felt, to love how she loved. In a way, I am comforted by them, though nothing will ever dull the ache of her physical absence.

When the service ends, Papa puts his arm around my shoulders. We've had plenty of time to talk during the past few days. We talked about Jackie Beitner and Mama and Jordan. We spent an afternoon with Robert and Marie Beitner where we looked through photo albums and drank our fill of lemonade. I told him about my feelings for David, and he told me about his plans for the future. But mostly we just made time to be together.

284

The other guests are dissipating, much like those rotten clouds. So eager to move on, to move away. They walk slowly toward their cars, hugging each other and speaking in soft, low tones. They will drive home and forget. But I can never forget.

"Mira, would you like a moment alone?" Papa asks.

"If you wouldn't mind," I answer.

He gives me a gentle squeeze. "I'll wait for you by the car."

I watch him as he joins the other mourners, then I turn to face Mama's grave. Her glossy rose-colored casket is draped in white and pink carnations. I pluck one from the arrangement and hold it against my breast. Slowly, I draw the now creased photo of Papa and Jackie Beitner from where I've kept it tucked in my sleeve. I think of everything that has happened these past few weeks and what I might have done to prevent it, but it was really out of my hands from the very beginning. I couldn't save Jackie, and I couldn't save Mama. Jordan's psyche showed me more than I ever wanted to know. I was an experiment to him, nothing more. And I *can* do something about that. I'll call Dr. Felton. Maybe he can help me, maybe not, but I have to start somewhere.

I toss the carnation into the grave. I look at the photo for a moment and then tear one end of it off and toss it in too. I tuck the remaining piece adorned with my father and real mother's faces back into my sleeve.

There are some things I wish I'd never known. I would love nothing more than to erase Jordan's memories, to somehow untangle them from my own and permanently delete them. But to do that would mean abandoning those who need me the most. The babies from the lab. David. Papa. But what I haven't told my father, or anyone else, is Jordan's deepest, darkest secret—Jackie Beitner wasn't the only test subject who was pregnant, and I wasn't the only child born to one. There are others out there like me.

I have to find them.

# ABOUT THE AUTHOR

**LAURISA WHITE REYES** is the author of the SCBWI Spark Award winning novel *THE STORYTELLERS* and the Spark Honor recipient *PETALS*. She is also the Senior Editor at Skyrocket Press and an English instructor at College of the Canyons in Southern California.

**www.LaurisaWhiteReyes.com**
**www.SkyrocketPress.com**

# ACKNOWLEDGEMENTS

I first fell in love with young adult fiction in 2012, the year my debut middle grade novel, *The Rock of Ivanore*, was released with Tanglewood Press. As a debut author, I was part of the Apocalypsies, the collective of debut middle grade and young adult authors that year. Through them, I was introduced to some of the best YA books I've ever read. *Contact* began as an experiment, actually. First, I wanted to try my hand at YA fiction, and second, I wanted to see if I could write as a pantser (writing without an outline). I'm so glad the experiment was a success.

I also wish to thank those who contributed invaluable feedback that helped shape the story: Carissa Reyes, Marc Reyes, my husband Gonzalo, Dorine White, Maddie Bennett, Kynzie Bair, and Jane Foster. Also to Hallowed Ink Press & Evernight Teen for giving this book a chance.

Thank you to my mom, Cyndi White, who has been my sounding board for all my ideas and who shares my passion for books. To my dad, Ray White, my fellow storyteller and writer-in-arms. To my family for their unending patience and support. And finally to God for the amazing opportunities and blessings he always places in my path.

Thank you for reading

# CONTACT

We invite you to post a review on Goodreads & your favorite online book retailer.

For a free e-book, join our mailing list at:
**www.SkyrocketPress.com**

www.ingramcontent.com/pod-product-compliance
Lightning Source LLC
Chambersburg PA
CBHW021957010726
47494CB00003B/769